CHASING RAINBOWS

Recent Titles by Rowena Summers from Severn House

The Caldwell Series

TAKING HEART
DAISY'S WAR
THE CALDWELL GIRLS
DREAMS OF PEACE

The Hotel Saga

SHELTER FROM THE STORM
MONDAY'S CHILD

BLACKTHORN COTTAGE
LONG SHADOWS
DISTANT HORIZONS
CHASING RAINBOWS

CHASING RAINBOWS

Rowena Summers

This first world edition published 2009
in Great Britain and in the USA by
SEVERN HOUSE PUBLISHERS LTD of
9–15 High Street, Sutton, Surrey, England, SM1 1DF.
Trade paperback edition published
in Great Britain and the USA 2009 by
SEVERN HOUSE PUBLISHERS LTD

British Library Cataloguing in Publication Data

Summers, Rowena, 1932-
  Chasing rainbows
  1. Love stories
  I. Title
  823.9'14[F]

ISBN-13: 978-0-7278-6758-2   (cased)
ISBN-13: 978-1-84751-123-2   (trade paper)

All Severn House titles are printed on acid-free paper.

Typeset by Palimpsest Book Production Ltd.,
Grangemouth, Stirlingshire, Scotland.
Printed and bound in Great Britain by
MPG Books Ltd., Bodmin, Cornwall.

One

Upstairs in the attic room they shared, the two girls excitedly changed out of their working clothes on their Friday night off. They took turns to wash themselves in the bowl of tepid water poured out from the jug they had laboriously carried up from the kitchen, and generously dabbed talcum powder beneath their armpits in their eagerness to get ready. Finally, they twirled around in front of the cracked dressing-table mirror, trying to convince themselves that nobody would take them for the kitchen maids they were.

The taller of the two girls studied herself, taking in the bronze chiffon dress that couldn't quite flatten her ample bosoms, and draped several long strings of shiny beads around her neck. In any case, by now she had cheerfully given up the flapper fashion that was never going to suit her shape. Her hair, almost the same dramatic colour as her dress, was twisted up in a topknot and fastened with a tortoiseshell comb, leaving flattering tendrils to frame her face. The new dance hall in town was going to see the best of Cherry O'Neil tonight, she thought exuberantly, and she felt more than a little flutter inside at the thought of the boys who might partner her for the charleston.

With a giggle, Cherry turned to her companion. 'You may help me decide which tiara I shall wear tonight, Jones,' she said, adopting an imperious voice that was so reminiscent of the lady of the house that her friend Paula screamed with laughter.

'You'll be the death of me one of these days, Cherry, and you'd better not let her ladyship hear you aping her voice like that. She'll think she's got a twin sister somewhere, and I always said you were more suited to being on the stage than a kitchen maid!'

'Oh yes! Fat chance I'd have for that,' Cherry said, reverting to her normal soft West Country voice. 'Anyway, you look a treat in that blue dress, Paula,' she went on generously, 'so how do I look?'

Paula grinned back at her. 'If you're fishing for compliments, you know blooming well you don't need me to tell you. You'd pass for a lady any day if it wasn't for your hands.'

Cherry inspected her outspread fingers for a moment and then shrugged. 'That goes for us both, but we've done our best to look presentable so there's no use fretting over something that can't be changed. Besides, the boys aren't going to be taking too much notice of our hands when we're dancing, are they?'

They'd spent long enough with their hands dipped in lanolin cream the night before, and then they'd worn cotton gloves while they slept, in the hope that the chaps and redness would soften. It had, too, until they'd had to do the usual menial tasks below stairs early that morning, cleaning out the ashes in the grates and scrubbing at the washboard. But Cherry had the right idea, thought Paula. She never wasted time in moaning over things that couldn't be changed, and she often envied her friend's optimism. In any case, tonight was for fun, not work.

'Come on then. Let's go! We don't want to be late.'

The Melchoir mansion and estate stretched out into the countryside on the outskirts of Bristol, so the girls had a fair walk to the bus stop to get their ride into the city and the dance hall. It wasn't one of the posher places in the city – the type that only admitted those who were born with a silver spoon in their mouths, and were undoubtedly far more sedate affairs. They were probably the kind of places where Captain Lance Melchoir, the son and heir of the family they worked for, went on a Friday night to meet his cronies.

Cherry sometimes imagined him dancing the light fantastic, or whatever they called it among the toffs, and couldn't resist a small twist of envy that she kept strictly to herself. Although she remembered Cook once saying she'd heard that Captain Lance usually went to his gentlemen's club in the city on Friday evenings – and that sounded toffee-nosed as well.

Cherry gave a small sigh, knowing Paula would think her totally mad to have even the smallest crush on the likes of Captain Lance. She put him out of her mind now as they put on their jackets and slipped their crocheted gloves in their evening bags, knowing it would be cold by the time they left the dance hall later that night, even if the lingering warmth of the April day was still pleasant in the early evening.

Spring was late in making an appearance that year, and there was still a chill at night, despite the hustle and bustle of the city and the crowded buildings that retained what heat there was. But the busy and tidal River Avon offset it all, winding through the city with the splendid suspension bridge crossing it so delicately. There was always a chill from the river, and frequently quite a stench from all the river traffic that criss-crossed it.

'I wonder if old Mr Brunel thought his bridge was going to last so long,' Paula said, looking down at the mud banks on either side of the river far below the bridge, with many small boats clustered together and sprawled impotently at angles until they could be refloated on the incoming tide.

'It's a good thing it did, or it would have clogged up the river for good if it fell in,' Cherry said smartly. 'He knew a thing or two about engineering, did our Isambard!'

'A friend of yours, was he?' Paula mocked. 'That must make you more than a hundred years old instead of twenty.'

'Don't be daft. I know a bit about him from a book I read, so my schooling wasn't all wasted, thank you very much.'

She was proud of that, too. She wasn't a dunce and her parents had made her take her schooling more seriously than Paula's seemed to have done. Either that or she hadn't been that interested in learning. Paula could get by, but Cherry was a competent reader. She was a thinker too, and she didn't see why a girl shouldn't be as well read as a boy. The days were long gone when girls were seen as second-class folk – Mrs Pankhurst had seen to that, and what she and her like had done for women shouldn't be forgotten or abused.

It sometimes made Cherry indignant to see how many girls simply ignored the sacrifices and pain that had been endured by the Suffragettes, but she knew better than to start reading the riot act to Paula when they were out for a night of fun. Besides, kitchen maids weren't really supposed to think, only to do as they were told.

Cherry was very fond of Paula. They had a lot in common, both growing up during the Great War, and both losing their fathers at a young age at the Battle of the Somme. Cherry shivered every time she remembered those dark days of despair. Even now, she couldn't forget the memory of her mother weeping inconsolably every night, and of herself creeping into her mother's bed to try to comfort her where no comfort was to be had. When the war finally ended and it seemed as if they could all turn a corner in their lives, Cherry's mother had died from the flu epidemic that had followed the war.

Cherry had been left in the care of her older brother, Brian, a good-for-nothing who earned his money by bare-knuckle boxing. He didn't care for the role of pseudo-parent, and as Cherry didn't care for it either, he soon left her, and only reappeared from time to time to check that she was all right – or more likely when he needed a bolthole from people he called bloodsuckers. Cherry never tried to find out exactly what that meant, or who such people were.

Shortly after the trauma of losing her mother, when Brian had done what he called his 'good deed' of seeing his mother decently buried and was off on his own pursuits, Cherry had met Paula, a girl about her own age who looked like a waif, unkempt and reduced to stealing scraps, as bewildered by everything that had happened as Cherry herself was. Cherry had been shocked at the other girl's appearance – knowing she could very well have been reduced to the same fate but for the few savings her mother had left her, and Brian's vague promise that he wouldn't let her starve – and she had offered her a cup of tea and a bite to eat.

She learned that Paula's father had also been killed in France, which gave them an instant bond, but Paula's feckless mother had soon got over it all and had run off with a soldier, leaving the young girl to fend for herself in any way she could. It was obvious that Paula hadn't had even the little education that Cherry had, but that was through no fault of her own, and it didn't detract from the close friendship they quickly formed. The two of them had stayed together from then on, and had eventually found employment as young kitchen maids in the house of Lord and Lady Melchoir. Lowly the work might be, but it was a world away from what they had left behind. They had a proper roof over their heads now, and security.

All in all, it had definitely been a good day when they had found each other, Cherry often thought loyally, and Paula was sometimes pathetically grateful to Cherry for lifting her out of the mire, as she called it.

As they saw the bus trundling into sight on that April evening, Cherry pushed all these gloomy thoughts out of her head as they joined the rest of the revellers on the vehicle that would take them into the heart of the city.

The dance hall was a modest little building, and was hardly the fanciest of places for a girl to find her true love, but the girls who frequented it always lived in hope. It was a cheap and cheerful place, to put it mildly, but it was ablaze with lights by the time they arrived, and excitement was running high. The band was blaring out the latest Charleston tune, and there was already a crowd of people on the floor, girls going wild with flailing arms and knock knees and flying beads.

As soon as Cherry and Paula had dispatched their jackets to the cloakroom they rushed out to the dance floor, eager to join in, partners or not. It hardly seemed to matter in this age of 'anything goes'.

Such a pace couldn't be maintained for too long, and after a while the band began to play a few slower melodies for people to get their breaths back, and for those more in tune with the foxtrot or the tango. There were also some good olde-tyme dances, which many of them still enjoyed, especially as it gave them the chance to change partners as frequently as the dances demanded. It was also a good chance for the girls, and for any boys who could dance at all, to see who took their fancy. Not that the slow dances would suit the clientele for very long. They wanted noise and fast-moving jazz tunes, and so did Cherry and Paula.

During the evening the Melchoir girls, as they liked to think of themselves, were never short of partners, making them giggle at some of their clumsy attempts to do the steps. Some of the young chaps knew what they were doing, and fancied themselves with their slicked-back, Brylcreemed hair, and others were just hopeless. Girls were taught the rudiments of social dancing at school, but many of the chaps simply hopped and skipped around the floor as best they could unless they found a willing female partner to show them how. But everybody was keen to learn the Charleston now, and most of the dance halls spent a little time giving a brief lesson during the evening.

'Good God, I didn't come here to get stepped all over,' Paula said, wincing as they sat out a while later. 'I'll have blisters on my blisters soon.'

Cherry laughed, her green eyes bright with excitement, despite the numbers of times her own toes had been stepped on. She had to admit that it was a rough and ready place. There were no toffs among the dancers, but Cherry was quite relieved about that, since her brother Brian turned up occasionally, usually with cuts and wounds on his knuckles and sometimes a gash on his cheek and ugly bruises on his forehead, which put most girls off dancing with him at all. 'It's just part of the job,' he'd always say when he made a point of trying to dance with his sister and with Paula. He was lumpy and awkward, and thankfully he wasn't here tonight to embarrass his sister. At least the toffs would know how to dance, Cherry thought ruefully, rubbing her sore foot. Captain Lance certainly would.

His name was in her head before she had time to think, and her heart gave a little lurch. She had no right to think of him at all, of course, and certainly not in the dreamy way she sometimes did, she thought guiltily. Kitchen maids didn't aspire to catch the eye of the handsome son and heir of the big house. And such eligible young men weren't supposed to look at kitchen maids – but that was where the truth of it differed, for the number of times it seemed that Lance Melchoir was just where she happened to be was surely more than coincidence. She hadn't even confided in Paula about that. There were some things that were too precious to share, and she knew the other girl would scoff and say she was chasing rainbows.

But if she was hanging out the washing on the kitchen clothes line, feeling less than spruce with wooden pegs clenched between her teeth and her hair all rumpled with steam from the wash-house, Lance would sometimes walk by, tipping his hat to her over the privet hedge. And sometimes when she was taking out the ashes to the dustbin she would catch sight of him riding by, sitting astride his horse as if he owned the world, his powerful legs tightly clad in pale suede jodhpurs, his back as elegant and straight as a ramrod and giving her an unaccountable shiver as he glanced her way, as if he couldn't resist it.

Of course, Paula would scoff and say she was mad to think he was even aware of her at all, and that it must be all in her imagination. If a toff took notice of a servant in that way it meant only one thing, and they all knew what that was. Rumours abounded of more than one young servant girl who had been sent packing in disgrace when she tried to say that a toff had interfered with her – and they knew of several, Paula would remind her darkly. At which point Cherry would defend Lance indignantly, even though they had barely exchanged half a dozen words in all the time she had worked for his family.

She knew he had a reputation of being a playboy these days, but according to Cook, who was the eyes and ears of the household below stairs, despite never going far from her domain, he was also an ex-army captain and had seen plenty of action during his service in the latter years of the war. Cook would never hear a word said against him. He had come home from the Front with honours, so if he preferred to play hard after all the terrible things he had witnessed in France, why shouldn't he?

Cherry secretly agreed, but knew better than to say so too loudly for fear of giving away her feelings. But it did no harm to dream occasionally, and if they were all she would ever have, she was determined to hang on to her dreams. She was quickly brought out of her dreams by a sharp nudge in the elbow from Paula.

'Oh God, look out, Cherry. Those two dock workers who were dancing with us earlier are coming our way again,' Paula hissed. 'Pretend you haven't seen them.'

It was a bit hard to do that when they were virtually standing in front of the girls now and blocking their view. The way they strolled arrogantly around the hall didn't endear them to anybody, and when they were close enough there was an unsavoury whiff of the river about them. Cherry and Paula might only be kitchen maids, but they were fussy about keeping themselves clean, and these two had already offended them with their uncouth manners and innuendos. The girls tried not to show their distaste as the dockers approached.

'Want another dance, sweethearts?' the one called Sid leered.

'No, thank you all the same,' Cherry said, adopting the classier tone that usually had the effect of quelling would-be admirers. 'We've decided to sit this one out to give our feet a rest.'

As she turned her face away from them, the two dock workers scowled, and Jim, the second one, imitated her voice badly.

'Oh, "no, thank you all the same", is it? That's not how you spoke earlier, if I remember. Think yourselves too good for us now, do you? Well, we can soon find somebody who doesn't think so much of herself, Miss Hoity-Toity!'

They swung away, with the other one muttering something beneath his breath that the girls couldn't hear, but which they were sure wasn't exactly complimentary.

'I don't think it was such a good idea to speak to them like that, Cherry,' Paula said uneasily. 'They're not the type to be made fools of.'

'Like what? Don't tell me you'd have wanted to dance with them. They're louts and you know it – and they smell!'

'I know they do, but you didn't have to sound so posh and make them seem so inferior.'

'Why not, when that's exactly what they are?' Cherry retorted.

But she didn't miss the fact that the two dock workers continued to hover near them from time to time, and Cherry began to wish she hadn't spoken as she had. She tried to put the incident out of her mind and to enjoy the evening, throwing herself into the dancing while keeping a watch on the time, as they couldn't afford to miss the last bus out of the city or they'd have to walk a few miles back to Melchoir House.

Reluctantly, the girls knew it was time for them to make a move. They went to the cloakroom to fetch their jackets, and out in the cool night air they found the two dock workers lurking outside.

'What's your hurry, girlies? There's still plenty of time for us to get to know one another,' Sid said lazily. They immediately blocked their path, and Cherry heard Paula give a gasp of fright.

'Will you let us pass, please?' Cherry said, not as haughtily as she had spoken before, but determined to let them know that she wasn't afraid of them – even if she was. For the first time in her life, she wished desperately that Brian was here, knowing that her brother would have taken on the two of them without a second's hesitation – and would have won, too.

'Now that's no way to behave when we're only being friendly, is it?' said his mate, Jim. 'Where's the harm in a little kiss or two?'

'Well, we don't want a little kiss or anything else, especially from the likes of you two,' Cherry snapped, since Paula seemed to have been temporarily struck dumb.

The dock workers were close enough to them now for the girls to smell the beer on their breaths and it was easy to tell that they had been drinking for a considerable time before they arrived at the dance. That would give them more courage than they had already, and they were a long way from the bus stop, Cherry thought desperately. It had been so hot in the dance hall that she and Paula had been drinking more cider than they usually did, too. It was supposed to be a refreshing drink, but it could be more lethal than she realized, and she felt far from steady on her feet now.

Just as she was wondering what to do, and sensing that she was going to get no help from Paula, the door of the dance hall opened and a crowd of people came out with their arms around one another, laughing and joking. This was the moment for the girls to take their chance. She grabbed Paula's arm, which seemed to have gone limp with fear.

'Run, Paula!' she yelled.

Their sore feet didn't make it easy to run as fast as they would have liked, but it was a typical Friday night, and with so many people on the streets it was easier for them to weave in and out of couples and groups of friends, who either laughed at the two girls or cursed them. Some even tried to grab them and ask where the fire was.

Cherry and Paula ignored them all as they tore along the streets and down back alleys, but there was always danger of a different kind there, and Paula shrieked that they would do better to stick to the main streets. They couldn't even be sure that the dock workers were still following them, but they didn't dare look behind them or stop running.

'I can't go any farther,' Paula finally rasped out painfully. 'I'll have to stop. I've got such a stitch in my side that it's killing me.'

'All right,' Cherry gasped back. 'I think we're safe now, anyway. Let's lean against the shelter of this wall to get our breath back. They won't see us here.'

It seemed a sensible thing to do, to let their breathing calm down a little – besides which, as they leaned against the high wall of a building, they realized they weren't even sure where they were any more. Foolishly, they had run off in a panic without any real sense of direction. Cherry's head was swimming by now, and Lord knew what Paula's was like. She felt a brief surge of sympathy for Paula, who couldn't drink even half a glass of cider without it going to her head, and they had both had far more than that tonight. She gave a small gulp, praying they would get back inside the house without Cook seeing them, or they'd be in for a right rollocking tomorrow morning.

But they couldn't stay here for ever, and at least the raucous sounds of the city revellers seemed far enough behind them now for them to think they were reasonably safe. All they had to do was look for some street signs that they could recognize, make sure they kept the river on their left-hand side, and they would eventually find their way back to Melchoir House. Ever optimistic, Cherry tried to jolly Paula into thinking the same way.

'Come on, it'll be all right if we keep our wits about us,' she said.

'If we don't get accosted by other chaps like those dock workers, you mean,' Paula said fearfully. 'Either that or the coppers will run us in for being street walkers.'

'Crikey, Paula, I'm doing my best!' Cherry said, annoyed.

'Yes, well, don't forget it was your fault that we've landed here in the middle of nowhere. If you hadn't made us run like that we wouldn't be in this position.'

'What would you rather we had done then? Given in to those horrible chaps? God knows where that would have landed us,' she said with a shudder. 'Anyway, it's not helping for us to start blaming each other, so let's just start walking.'

They moved reluctantly away from the protection of the wall, wincing again as their feet smarted even more after the brief rest. After a few moments, the lights of a motor car from behind them lit up the road, revealing them both. The car seemed to be slowing down, and Cherry groaned.

'Now we're for it. Don't turn around, Paula. If it's some kerb crawler we'll just keep on walking and take no notice, and if it's the police, well, we'll think about that when it happens.'

She tried to sound positive, taking command, even though she was shaking all over, but she knew Paula was wilting by the minute now, and it was up to her to deal with whatever was coming to them. Truth to tell, she had a horror of being hauled into the Bridewell police station and thrown in the cells for the night. Brian had experienced it more than once, and had relished relating colourful versions of his experiences to the two gullible young girls.

The only thing they could do was keep on walking as fast as they could, keeping their heads held high as if they knew exactly where they were going, and hope that the motor car would pass them by. The engine made little more than a soft purring sound, so Cherry guessed that it must be an expensive motor, which meant it probably wasn't a police car. The thought gave her a slight feeling of relief as the car seemed to gather up a little speed and then swept past them, into the darkness and around the corner ahead.

'Thank goodness for that,' Cherry muttered. 'We've had enough frights for one night.'

By the time they reached the corner of the road themselves, they were feeling relieved, even though they still didn't know where they were, and Paula was complaining that she was going to fall asleep on her feet if they didn't find the way home soon.

'You shouldn't have drunk so much cider,' Cherry said in annoyance. 'If you think I'm going to carry you, you've got another thought coming!'

And then they clutched each other's hands as they saw that the car was waiting for them in the next street. In the split second that it took to register the black Rolls Royce properly, and the well-dressed gentleman getting out of the driving seat, Cherry felt her heart leap.

'Bloody hell, it's him,' Paula croaked. 'We're really in for it now!'

Two

Cherry found it impossible to reply for a moment since her tongue seemed to be stuck to the roof of her mouth. Besides which, by now her heart was beating so fast she thought she was going to faint, and it was hard to say which of the girls was clinging harder to the other. They were both shivering with fright now, and it was the gentleman who spoke first, and with some annoyance.

'I thought I recognized you, if only by the colour of your hair,' he said, looking hard at Cherry. 'What the devil are the two of you doing out here? Don't you know you're in danger of being accosted by ruffians or God knows who?'

'We thought we were,' Cherry managed to stutter, furious that her hair seemed to have slipped out of all its pins now, and that it must be hanging down in rats' tails. And she had started out this evening thinking so well of her appearance. So much for false pride, she thought bitterly.

A moment later the man broke into an amused laugh and her world momentarily turned the right way up again.

'We're really sorry if we startled you, Captain Lance,' she went on, a mite more boldly. 'We've been to a dance and we seem to have missed the last bus, and knowing how Cook will rail into us if she catches us getting in late, we started to walk and lost our way.'

By now, she knew she was babbling, and she groaned inwardly, knowing what a naive fool she must seem to someone as worldly as Lance Melchoir. Paula, as ever, was saying nothing, letting Cherry do all the talking and just clinging to her side like a limpet, and acting twice as sloppy as usual.

'You'd better get in, then,' Lance said, opening the rear door of the car.

While Cherry gaped, Paula suddenly found her voice. 'In your motor? Oh no, sir, we couldn't do that. It wouldn't be proper,' she squeaked.

Cherry dug her in the ribs. 'Don't be stupid, Paula. If Captain Lance is kind enough to give us a lift home, we shouldn't be so ill-mannered as to refuse.'

Too late, she realized to her horror that she had spoken in the haughty tone she had used with the dock workers, the tone that was so like Lady Melchoir's own, and which was surely going to infuriate the son of the house. From Paula's gasp, Cherry knew she had noticed it too. Then they heard Lance's laughter again.

'My God, girl, you do my mother to a turn! Are you sure you're not some society deb disguised as a kitchen maid for the sport of it?'

Cherry felt her face burn with anger. 'There's no need to patronize me, sir, and I apologize for putting on airs. It's often the only way to deal with young chaps who think they can get away with anything with the likes of us. And thank you for the offer of the lift, but we prefer to walk.'

She grabbed Paula's arm and dragged her away from the car, despite Paula's protests that her feet weren't going to carry her one more yard. They heard the car doors close behind them, and her eyes prickled with furious tears, because now they were in the same predicament as before, and she had ruined everything. She felt Paula stumble against her and hissed at her to keep going. She heard something else too, as the Rolls Royce slowly cruised alongside them.

'Stop being so foolish and get in the car,' Lance called out irritably. 'That girl's going to collapse if you make her walk much farther.'

'Please do as he says, Cherry,' Paula said faintly.

Knowing there was no option now, Cherry stood still and waited silently as Lance stopped the car and opened the rear door again. Paula almost fell inside the soft, plush interior, and Cherry followed, freely admitting that this was a darned sight better than having to walk all the way back. Lance got back into the driving seat and the car began moving again, so smoothly that Cherry felt her taut nerves begin to relax a little. Paula's head had already lolled back against the headrest, and her eyes had closed.

'So you've been dancing, have you?' Lance said, glancing back at Cherry through the interior mirror. 'Are you any good at it?'

'Of course,' she said, bristling. 'Even kitchen maids can learn how to dance!'

If she had ever thought she had a chance of catching his attention – which, realistically, she never had done – she knew she was doing everything wrong now. She shouldn't be replying to his civil question in such a defensive way. She should be deferential, as befitted her status. But kowtowing to anybody had never been Cherry O'Neil's style.

'You'll have to show me some time,' he said, still with that laugh in his voice as if she had said something terribly witty.

She stared furiously at the back of his head. What a nerve he had, patronizing her like that! As if he would ever deign to dance with her. And then, for one brief, crazy moment, she imagined herself dancing with him. Not in the mad whirl of the Charleston in some cheap, smoke-filled dance hall where the riff-raffs tried to get off with the nearest girl, but held close in Lance's arms in an elegant ballroom, while they swirled around to some dreamy waltz music . . .

'Such an idea obviously doesn't appeal to you,' Lance continued as she clamped her lips together and said nothing. 'By the way, what the devil's your name? I can't just call you "kitchen-maid".'

'It's Cherry,' she mumbled.

It had suddenly become personal. He knew who she was. She was no longer just a menial servant in his home, but a person with a name. Maybe the dream was no longer quite such an impossible one . . . And she was far too tipsy to think sensibly, she realized.

The fantasy was interrupted by an enormous snore from the other side of the rear seat, and she was brought abruptly back to the present as Lance let out a laugh that was more of a guffaw.

'It sounds as if our little companion is well out of it. Have you two been drinking tonight?'

'No, sir,' Cherry said indignantly, despite the fact that her head was starting to swim now, although that could be due to the motion of the motor car. She was used to the rough and ready movements of the town buses, not this soft, gentle motion that must be more like the waves on a peaceful ocean.

'Well, perhaps a bit more cider than usual,' she admitted.

He had probably been drinking too, she thought suspiciously. He was uncommonly sociable, but then they had never been at such close quarters before, and that was going to her head as much as anything else.

'Have you been somewhere nice tonight, Captain Lance?' she asked, because if he wanted to talk, then why shouldn't she?

'My club,' he said briefly. 'I lost a packet at the gaming tables tonight, so it's a relief to have somebody different to talk to other than the stuffed shirts who only wanted to talk about politics or the stock market or their horses. Not that I minded the latter, but some of the members can be hideously boring old farts – begging your pardon, Cherry.'

She was almost more charmed by the fact that he had used her name than mildly astonished that he had bothered to apologize to her. She tried to think of something to say, and there was only one thing that she could think of now, since everything else he had spoken about was beyond her.

'I've seen you riding your horse. I don't know much about them but I'm sure you ride very well,' she said, finishing awkwardly as she realized how idiotic it sounded.

'He's a fine thoroughbred,' Lance conceded. 'Would you like to see him? We're nearly back at the house, and since your friend looks fit to sleep it off, we can leave her to it while I show you round the stables.'

Cherry gulped. 'We really should be getting indoors, sir. As it is, we'll have to sneak upstairs so as not to disturb the household.'

'Oh, ten more minutes won't hurt. And I can show you a way to get inside unnoticed – I perfected it years ago with some of my school chums.'

Cherry had a sudden vision of the young Lance Melchoir defying his stuffy parents' rules, and sneaking into the house with a group of friends. It sounded reckless and daring, and so unlike the usual conventions of a well-bred family that she found herself giggling.

'So, what do you say, Cherry-Ripe?' he went on persuasively. 'Are you game enough to leave our sleeping beauty here and come out to play?'

'All right,' she said breathlessly.

She realized they had arrived, and that Lance was driving the car smoothly around the back of the house to where the stables and outhouses were. He turned off the engine and they were in darkness, lit only by the moon. The house was quiet, and all they could hear now was the rhythmic sound of Paula's breathing.

Cherry was suddenly gripped by a wild sense of adventure, of going into unknown territory, and she told herself sternly not to be so foolish, or to make more of this than it was. Lance was merely going to show her his horse, of which he was obviously very proud, and if there might – well, there just *might* be a bit of a kiss and a cuddle – she wasn't going to object! Not that she really expected it, but you never knew.

Almost dizzy with excitement now, because this evening was having such an unexpected ending, she was aware that Lance was already out of the car and was opening the rear door for her. Such courtesy to a kitchen maid! She giggled again, and stumbled a little in the cool night air, until she felt his supporting arm around her.

'Steady, girl,' he said softly. 'I think perhaps your friend wasn't the only one to let the cider go to her head tonight.'

'It really wasn't that much,' Cherry protested, lest he should think she was accustomed to drinking. The fact that it didn't happen very often made the effect all the more pronounced.

'I'm not condemning you for it, Cherry. It always helps to relax you and loosen your inhibitions.'

She knew the word, but she wasn't quite sure what he meant by it. In any case they had reached the stables now, and they went inside, where the sweet smell of hay mixed with the earthy smell of the horses in their stalls. There were four of them, and Cherry wondered fleetingly why a small family needed so many. It was all to do with status, she supposed. They could afford them, so they had them. She felt a small stab of anger at the unfairness of life, when those who had so much compared so unfavourably with those who had little or nothing.

'This is Noble. Isn't he a beauty?' Lance said, still with his arm around her waist as they moved towards the last stall where the horse raised his head at their approach and nuzzled into Lance's hand. He had named all the other animals as they went past them, but this one was clearly his pride and joy.

'I never realized how big they were,' Cherry said, a little frightened.

'Don't let him scare you. Put your hand on his nose and let him smell you. It's not often he gets the scent of a pretty girl.'

Very gingerly, she did as she was told, and then gave a small gasp as the horse moved beneath her hand. She snatched it away quickly.

'He won't hurt you, Cherry,' Lance said. 'He's a big softie unless he's competing, and then he really shows his mettle. Besides, I took you for the kind of girl who wasn't afraid of anything.'

'Oh, really? And what kind of girl is that?' she mumbled.

He had turned her to face him now and her heart began to pound.

'The kind who wouldn't say no to a bit of creature comfort.'

Then the impossible dream because real as she felt his mouth on hers, and she couldn't help winding her arms around him and kissing him back. It must be a dream, she thought faintly, because such things couldn't happen . . .

'If we go up into the hayloft you can see these magnificent beasts in all their glory,' Lance was saying now, still in that soft, seductive voice.

It was what she had come here for, she told herself. She had come to see the horses, not to be persuaded by a suave, sophisticated man of the world to climb the wooden steps to the sweet-smelling hayloft, nor to find herself being gently pushed down on to a rug – and where had that come from, she asked herself dizzily. But the mingled, evocative scents of the hay and the horses were oh, so seductive, and so was he . . . This was the man of her dreams who was covering her with his body now, and whose hands were pushing up her skirts and caressing her soft flesh so gently.

Some semblance of sense rushed into her head then, and she gasped as she realized exactly where this was leading.

'Please don't. *Please*, Captain Lance.'

'For God's sake, forget the formality, my Cherry-Ripe,' he said, his voice oddly thick. 'You're the prettiest girl I've seen, and I've seen you many times, but never like this, so sweet and compliant in my arms. Just for now, forget the differences between us, because tonight we're just a man and a woman.'

She knew then that there was no turning back. It was too late for that, because he was surging inside her and after a few moments she was moving with him until she felt a burst of exquisite sensation that she had never known before. She was gasping for a different reason now, and he buried his face in hers as he lay heavily on her, murmuring words her dazed senses couldn't comprehend.

Later, Cherry couldn't recall how or when they had left the hayloft, or how they had persuaded the half-conscious Paula that she had to walk, or be half-dragged between them while they got her upstairs through a passage and stairway that the kitchen maids didn't know even existed. She couldn't recall the moment when Lance had left them and she and Paula had fallen across their beds without bothering to undress and slept for hours until the first fingers of dawn light awoke them.

It was only then, staring into the dim light thrown across the attic bedroom through the small square of uncurtained window, that Cherry realized what she had done. And what had been done to her. She was alternately caught up in the magic of having been loved by Lance Melchoir – if love was the right word for their brief lustful coupling – and her horror that she had let it happen. It was what the lowest of servant girls did, to let themselves be seduced by their betters. It wasn't love. It was no more than a moment's sport to them, no more than what the beasts in the fields did, and a slow trickle of tears ran down her cheeks.

'Cherry,' she heard a weak voice say from the other bed. 'How the bloody hell did I get here, and where's the bloody chamber pot? Any minute now I'm going to be sick.'

If there was anything guaranteed to shatter any romantic thoughts of the previous night, that was it. Cherry held Paula's head while she puked into the chamber pot, which was thankfully empty, and prayed that there would be no consequences of what she had done.

When Paula had recovered, she told her briefly that Captain Lance had helped them get indoors without being seen.

'Blimey, I remember now,' Paula said. 'We ran from those dockers, didn't we, and Captain Lance gave us a lift back in his motor. That was a turn-up, if you like. But I still don't know how I got up here, and still in my best dress too.'

She looked down at herself, her blue dress crumpled and slightly smelling of sick, and wrinkled her nose.

'I'll have to take it off,' she went on, without waiting for an answer. 'It's making me feel worse just to look at it – and to smell it. We'll have to get ready to start work soon, anyway, even if my head feels as if I've got a football in it. You don't look so bad,' she added, almost accusingly. 'So tell me what happened last night.'

Cherry swallowed. She and Paula usually confided everything to one another, sharing secrets in good times and bad. But there was no way she was going to tell Paula everything this time. Some things were too private, too wonderful – and too shameful – to reveal, even to a best friend.

'You sort of passed out in the back of the car,' Cherry said quickly, as Paula struggled to get her arms out of her dress and tottered over to the wash basin. The water was stone cold, but at least it would help to revive them.

'And then what?' Paula asked. 'Did your dream man actually talk to you?'

He did a darned sight more than that, thought Cherry.

'Well, he couldn't leave you in his car all night,' she said, ignoring the question. 'I managed to wake you up, and he helped us indoors like I told you, up some stairs and a passage that he and his school friends used to use.'

With every word, it only emphasized the distance between his world and hers, she thought, her heart sinking. She was perfectly sure that by now he would be regretting what had happened and would want nothing more to do with her. Or it would have meant so little to him that he would already have forgotten it. There would be no more special glances between them, and maybe even all of that had been in her imagination after all. But he *had* noticed her before, because he'd said he recognized the colour of her hair. It gave her a small crumb of comfort to remember that, though what good it would do her, she didn't know.

'So he actually came up here with us?' Paula squeaked. 'Blimey, I bet he didn't know such cramped little rooms like this even existed.'

Cherry pulled her own dress over her head and let the long strings of beads fall to the floor. She had always loved their bright, glittery showiness, but now she could only see them for what they were: cheap and tawdry, and little more than fairground baubles.

Such finery was a mockery, compared with the ladies Lance Melchoir must know, dressed in their diamonds and pearls. He had only wanted her for one thing, and he was never going to have her again, she thought fiercely, with the first semblance of her pride and self-preservation returning.

'He didn't try it on, did he?' Paula asked mischievously, her voice muffled by a rough towel as she dried her face and neck from her morning ablutions.

'Of course not,' Cherry said crossly.

'Oh well, better luck next time!'

'Next time we'll be damn sure to catch the bus back and not be so embarrassed. I'll never be able to look him in the face again.'

Paula sniffed. 'Well, you're not likely to, are you? So you needn't let that worry you.'

By the time they were dressed for their morning duties, they tried not to notice their throbbing heads, knowing that Cook was just as likely to box their ears for their stupidity in drinking too much cider, making their heads spin still more. In any case, when they went downstairs it was to find the whole kitchen staff agog with news. Even the stately butler, Mr Gerard, seemed unduly agitated. But it was Cook who badgered them to start work almost before they'd got their breath back from running downstairs.

'Come along, you two, we've been told there's going to be a special birthday party for Lord Melchoir at the beginning of May, so every bit of silver has to be cleaned and polished, and as there's no time like the present we need to get on with it sharpish.'

'We might have known we'd get all the donkey work,' Cherry muttered to Paula. 'How old do you reckon he's going to be? Sixty-five or seventy?'

Cook had sharp ears. 'Now then, you girls, it's not for us to speculate on how old Lord Melchoir is. But, for your information, before you go putting years on him, I happen to know he'll be sixty-five.'

'Trust her to know,' Paula said with a wry grin. 'How many people are they expecting to this birthday party then, Cook?'

'I'm told there will be about fifty, all toffs and their families, of course, and I daresay a good few young ladies among them hoping to catch Captain Lance's eye. It's about time he settled down and found himself a wife.'

Mr Gerard rebuked her at once. 'Now then, Cook, it's not for us to speculate on when the upper classes decide to get married. If Captain Lance decided to remain a bachelor all his life, it's no business of ours.'

'It'll be Lord Melchoir's business, though,' she retorted. 'He'll want to see his son married off and the estate settled with an heir of his own before the old gentleman snuffs it.'

Paula giggled. 'I don't know how she gets away with talking like that,' she whispered to Cherry as they made their way to the small pantry where all the special silver was kept. 'Mr Gerard would never let us be so disrespectful.'

Cherry wasn't listening. Ever since the butler had mentioned Captain Lance finding himself a wife she had felt a familiar pain around her heart. It had nothing to do with heartburn, and more to do with the fact that such a person could never be her. And, too late, she knew that even though she was well aware that she had been taken advantage of last night, she was more than half in love with Captain Lance, and had been for a very long time.

She snapped at Paula before she stopped to think what she was saying. 'Well, I think it's a lot of blooming fuss for an old man to have an elaborate sixty-fifth birthday when ordinary folk like us make do with a slice of cake and a drop of brandy in our tea if Cook's got a mind to give us a drop – and we enjoy ourselves just as much without all the fancy trappings.'

Paula's eyes opened wide as she lifted down one of the heavy boxes of silver to put on the pantry table, along with the silver polish and rubbing cloths.

'Blimey, Cherry, you were always partial to sneaking upstairs and taking a quick look at all the toffs in their finery. Got a touch of the green eyes now, have you? I reckon it's having that ride in Captain Lance's Roller last night that's done it. You want to mind yourself, girl, or you'll be getting above yourself.'

'Don't be so stupid, and if you can't think of anything more sensible to say, you'd be better saying nothing. You can start on this cutlery while I go and ask Cook for some headache powders. I daresay you could do with one as well, if only to clear out some of the rubbish in your noddle.'

She swished out of the small pantry with her eyes smarting, knowing she was taking her frustration out on Paula when none of this was her fault. Well, only the part where she had virtually passed out in the back of the car, because if she hadn't, none of it would have happened. Not the visit to the stables to see Lance's horse, nor what had happened afterwards.

She leaned against the wall for a moment, unable to resist reliving it all, as if she were seeing it as one of the romantic flicks at the Roxy cinema . . . It was more like looking at it all through rose-coloured spectacles, she thought bitterly, as Cook appeared as if from nowhere and asked her what she thought she was doing, idling there.

'I was just coming to ask you for some headache powders for me and Paula if you please, Cook, and some water to take them with,' she said swiftly. 'It gets so hot and stuffy in the pantry and the smell of the cleaning stuff gets down our throats. Paula wasn't too well this morning but she don't want to slouch in her work.'

She knew she was putting part of the blame on Paula, and she might be saying it with her tongue in her cheek, but it was true, all the same. A heavy morning of cleaning silver was going to do their heads and throats no good at all. And Paula was a bit of a pet as far as Cook was concerned.

'All right, my girl, and when you've had a bit of dinner later, you can both take a turn around the kitchen garden to get some air in your lungs before you get on with it this afternoon. I don't want you falling by the wayside while we're going to be so busy for the next few weeks. In fact, I may send you out to get me some flour and sugar and other goods from the grocery shop later as well.'

Once Cherry had been given the headache powders and a jug of water and glasses, she escaped back to the pantry again. By now Paula was rubbing half-heartedly at the first batch of forks and spoons.

'You'd better put more elbow grease into it than that,' Cherry told her, 'or we'll be here till Domesday – if you know when that is!'

Paula looked at her speculatively. 'I've been thinking.'

Cherry gave a mock groan. 'Oh Lord, wave the flags!'

She tipped a powder into each glass and half-filled it with

water and handed one to Paula before swallowing hers as fast as possible, while shuddering at the bitter taste as she waited for Paula's thoughts to materialize.

'You and your dream man went off and left me in the car last night, didn't you? I don't know how long it was, but I remember snoring so loudly that I woke myself up, and you weren't there.'

'Don't be so daft. You must have been imagining things. Of course we were there. I told you, we had to half-carry you up the stairs and it was lucky that Captain Lance knew a way to do it without us getting caught.'

'I know that's what you said, but it's not what I remember.'

'Well, I think your memory's playing tricks with you, because that's the way it happened,' Cherry snapped, more unnerved than she let on, because she couldn't bear it if Paula thought badly of her. Paula had always looked up to her from the day they had met, and if she even half guessed what had happened last night, Cherry would no longer be her heroine, that was for sure.

Three

Lord Francis Melchoir had always wanted more than one child. As the Royals had long been known to decree, 'an heir and a spare,' and even a few more, would be far preferable to having an only son, even though he was well satisfied with the one that he and Elspeth had produced. Lance had turned out to be a chip off the old block, doing his duty in the army like his father, and coming out of it with honours. Francis knew what army life could be like, and he didn't begrudge his son a moment of the time he spent enjoying life to the full nowadays. But if he'd had his way, Lance wouldn't have been the only Melchoir sprog.

Unfortunately, Elspeth hadn't been so amenable. After a lengthy and miserable time giving birth to Lance, she had vowed that she wanted no more of it, and when the strong-minded Elspeth decided on something that was the end of it. For years afterwards, even his occasional forays into her bedroom had been met with frowns and expressions of annoyance, and had gradually diminished to nothing. Not that he really cared any more. At his age, and becoming increasingly aware of the passing years, the urges in his loins had also diminished.

No, it would be up to Lance now to secure the continuity of the family fortunes, and this coming birthday party might see a few suitable girls who would fit the bill. They would have to be practically blue-blooded to suit Elspeth, of course, although in his opinion, that didn't always make the kind of wife a man yearned for. Cold as charity, most of them. He'd had the pleasure of dallying with a few little fillies himself in the past, and they were the ones who could stir a man's blood, not the well-bred daughters of the town.

Halfway through the morning he put down his copy of *The Times* as his son came into the drawing room, looking surprisingly alert after a late night out.

'Ring the bell for some coffee and biscuits, my boy,' he said genially, 'and then tell me how much of my hard-earned cash you lost last night while your mother's out at one of her coffee mornings in town. God knows what these women have to talk about, but it keeps her busy.'

Lance grinned. Life was always more comfortable when his mother was out, and the two men could take their own morning coffee together in a relaxed atmosphere. Lady Melchoir was a stickler for the conventions, and if she ever guessed that her husband enjoyed dipping his biscuits into his coffee when she wasn't around to witness it, she would throw a fit – if it wasn't too unladylike to do such a thing. Lance loved his mother as much as any son did, but he would never understand her aristocratic ways.

'I lost quite a bit at Darwin's Club,' he admitted. 'But don't worry, I'll get it back next week. And it wasn't your cash, Father. I parted company with my own last night. Since when was yours so hard-earned, anyway?'

Lord Melchoir laughed, not in the least put out by the free and easy way his son addressed him. He welcomed it as a breath of fresh air in the rarefied atmosphere in which his wife seemed to thrive.

'*Touché*, Lance! So what was it, roulette or poker?'

'Roulette. My damn numbers kept letting me down, and in the end it was a relief to get out of there.'

The drawing-room door opened at that moment, and a house-maid brought in a tray of coffee and biscuits. Francis waved her away, saying they would pour it themselves, and immediately left his son to deal with it.

'So tell me, what else did you get up to last night?'

Lance's hand wavered for the slightest moment over the coffee pot. The sight of the maid in her crisp white cap and apron over her black morning dress reminded him all too vividly of another girl who was normally dressed far more drably, as befitted her kitchen duties. Her dramatic hair and green eyes could melt a man at ten paces, even when she was flustered from hanging out the clothes in the kitchen garden. She had looked quite the charmer last night in her bronze-coloured dress. She had a deliciously rounded shape too, not flattened out of all recognition like one of those appalling flapper women. He stilled his thoughts, and handed his father a cup of coffee and the plate of biscuits.

'What makes you think I got up to anything else?' he countered his father's question. 'Wasn't losing a packet enough for me to want to come home and lick my wounds?'

'I'm sure it was, if only for a little while. But I've seen that look in a young man's eyes before, and I'm guessing it wasn't only the thrill of the tables that excited you.'

Lance laughed, stirring two lumps of sugar into his own cup of coffee.

'Maybe not, but I'm too much a gentleman to tell, and you're far too much of a gentleman to insist on it, Father.'

'God damn it, you've got me there, boy. All right, but was she worth it?'

'More than worth it,' Lance replied, no longer looking at his father.

Francis felt a small flicker of alarm. It was right and proper for a young man to sow his wild oats, as the saying went, but falling in love with the wrong girl could only lead to disaster. For once, he was in tune with his wife on that score. It was time his son was married and secured the succession of the Melchoir estate and fortune. He wasn't immortal, and it was important to see things settled before he popped his clogs. He cursed himself for thinking a cliché better suited to the riff-raff – and one that Elspeth would certainly despise – but nevertheless, it said it all.

'You do know that there will be some eligible girls at my birthday party, don't you, Lance?' he said casually. 'Your mother and I are both hoping that one of them will make a suitable bride for you.'

'For God's sake, Father, this isn't the Victorian age,' Lance said, suddenly angry. 'If you're planning on making this party a cattle market for me to pick and choose the one with the best hocks or whatever, you can think again. I'll marry when I'm good and ready and not before.'

'All right, there's no need to fly off the handle. Naturally, we both want the best for you, and nobody's trying to force you into anything. Just remember that I won't live for ever, that's all, and I'm saying no more about it.'

'You're not ill, are you?' Lance said sharply.

It was tempting for a moment for Francis to say that he was, or that he'd been having a few chest pains recently, if only to speed the boy into finding a wife. But it wouldn't be true, and it was far too much like tempting fate to play around with his health like that. So he shook his head firmly.

'I've never been in better health, so forget about all that and take a look at these stock exchange figures in *The Times*, and tell me whether you think I should buy or sell, and what looks like being a good prospect.'

They studied the newspaper together, although Lance's attention wasn't entirely on it. If his father had any idea just where his thoughts were straying, he'd have had palpitations there and then. It was damn stupid, of course. The O'Neil girl wasn't the first one he'd pleasured, but for some reason he couldn't get her out of his mind. He remembered the startling moment when she had spoken in an imperious accent so like his mother's that he could still laugh out loud at the memory, but right then, what really started to tickle him was the thought of a charade like no other.

He had the weirdest vision of imagining her dressed to kill and turning up as a mystery guest at his father's birthday party. If it could be pulled off, it would be a lark like no other. He tried to picture it now . . . Cherry dressed in delicate silks and glittering jewels, her glorious hair properly coiffured, and that soft voice, removed from its usual attractive West Country accent, so cultured and correct, charming everyone around her, even his starchy mother.

Christ Almighty, it would be the coup of the century . . . Lance couldn't resist a sudden involuntary snort of laughter, causing his father to look up from the newspaper and stare at him.

'Well, I don't know what's so funny about stocks and shares, boy, but I can see your mind isn't really on it today. I think I'll leave any decisions until I can concentrate on it properly.'

He closed the pages and put the newspaper to one side while he finished drinking his coffee.

'So what else is on your mind?' he said at last. 'I can see there's something, so out with it.'

'Absolutely nothing, Father. I was dreaming, that's all, and I apologize.'

Francis gave a low chuckle. 'Oh well, I won't press you. But when a healthy young man gets the kind of look in his eyes that you have, I'd say there was a filly involved. Just be careful, that's all.'

Lance felt the need to get out of the drawing room before he let something slip, and his father had inadvertently given him the lead.

'I'm always careful. But after last night's gambling losses I suspect the look in my eyes is more the need for fresh air than anything else. I'm going to give Noble an airing this afternoon, so I shall go for a ride across the Downs to clear my head. I'll see you later.'

He escaped before there were any more probing questions. The absurd notion that a kitchen maid could be dressed in silks and pass herself off as a lady just for his amusement was fast disappearing now. It was demeaning to her to even think of it. And it could never have worked. He didn't know a great deal about what went on below stairs, but he guessed that the girls who worked there were kept on a pretty tight rein by the butler and the formidable cook, and she could never have got away with it, even if she had the means to find the clothes and the jewellery – which, of course, she didn't.

Besides, he wasn't sure that he would have wanted it to happen. It was a stupid idea. He was alternately intrigued by it and angry with himself for even considering it. Parading the girl in company as if she were some kind of puppet for his amusement was all wrong. She deserved more than that.

God, what was he thinking of! She was a bloody kitchen maid, one of the servants, and nothing more. Lance put her strictly out of his mind and got on with the business of the day. There was some paperwork to deal with in his study, which took some of the load from his father, but as he worked it only served to dull his brain further, so he eventually abandoned all thought of work.

After a light lunch, he changed into his riding clothes and strode towards the stables, determined to think of Cherry O'Neil as just another conquest who meant nothing to him. He wished he'd never asked her name, though, because she became all too real whenever he thought of it. He saddled up Noble and led him outside, and once the stable boy had helped him mount, he trotted the horse away from the estate grounds and on towards Clifton Downs where he could let the animal have his head and feel the wind in his face, and rid himself of the wild notion that a kitchen maid could ever pass as a lady.

'Did you see him?' Paula asked Cherry slyly, early that afternoon when they had slipped outside the pantry room for a few minutes to get some air into their lungs instead of the pungent smell of the silver polish.

'Who?' asked Cherry vaguely.

'Don't give me that innocent look, Cherry O'Neil! You know who! His lordship, of course, going out to the stables to ride his nag.'

'He's not "his lordship", and he won't be Lord Melchoir until his father dies,' Cherry corrected her. Without thinking, she added, 'And the horse is not a nag. His name's Noble and he's a thoroughbred.'

Paula grabbed hold of her and bundled her back inside the pantry room, where she held on tightly to her shoulders, forcing Cherry to face her. For a slightly built girl, she was surprisingly strong when she needed to be.

'And just how did you come to know anything about that horse, may I ask? I *knew* there was more to it last night! I didn't dream about being left alone in the motor, did I? You went off with him, didn't you? Don't lie to me, Cherry.'

Cherry gave a shrug. 'Oh well, what if I did? It was only for a few minutes, and you were dead to the world. You didn't come to any harm.'

'But did *you*? You know what I mean . . .'

'Of course I didn't. He was the perfect gentleman as you would expect,' she said crossly. She pulled away from Paula and turned back to the polishing table, grabbing a handful of spoons that had already dried white with the polish and rubbed them with a cloth as if her life depended on it.

Paula's voice relaxed a little from its earlier quivering excitement.

'Oh well, as long as he didn't try anything on. I don't know what was so interesting about getting up close to a horse, though. Nasty, smelly things, if you ask me.'

'Well, I didn't ask you,' Cherry retorted.

This was just what she didn't want. The aura of last night's encounter was still magical in her mind, and she simply refused to think badly about any part of it. For that small space of time, the man of her dreams had wanted her as much as she wanted him, and she was not going to let anything spoil it, least of all by dissecting every moment with Paula. She rubbed even more furiously at the silver, trying to find the usual satisfaction in seeing it come to gleaming life in her hands, but somehow failing. She should never have let her words run away with her and mentioned what she knew about Lance's horse. Trying to be too clever, as always, she thought in annoyance.

They worked in silence for a while until Paula could stand it no longer.

'Look, Cherry, I'm sorry if I upset you. I know you wouldn't do anything foolish. You've got far too much common sense for that, and you always said I'd be the one that blokes would take advantage of, didn't you? That's why you've always looked after me like a sister.'

'Oh, for goodness' sake, let's forget it,' Cherry said, embarrassed at the way the girl was going on, when she knew she was the foolish one. 'We'd better get as much done as we can now, because Cook's sending us into town to buy some extra dry goods later, and she'll skin our hides if it looks as if we've been slacking.'

It was enough to make Paula work more diligently, and enough to make Cherry feel shamefaced at the way she was deceiving her friend. But it was better that way. There was no need to tell her everything when there was nothing to tell. Well, only the most important event in her life . . . But that was a secret she was keeping to herself, and nobody else need ever know.

She tried to think realistically, and to remember her place. Men like Captain Lance probably thought no more of a dalliance with a servant girl than having an occasional change of diet. He would have forgotten all about it by now, even if she hadn't, and couldn't, and never would.

By the time the girls were relieved from their silver-cleaning duties, they were glad to put on their boots and take the long walk into town to fetch the goods Cook needed. With any luck they might be able to catch a bus part of the way back, otherwise their arms would be hanging out of their sockets by the time they returned. The majority of the kitchen supplies were delivered once a week, and there was always a good assortment of vegetables in the kitchen garden to suit most of the household's needs, but occasionally Cook decided she needed more, and when she needed it, she needed it *now*!

It was a pleasantly warm afternoon for late April, and it felt good to be out of the house and into the spring sunshine. Cherry had put Captain Lance firmly out of her mind by now, but they had another glimpse of him riding hard across the Downs, and it made her heart skip a beat that was almost painful, before it raced madly on. He sat astride the horse so magnificently, as if they were truly part of one another, and if ever man could be called beautiful, that was exactly what he was, she thought, a little incoherently.

'My God, you really are smitten, aren't you, girl?' she heard Paula say, noticing her look and her indrawn breath. 'You know no good will come of it, don't you?'

'Of course I know it,' Cherry replied in a slightly strangled voice. 'But you can't help your feelings, can you? Don't worry, I'll get over it. I'll have to.'

It hadn't been so hard to do when there were no more than occasional glances between them, and never the chance of meeting and talking properly. That was only foolish dreaming. But that was before last night, and last night had changed everything. He was no longer a stranger, a knight in shining armour who was completely unattainable . . . He was still that, of course, but he had also become flesh and blood in a more intimate way than Cherry could ever have dreamed about. In the most intimate way a man could be to a woman. She knew his body, just as he knew hers. She drew in her breath again, reliving for one blissful moment that sensational feeling of oneness with another human being that she had never known before.

'Well, you'd better get over it,' Paula said grimly. 'It can't be very long before they marry him off and then you'll have to put up with seeing him bring a bride to the house, and eventually having kids of his own.'

Cherry felt her heart flip in a less than comfortable manner. 'I wish you hadn't said that, Paula. But I'll deal with it when it happens.'

'What will you do? Hand in your notice and leave me to it?'

Paula teased, not really believing it for a minute until she saw Cherry's face. 'You wouldn't, would you?'

Whatever Cherry might have said to that was left in the air as they both saw a familiar figure swaggering towards them across the Downs.

'Oh Lord, what does he want now?' Cherry muttered.

'Don't give him anything, Cherry. He's big enough and ugly enough to earn his own money.'

'He's that all right,' Cherry said with a grin as her brother sidled up to them and stood with his legs apart and his hands on his hips. There was a swelling beneath his left eye and his lip was cut, which could have accounted for his unshaven and generally unkempt appearance, Cherry thought, prepared to give him the benefit of the doubt.

'Well, here's a sight for sore eyes,' Brian O'Neil said as best he could, considering how his lip smarted with every word. 'Where are you two off to this fine afternoon?'

'We're going to get some groceries for Cook, so we haven't got time to stop and chit-chat, Brian,' Cherry said crisply.

His face darkened. 'Is that any way to talk to your only brother? Aren't you even going to ask how I am?'

Paula spoke up. 'I think we can see how you are. What was it this time? A run-in with a seaman at the waterfront, or trying to dodge a constable?'

He turned his attention to her, his eyes cold and full of dislike. 'Why don't you mind your own business? I don't want anything, Miss Know-it-all. This is between me and my sister.'

Cherry put her hand on Paula's arm. 'Well, since I don't know what it is you want, Paula's got a perfect right to say what she thinks. It's a free country, in case you hadn't noticed.'

'I know all about that, and I haven't had a run-in with anybody, except the bloke I was fighting last night, and for your information he came off worst, despite the way I look. So I've got a few quid in my pocket and don't need your handouts. I was only saying hello, since I saw the two of you tripping across the Downs, and now I'll say goodbye!'

He strode off in the opposite direction, and Paula giggled.

'For a cheapskate like him, he can put on a few airs and graces when he likes, can't he? Not like you, mind. He can't talk the talk.'

'Oh, well, let's just be thankful he wasn't on the scrounge for once,' Cherry said as casually as she could.

She admitted that the small encounter had unsettled her as always. There was never any knowing what kind of mood her brother was going to be in, and she was just glad to hear him say he didn't need anything from her – this time, at least. Whenever he was skint he was just as likely to turn up at Melchoir House, annoying Cook and scaring the housemaids with his appearance, and she always felt obliged to give him some of her paltry wages, just to get rid of him.

But seeing him always made her remember who she was, and the stock that she came from. She might be able to talk the talk, as Paula put it, putting on different accents – and not just Lady Melchoir's – to amuse the other servants, but it made no difference to who she was. She was the daughter of a working-class couple, and as far as the arrogant lady of the house was concerned, she was a nobody. Cherry tightened her lips and squared her shoulders, knowing there was nothing she could do to change that, so she might as well make the best of it.

'Are you all right, Cherry?' Paula said nervously. 'Only you're walking so fast now, my feet are hardly touching the ground, trying to keep with you.'

'Sorry,' she said, slowing down. 'It's just our Brian. You know how he gets to me, even when I don't want him to.'

'I don't know what you can do about that, but I know it makes me glad I haven't got a brother. You can't ignore him completely though, can you? He's your flesh and blood after all.'

'I know,' Cherry said with a sigh, and felt her eyes unexpectedly blur for a moment. 'There was even a time, when I was very small, when I thought the sun shone out of his backside. He was just my big brother, and he hadn't taken up the bare-knuckle fighting then. That was before Dad was killed, and he went a bit wild after that. Still, we don't want to spend the afternoon talking about him,' she said determinedly.

'But you'll always have a soft spot for him, won't you?'

Cherry laughed. 'Don't be so daft! You know very well I can't stand the sight of him most of the time!'

Despite her protests, she thought ruefully that Paula was probably right. People said that blood was thicker than water, and you couldn't change your family. If only he didn't keep turning up like the proverbial bad penny. If only he looked reasonably normal when he did so, and not covered in cuts and bruises, which made him look more like a thug, yet didn't seem to worry him at all! Life was far too full of 'if onlys', however, and now she felt guilty for even thinking that way about him at all, damn it!

It was a relief when they reached the supply store and collected the goods that Cook wanted, and she could think of something other than her brother. The shopkeeper knew them well and greeted them cheerfully.

'From the size of the next order that's been sent, it looks as if there's going to be a big shindig at your place sometime soon,' he said, ready for a bit of gossip as usual. 'What's it to be – is young Captain Melchoir getting himself engaged at last? He'll be a catch for anyone, what with his good looks and his family background. Any idea who the lucky woman is, girls?'

Cherry felt the roof of her mouth go dry at the artless question, and it was Paula who answered quickly.

'It's nothing like that, Mr Forester. It'll be Lord Melchoir's sixty-fifth birthday on May the eighth, so it's going to be his birthday party.'

'Lord love us, it's all right for some, isn't it?' the man said. 'I daresay the likes of you and me would be happy enough to make do with an iced bun or two when our birthdays come around. Parties are all right for young 'uns, but I suppose the aristocracy see things differently – as well as having the money to pay for it.'

With every word he said, Cherry was more and more aware of the distance between the privileged lives of the Melchoir family and her own. She knew it every single day when she did her menial kitchen maid tasks, but Mr Forester only emphasized it more. Most of the time she accepted it, because that was the way it was, but last night their two worlds had collided in a spectacular way that she could never have dreamed about, a precious secret she shared with nobody else except Captain Lance.

Four

The night of Lord Melchoir's birthday party had arrived, and the gardens were decorated with Chinese lanterns, and fragrant with the scent of spring flowers. Motor cars were arriving, driven by the gentlemen in each group or by their chauffeurs. The sound of excited chatter filled the air as hosts and guests greeted each other, and cards and gifts were bestowed upon the man of the hour.

Below stairs there was a different kind of frantic activity. Cook was flustered as always, ordering everyone about in her efforts to get the food ready in good time. The first course consisted of smoked salmon and warm toast, followed by venison with port and redcurrant sauce, boiled potatoes, spring cabbage, carrots and onion gravy. The dessert course was a choice of a delicate lemon mousse to cleanse the palate, or a hot apple pie and fresh cream for those with a heartier appetite. It was all to be served with great precision and timing, sent up through the serving lift in huge tureens and served at the table under the direction of Mr Gerard. Wines and clarets would also be served according to everyone's taste.

Afterwards, when the party adjourned to the drawing room to drink coffee and liqueurs, a birthday cake would be served, adorned with the simple words *Happy Birthday* rather than referring directly to Lord Melchoir's age. Mr Gerard had decreed that this would be the time for the kitchen staff to take a sneaky look through the doors to see the company's finery and their after-dinner entertainment. As usual, one or other of the guests would have already agreed to take part, either with a tune on the piano, or a song, or to recite a poem. Very often a humorous poem or limerick would have been written specially, in honour of the host and the occasion.

'It's all right for some, isn't it? The smell of all this food fair makes my mouth water,' Paula breathed to Cherry, when the bulk of the work had finally been done. The first course dishes had

already been sent up to the dining room, the second course was
ready to be delivered as soon as the empty dishes were returned,
and then they could all breathe a small sigh of relief.

'Don't you worry, my girls,' Cook said, more expansive now
that everything was under control. 'We'll have our own bit of
dinner when them upstairs have finished theirs, so you just be
grateful that at least you won't starve! There's a lot to be said for
being in service in a good house. There might even be a drop
of wine for us if Mr Gerard feels inclined enough to bring up
a bottle from the cellar,' she added with a wink.

'I'm not sure I feel like eating or drinking anything,' Cherry
said. 'It all smells wonderful, Cook, but it's been enough to fill
my stomach already.'

The woman looked at her quizzically. 'And you with such a
good appetite as a rule! You're not ill, are you? The day when
any of you girls says no to my cooking will be the day I pack
up my pots and pans.'

'I'm not ill,' Cherry told her. 'I just feel full already, that's all.'

'Well, that's what comes of picking when you should have
waited for a proper meal,' Cook went on. 'But I guarantee that
by the time the nobs have finished theirs, you'll be thinking twice
about it.'

Cherry doubted it. She had had an uncomfortably full feeling
in her stomach all day, and even longer than that if she thought
about it. But she didn't really care to think about it too much,
because another thought had also occurred to her lately, and one
that was likely to send her off into a bundle of nerves. It wasn't
a good thought, and so far she hadn't confided any of it to Paula.
If what she feared came true, everyone would know it soon
enough. But as always, she willed the thought away before it was
properly formed in her head.

She wished she hadn't mentioned this evening to her brother
the last time she had seen him, because he just might turn up
to have a free meal with them, and she didn't feel like hearing
his jokes, which were usually a bit too saucy for comfort. But
for some reason that Cherry couldn't fathom, Cook had taken a
bit of a motherly shine to Brian O'Neil and thought he was a
brave young man for doing what he did, so when he turned up
he was never sent packing.

Cook was even tickled by his new name, although Cherry knew very well that Mr Gerard thought it more common than appropriate. Knuckles O'Neil, indeed! She admitted it had a certain swing to it, but she could just imagine her mum giving him a swipe around the ears if she had known of it. Cherry gave a small shiver. She didn't consciously think of her mum too often these days, but when she did it always sent a wave of sadness through her.

'What's up with you today?' Paula demanded a little later when the first course dishes had been returned, and she and Cherry had set about washing them up in the big stone scullery sink. 'I can tell there's something. I thought you'd be excited about going upstairs to take a look at the party, especially to see your precious Captain Lance, but you haven't said a word about it – nor about him lately, come to that.'

'Maybe it's because I'm not so keen to see how other folk live when it's out of our reach. We don't belong with them, and our place is here.'

Paula's arms were up to the elbows in soapy water. She stopped swishing it about for a moment, and then she yelped as Cherry dumped a pile of dirty dishes into the sink, sending the soapsuds flying up into Paula's face.

'What did you do that for? Don't take it out on me because you weren't born with a silver spoon in your mouth. I don't know what's got into you lately, Cherry. Besides, we're all looking forward to later on, and relying on you giving us all a show of our own, mind, aping the plum-in-the-mouth talk from upstairs, so you'd better not disappoint us!' She wiped her face with her sleeve and glared at Cherry.

'Well, perhaps I won't feel like doing it,' Cherry snapped. 'Perhaps it's wrong to mock our betters, anyway.'

'God Almighty, now you're getting really stupid. Since when did it do them any harm? You're getting a bit above yourself, talking like that.'

Cherry gave in as she knew she would. 'All right, I'll see how I feel when the time comes. I can't help it if I feel out of sorts, can I? Anyway, right now, we've got better things to do, so let's get on with washing these dishes.'

Paula's eyes were suddenly suspicious. 'You're never out of sorts except when you've got your monthly, and I'd know if it was that. You ain't . . . Oh, my good God, you ain't late, are you, Cherry?'

'Maybe a couple of days, that's all. That's probably why I've got the gut's ache. The cramps have been griping me all day.'

'Well, as long as you're sure that's all it is!'

'Of course I am, so stop making such a fuss,' Cherry snapped. 'I wish I'd never said anything, so forget it.'

She wished it was as easy to forget it herself, but the unwelcome thought kept nagging her. If she really was up the spout, God knew what she would do. But you didn't get caught from one encounter, did you? Not from the first time you did it. She constantly told herself that it had been such a brief, fumbling few minutes that it was unlikely that anything could have happened. She tried to convince herself with all the old wives' tales she had ever heard.

Anyway, there was too much work to do tonight to dwell on something that might never happen. The dirty dishes kept coming, and she and Paula took turns in the washing and drying, until her arms ached, and she felt more like going to bed than having a glimpse of the gentry enjoying themselves. But if she was the only one to say she didn't want to do it, there would be a hue and cry, especially when there was their own dinner to come later, and she was expected to put on her usual mimic show for them to laugh and jeer at. She was a little star, Cook always told her admiringly, and at least it was something she could do that the others couldn't.

As another cramp twisted her gut, she reminded herself that this was probably how actresses on the stage must feel sometimes, when they were out of sorts and would much prefer to be tucked up in bed rather than perform. But they didn't have any choice when they had a large audience waiting for them, and neither did she. Her audience might be far smaller and far more modest, but Cook and the rest of them still enjoyed her act. In fact, she knew damn well it was the one time she had a bit of extra status among them. She gritted her teeth and told herself not to be so selfish, because they had all had a blooming hard time below stairs in getting ready for tonight, and she wasn't going to disappoint them. She'd act her blooming heart out, if she had to.

*   *   *

Lord Melchoir was well aware that the kitchen staff made their rare little jaunts upstairs on these occasions, and after much persuasion, his wife had agreed that the drawing-room door should be left ajar at such times. So by the time all the kitchen duties were finished, and their own dinner was simmering nicely on the stove, they were finally allowed to take a peek at the jollifications upstairs.

The party guests were well away with good food and drink by now, and a portly gentleman was coming to the end of reciting a very long and well-known music-hall poem called 'Albert and the Lion', which had them all shrieking with laughter and applauding madly at the end of it. Any upper-class inhibitions had obviously been loosened long ago.

'Poor Albert,' Paula whispered in Cherry's ear as they jostled to get a good look at the company in their finery. 'It's a funny poem, but nobody thinks about the kid, do they?'

Cherry wasn't listening. She was more interested in the fact that Captain Lance was sitting very close to a stick-thin and very fashionable young woman with blonde hair, who was wearing a lilac-coloured, fringed silk frock and a band of matching silk around her head fastened with a short peacock feather. She wore strings of pearls that reached almost to her waist. Her skin was pale and white, including her hands, with fingernails that were long and well-manicured and had probably never seen a day's work. She could have been one of those elegant models in a magazine, or a snotty-nosed mannequin in a shop window, Cherry thought, with an acute surge of jealousy. As Lance leaned towards the girl and said something to amuse her, Cherry heard her tinkling laughter, followed by whatever she was saying in a high-pitched, educated voice, without the merest hint of a Bristol accent.

By now Cherry felt hot and lumpy from all her exertions below stairs, and her own grey dress seemed to strain against her bosoms that would never be as flat as that other girl's, who was exactly the type of chinless society girl that Lord and Lady Melchoir would want to see married to their son, she thought, torturing herself even more. But why shouldn't this girl be his choice too? It was never on the cards that Lance was the one for *her*. Never in a million years. He had to get married to some-body, some time, and she certainly didn't fancy being around on the day of *those* celebrations!

'That's Lord Hetherington's daughter,' one of the housemaids whispered, giving Cherry a nudge. 'She's a corker, isn't she? I think her name's Cynthia Hetherington, and I reckon Captain Lance has got his eye on her all right. They'd be quite a match, what with him so dark and dashing, and her so fair. I can just see the pictures in the society magazines.'

As she prattled on, Cherry felt sick. The atmosphere in the house was very warm tonight, and with so many people in the drawing room and the small crowd of kitchen staff pushing ever forward for a good view, she was beginning to feel stifled. She made a sudden movement to get away, and as she did so, it was at that moment that Lance Melchoir looked up and saw her. It gave Cherry a weird sensation. It was as though for that split second there was nobody else in the world but the two of them as their glances locked. She was sure she saw a flicker of recognition in his eyes, just for a moment, but she doubted very much that he had the same feeling as she did, because almost immediately he had turned his head to hear something his companion was saying, and Cherry's eyes smarted at her own foolishness.

'I think I've had enough,' she almost gasped to Paula. 'I need some air.'

She pushed past the others, and Paula followed her down the long staircase and into their own domain. Once there, Cherry rushed for the kitchen door and went outside into the garden, to breathe in great gulps of the soft evening air since she was in danger of throwing up and disgracing herself. She couldn't keep still, and she walked around in agitation, unable to stop her thoughts winging ahead to the thought of seeing Captain Lance bringing the Honourable Cynthia Hetherington home as his bride, with their photographs splashed across the society magazines. She would definitely have to leave if that happened, she thought almost hysterically, steeped in misery and melodrama.

'You don't want to take any notice of what that stupid Gwen says, if that's what's bothering you,' Paula said roughly, referring to the housemaid, and sensing Cherry's feelings. 'She don't know nothing, and she's away with the fairies half the time.'

'Like me, you mean,' Cherry said with a small sob.

Paula sighed. 'Look, Cherry, I know you couldn't help falling for him, but you knew nothing was ever going to come of it, didn't you? You didn't expect him to stay a bachelor for ever, either. That's not what the gentry do, is it? They have to find a wife for their offspring, and even if the wife's a cold fish, the bloke just finds himself some other bit of pleasure on the side. That's how their sort live, and there's nothing you can do about it.'

'Well, it's not how I was brought up – nor you, neither, I bet,' Cherry said savagely. 'I wouldn't want to be just anybody's bit of pleasure on the side.'

'Well, you ain't going to be Captain Lance's wife, neither. Not even if you was in the pudding club, so get that stupid idea right out of your head.'

'But what if I *could* be?' Cherry said forcefully. 'What would I do then, Paula?'

Paula sniffed, not prepared to accept for a moment that it could be true. 'You could always ask him to make an honest woman of you, but the nobs would never believe you, and they'd think you were just trying to get money out of them because you'd been playing around. Most likely you'd be packed off in disgrace and have to fend for yourself and I'd never see you again. But since none of it's going to happen, just shut up about it and let's go back inside before the rest of them come down and wonder where we are. I'm hungry even if you're not!'

She sounded so forceful and so positive that Cherry found her nerves relaxing the smallest amount. Trust Paula to put it all into perspective, and it was only her vivid imagination that was making her talk so daft. She linked arms with her friend and went back to the kitchen, determined to put it all behind her for tonight, anyway, especially to forget any idea that Captain Lance might be attracted to some blonde twig, and to be ready to be her usual entertaining self after their meal.

Neither of them heard the stealthy movements in the bushes behind them as they went back indoors. Neither of them was aware that Brian 'Knuckles' O'Neil had arrived on the scene hoping for a free dinner and maybe a drink or too, and a chance to sleep it off in the stables. But right now he was relatively sober, and mulling over in his mind everything he had just heard. If he had got his assumptions right from what he'd overheard, the son of the house had had it away with his prissy sister, and now it sounded like she might even be in the pudding club. Brian's eyes sparkled with the possibilities the news had given him, but it needed a lot of thinking over, without doing anything rushed. For the time being, he was going to watch his sister closely. She had always been a well-rounded girl, but it would be useful to see if there was any hint of a little extra bump appearing beneath her dress.

A few hours later, all the party guests had gone home, and Lance was on the balcony outside the drawing room, smoking a last cigar, and glad to be alone for a while. It had been a good party, and they had done the old boy proud on his sixty-fifth birthday. He drew on the fragrant Havana, smiling to himself as he remembered the less than subtle attempts on his mother's part to push him near to one or other of the pretty young women guests, and towards one in particular, whose parents had even more wealth than his own.

But whatever his mother's hopes, he had no intention of marrying the Hetherington girl. She was pleasant enough company, but as shallow as a drop of piss on mud, he thought, the amount of drink he had imbibed that evening making his thoughts coarser than usual. He knew he was being unkind to the daughter of one of his father's old friends, but to hell with that. The girl was so skinny she'd end up thinner than cardboard the minute a fellow lay on her, and she'd need signposts to mark out the relevant parts of her body. It wasn't a prospect that appealed to him. A red-blooded man needed more than that in a woman.

Not even for his father's sake, and especially not for his mother's, did he intend getting wed to a woman of their choice just for the convenience of carrying on the Melchoir name. It might be against the notions of well-heeled families like his own, but when he married, it would be for love, and nothing less.

He listened to his own thoughts with something like amazement, wondering where the devil all this poetic and romantic nonsense was coming from. What did love have to do with a good marriage? It never lasted, anyway. He'd seen enough evidence of that among his parents' friends and his own contemporaries. He'd seen chaps in the army under his command who had married in haste because of love, and then been cut down to die in blood and filth, leaving him and officers like him to write the trite words that told a grieving young widow that their husbands had been killed instantly without pain, and always like a hero. It had been hard enough to do that, let alone receive the occasional grateful letter back from the widow, usually written in less than grammatical sentences, but filled with shock and grief nevertheless.

It was one of the duties of an officer that was never talked about, but it had often turned his stomach to receive their pathetic gratitude, and it had hardened him, as it had hardened everyone in that war to end all wars, even though he himself had been involved in it for so short a time.

No, marrying solely for love was a fool's game. It was more likely to be a mutual attraction that produced the necessary offspring. Too many couples he knew lived virtually separate lives within the outwardly respectable bounds of the marriage contract. If it was a sad fact of life, it was also a cynical one, but folk with enough wealth could afford these little extras that did nobody any harm.

On the drawing-room balcony now, he blew smoke rings into the air and watched them dissipate and then disappear. He was about to go back inside and have a last tot of brandy before he went to bed, when he heard the strains of music floating out of the night, and of people singing. It came from somewhere below, and the evening air was so still that it reached him easily, coupled with the distant sounds of laughter that followed. Lance smiled wryly. The servants were clearly enjoying themselves in their own way, and it was probably far more lively than some of his own evening's entertainment. Despite the last hour or so, when most of them had finally managed to let their hair down, it had still been quite a stilted affair, due in no small part to his blessed mother's keen eye on the young fillies in the party.

That she had finally decided on Cynthia Hetherington for him was so blatantly obvious it had made him want to vomit. But just to keep her off the scent he had paid extra attention to the vapid Cynthia with no compunction whatsoever. He and Cynthia were old friends, and were never destined to be anything more, and he was perfectly sure that she had no more desire to marry

him than he had to marry her, because Cynthia had once made
it perfectly clear that she had no intention of marrying anybody
for years and years.

But if it kept his dear Mama quiet for a while to think they
were stuck on one another, so be it, and it had amused him to
flirt mildly with the girl, just for appearances' sake. If he had
thought for a minute that Cynthia was getting the wrong idea,
he would have stopped it at once. But he knew she was not, and
she had cheerfully joined in the game.

Lance leaned further forward on the balcony as the music
below stopped, filled with an irresistible curiosity to see what
these other folk got up to. He left the house silently and went
out into the gardens, ostensibly to continue his smoke and take
a turn before retiring for the night. In reality he was near enough
to the windows of the kitchens, open now to let out the heat
of the cooking, to hear what was happening and get a glimpse of
the fun. It had to be fun from the sound of raucous laughter
and applause now, and for a startled moment he thought his
mother must be there, reading them the riot act. But if that
were so, they wouldn't be laughing, would they? And Lady
Melchoir would never lower herself to do such a thing in person
anyway.

He crept closer, feeling faintly ridiculous for skulking around
his own house, but curiosity was winning, and he got his first
glimpse of Cherry O'Neil holding court and giving the rest
of the servants a mock dressing-down in the finest mimicry of
his mother that wouldn't go amiss on any stage. The rest of
them cheered and egged her on, and he found himself wanting
to do the same. She was a fine specimen of womanhood, he
thought admiringly, with her copper hair loosened now. She
was looking decidedly warm from the earlier exertions of
the evening, and those fine breasts, which had no intention of
being confined in the current fashion, were peaked with her
own excitement.

Lance felt himself quickly getting warmer in certain regions,
and the sudden memory of that one night in the hayloft, when
she had lain so deliciously beneath him, swept into his mind.
Whoever won this girl in marriage wouldn't go short of passion,
he found himself thinking.

A sudden rustling sound behind him made him withdraw quickly from the vicinity of the kitchen windows. If one of the stable lads was hovering about, he certainly didn't want to be caught gawping at his own servants.

'She's a fine bit of stuff, ain't she?' he heard a rough-edged voice say close by, and he finally registered that there had been footsteps following him. 'A man could do a lot worse, wouldn't you say, sir?'

Lance frowned. The echo of his own thoughts from the mouth of this ruffian, whoever he was, didn't sit comfortably on him. He snapped as loudly as he could, not wanting to alert the servants indoors.

'What are you doing here? Get away from this estate at once or I shall call the constables and have you thrown in the Bridewell for the night.'

'Oh, I'm going, don't you worry, but I'm sure I shall be seeing you again some time, sir. You and me may have some unfinished business to discuss.'

'I don't know who the hell you are, but I can't think what possible business I could ever have to discuss with you. Now, are you leaving of your own accord or do I have you thrown out?' Lance demanded again.

Knuckles O'Neil reckoned it would take more than a namby-pamby snob to get the better of him, despite the chap's reputed army training, but right now he had no desire to fight with him or put it to the test. He had bigger and better things to think about.

'There's no need for that,' he said sneeringly. 'But you might think about what you've been doing recently, and what the conse-quences might be.'

He swaggered off into the night, leaving Lance incensed by the chap's insolence and the underlying threat in his voice. The words were completely incomprehensible to him, but he was furious to have been caught like this, especially by some down-and-out. Everyone knew that servants in wealthy houses weren't averse to passing on the odd meal to the needy, and most owners turned a blind eye to it. But from what he could gauge, this ruffian had a powerful physique and didn't look as if he had been short of a good meal.

Quickly, Lance turned away and went back inside the safety of his own four walls, hardly knowing why he should be thinking of them in such terms. God knew he had nothing to fear from such a scoundrel, and once indoors, he had the final drink of brandy he had promised himself, and put the fellow right out of his mind before retiring for the night.

Five

'Now then, Lance, I want to have a serious talk with you,' Lady Melchoir said several days later, cornering him in the summer house.

He groaned, knowing all too well what this was going to be about. When his mother got that determined look on her face it meant one of two things. Either he had been caught out in some misdemeanour, which at his age would be faintly ridiculous to have his mother reprimanding him for, or it was about his matrimonial prospects. He guessed rightly that it would be about the latter.

'Whatever it is, can't it wait, Mother? I was about to take Noble for his exercise across the Downs.'

'No, it can't wait, and you're not dressed for riding, so you can stay here and talk to me for a while,' she snapped, eyeing his finely turned-out appearance. 'I want to know what you intend to do about Cynthia Hetherington.'

'I don't intend to do anything about her. I didn't know there was anything wrong with her that needed my attention. Is she ill? If so, she needs a doctor,' Lance replied innocently, knowing very well his casual attitude would annoy his mother, but unable to resist teasing her.

'Lance, please don't be so obtuse. You know very well what I mean. The girl has a pleasant manner and is quite attractive and obviously well-connected. You and she seemed to be getting along very well at your father's birthday party, and we both feel that she would be a suitable partner for you.'

'Oh, I see,' Lance said, feigning surprise. 'You want me to go into some kind of business partnership with her, do you? Well, I know she's interested in horses. Do you suggest that we start up a racing stable together or some such?'

Lady Melchoir stood up in annoyance. 'I most certainly do not. Really, Lance, you can be the most irritating young man sometimes. You know I would never be referring to a business partnership, and I shall get your father to talk some sense into you, since it's obvious that I can't. In any case, he should be the one dealing with this, man to man.'

Lance watched her walk stiffly back to the house, every inch of her unbending shape resembling the autocratic manner of Queen Mary. He felt momentarily sorry for mocking her, thinking, as he often did, that she had been born into the wrong age. She should have been a Victorian Mama, not one in the progressive first quarter of the twentieth century. Wanting to get a son married off in order to produce grandchildren – which was what this was all about – was as outdated as crinolines. It was also to secure the inheritance of the estate, of course, but for all his family pride in it, Melchoir House wasn't such an impressive pile as many other great houses, and Lance had no intention of marrying anyone just for the sake of it.

He stretched his legs in the summer house, relishing the sunshine before he went for a canter across the Downs, which had certainly been his plan for this fine May morning. He smiled to himself, remembering the scandalous look on his mother's face when he mentioned starting a racing stable with Cynthia as his business partner. Such a commercial venture would offend her sensibilities to the core and truly give her the Victorian vapours.

His face softened a little. He really shouldn't upset her so, but sometimes he was simply unable to resist teasing her. It gave a little fillip to his days, and he had to admit that he was becoming tired of the idle life he had been leading since giving up his commission. A man needed to have some purpose in his life, and he frequently felt that he had very little. No wonder the old music-hall turns had made such a mockery of the fine English gentleman strutting about his estate with nothing in his head but what to wear that day. It demeaned every one of them, and made them all sound like Little Lord Fauntleroys . . . but Lance had to admit that there was more that a bite of truth in their mocking songs.

The sound of female laughter caught his attention, and he left the summer house to stroll towards the stables, but also to follow the sound of the laughter, which was like a dose of fresh air in the lungs. It came from the kitchen garden, and he caught sight of Cherry O'Neil and her friend wrestling with one of the large damask tablecloths that had been used at the party, and trying to hang it over the washing line without much success so far. His heart gave an unexpected lurch at the sight of Cherry, arms lifted high with the weight of the wet fabric, and the upthrust of her breasts a delight to behold. God knew who had decreed the current fashion of flattening them to boyish proportions, when it was part of man's nature to want to bury his head between a pair of luscious mounds.

He caught his breath, wondering where such a thought had come from. It wasn't in his nature to be unduly coarse, although it wasn't unheard of either, he admitted. He realized Cherry's companion had seen him watching them, and was hissing something to her, since she had momentarily disappeared beneath the wet folds of the tablecloth. She emerged with her hair damp and her face flustered as she saw him too. He was too polite to turn and stride away, so he said the only thing that came into his head at that moment.

'Good morning to you. I trust you enjoyed your festivities the other night.'

Paula giggled uncertainly, too tongue-tied to reply, and Cherry knew it was up to her to say something, since it was ludicrous for the two of them to stand transfixed like a pair of idiots.

She gave the smallest nod. 'Thank you, sir, we did, and I hope you and your guests did the same, and that Lord Melchoir enjoyed his birthday,' she added.

She wasn't at all sure if this was the right thing to say, but she had said it now and he didn't look offended. She wished he would go away, since the heavy weight of the wet material was making her arms ache. Besides, she felt such a fool, standing here draped in a tablecloth, and she couldn't quite interpret the smile playing around his lips. Perhaps he thought she was a fool too, a fool for giving into him the way she had. Not that she had had much choice, except to cry rape, and to her shame she knew that such a thought had never entered her mind.

Her chin lifted. 'If you don't mind, sir, we do need to get on with our work,' she heard herself say, and to her horror she knew her voice had assumed a posher tone that almost matched his own.

'*Touché*, Cherry-Ripe,' he said with a laugh, and turned and walked away before he gave himself away and told her how delightful she looked with drips of water dampening her dress and apron and emphasizing those delicious curves still more.

'What the dickens did you talk to him like that for?' Paula said, almost howling with laughter once they were on their own and had finally managed to haul the huge tablecloth over the washing line. 'He'll think you were taking the mick, and he'll probably have you sacked.'

'No, he won't,' Cherry said, with an almost visionary sense of Lance Melchoir's feelings. 'He'll think I'm clever and amusing and that there's more to me than just a kitchen maid.'

She pushed the wooden clothes pegs over the cloth almost viciously, because he knew that all right. He knew it already. He knew she was nothing more than a trollop, ready to open her legs when she saw a good opportunity to get a few quid out of a gent for the privilege. But it hadn't been like that. There had been tender moments between them, and there had never been any thought of money on either side, and she shouldn't condemn herself so.

As always, Paula brought her down to earth. 'Blimey, Cherry, you ain't stupid enough to think he really fancies you, are you? You'd better get those ideas right out of your head, because nothing's ever going to come of it. You saw that for yourself the other night, when he was fussing over that Hetherington tart, and we'll probably be hearing wedding bells soon.'

'I know,' Cherry said crossly. 'I was just being daft, that's all.'

But she couldn't deny that her heart had turned over at Paula's last words, and she repeated what she had already told herself. She couldn't bear it if Lance married the Honourable Cynthia Hetherington, or anybody else, but if and when it happened, as it surely would, realistically she would simply have to grin and bear it, or change her job.

As she and Paula got on with the rest of their morning's work, she tried not to think of such a bleak prospect as leaving Melchoir House. She had been here for nearly half of her life now, and the people she worked with were her family, since she had no other except for her brother. And he didn't count for much. Before her mum died, for all that she had begged Brian to look after her, she could count on the fingers of one hand the times he had shown up without wanting something. She would miss this house and everything about it so much if she ever had to leave it, not least Paula, who was like a sister to her.

She gave her an unexpected hug as they finally went back indoors with the empty laundry basket and with the washing blowing merrily on the line.

'What was that for?' Paula said suspiciously. 'You ain't going queer, are you? I've heard of girls having crushes on other girls, but I never thought you was one of them.'

Cherry laughed. 'Not likely! Give me a bloke any day! I just decided it was good to be alive on this lovely day, that's all.'

'Thank goodness for that. At least you seem in better spirits than you have been lately. Got rid of the gut's ache, have you?'

'More or less,' Cherry said airily, having decided during many sleepless nights that there was no use worrying over something that might never happen. And no use worrying Paula with it, either, who would never stop probing until she got every little hour-by-hour detail of anything happening below yet. It hadn't, but that was nobody's business but her own.

'I'm thinking of getting my hair cut,' she announced later. 'I'm tired of having it all hanging down my neck and it's old-fashioned now, so I'm going to have it bobbed like that girl at the party the other night.'

Paula's mouth fell open. 'Blimey, you're not trying to turn into her, are you, Cherry?'

'Of course not. I just want to be up to date and look a bit smarter, that's all. What's wrong with that? Gwen's had hers done, so why don't we both do it? I dare you. Are you game?'

'Well, perhaps,' Paula said warily. 'But you always said you'd never have it cut just to suit the current fashion, so don't start crying when you're shorn like a sheep and you see it all on the floor ready to be sold for wig-making.'

Cherry shrugged. 'So I've changed my mind. And at least I'll be doing something for some poor soul who needs a wig, won't I!'

'Or it'll be on the head of some cheap actress who fancies herself with red hair, more like,' Paula retorted.

But Cherry had made up her mind now. And of course she damn well wanted to have her hair bobbed to be as fashionable as Cynthia Hetherington. It was all the rage nowadays, but because her glossy long red hair had always been her pride and joy, she had resisted it for far too long. But that was pride talking, and pride never did anyone any good.

They had a couple of hours off that afternoon, so before Paula could change her mind, Cherry insisted that they went into town to the nearest hairdressing establishment and asked for the latest cut, just as if they were toffs who knew exactly what they were talking about, and visited such places every day. But she had to admit that it was just as Paula had said. As the first chunks of her hair were lopped off and fell to the floor, Cherry closed her eyes for a few minutes, for fear that she would cry out loud and tell the girl to stop at once. A fat lot of good that would be if she went rushing out of here with one side bobbed and the other side still hanging down past her shoulders. It had to continue now, and she gritted her teeth and let the girl do her work, guessing that Paula must be feeling the same as herself.

'There you are, miss,' the girl finally said. 'And you look a fair picture now, I must say. I hope you're pleased.'

Cherry stared at the girl in the mirror, hardly able to believe that she was looking at herself. Gone was the rumpled hair of the kitchen maid, often failing to escape the confining hair pins, and in its place was a girl with a sleek fashionable bob with a fringe that showed off her wide green eyes and made them glow. Or maybe that was just the thought of the effect this new Cherry O'Neil might have on a certain Captain Lance Melchoir!

'Blimey, Cherry, you look like a film star!' she heard Paula squeak.

She turned to look at her newly coiffed friend, anxiously waiting for a reaction, and smiled with approval.

'And you look a smasher as well. Cook will never recognize us when we go back. She'll think she's hiring two new girls, looking so smart that she'll have to raise their wages!'

'That'll be the day!'

But the teasing was enough to satisfy Paula, and they went out of the hairdressing establishment with linked arms, feeling ten feet tall and ready to face the world. If Cherry had ever imagined what a change of hairstyle could do she would have had it done long ago! It didn't just do something to your appearance, it gave

you confidence and changed the entire way you felt about yourself, and that was something that money couldn't buy.

On the same day, following the unwelcome talk with his mother,
Lance had changed into his riding clothes and was giving Noble
his ride across the Downs, trying to put the little incident with
her out of his mind. But for the life of him, he couldn't stop
comparing two girls who were as unlike one another as chalk and
cheese. On the one hand, there was the well-connected girl his
parents had now earmarked for him as being an admirably suitable bride; and on the other, there was that kitchen maid . . .

Cherry O'Neil, who in his own mind he thought of as Cherry-
Ripe, with all the delightful connotations it implied. Ripe in
shape and ripe for loving . . . as she certainly had been, he thought,
with a stab of pleasure in his loins. And just for an instant he
thought of the shock and horror on his mother's face if he ever
announced that Cherry O'Neil was the woman he intended to
marry.

The idea was so ridiculous that he laughed out loud, startling
several nursemaids out with their charges in their perambulators
on this glorious May morning. He nodded to them and received
their admiring smiles in return at the fine stance of the mounted
gentleman as he galloped on across the Downs, pushing such
stupid notions right out of his head.

Away in his rented lodgings in a seedy part of the city, Brian
'Knuckles' O'Neil was still lying in bed, even though it was
nearing midday, still trying to make some sense of what he thought
he'd overheard that night. By now, he was wondering if he had
really heard it at all. He had had a fair few bevvies with his pals
before lumbering up to the Melchoir estate feeling decidedly
squiffy already. Sleeping it off had done nothing to quell the
queasy feeling that there must be nigh on a regiment of soldiers
beating their drums inside his head. A few days later, they were
still hammering away at him.

But had it all been in his imagination, or had his sister all but
confessed to the pasty one that she'd had it away with the
snot-nosed captain? It seemed pretty far-fetched now, and his
recollections were making a mishmash of it all, but he knew he'd

come face to face with the bugger later on. At least that much was true. He'd been told to clear off or risk being thrown in the Bridewell, and he couldn't afford that, with another fight coming up soon. So he'd done the right thing, but it hadn't improved his temper, since it had also prevented him from having a bit of Cook's tasty meat pies and a swig of good ale, and a doze in the stables for the night. Instead of which he had staggered back to his lodgings with his head swimming, and fallen across his bed in his clothes, which was exactly the state he found himself in now.

He got up and sloshed some cold water over his face and neck to revive him a little, and with daylight common sense returned. No, it couldn't have happened. It was all in his imagination. Pity. If it had been true, what capital he could have made out of it! Still, . . . The hell of it was the remote possibility wouldn't leave him alone, and he decided to keep a closer watch on his sister over the next weeks. It wouldn't hurt to say he'd been remiss in caring for her – even to give her a few quid out of his winnings on the next fight, though perhaps that was going a bit too far. His natural feelings of self-preservation and looking out for number one quickly asserted themselves, and he decided a general pretence of affection was all that was needed. Who was to say she wouldn't even confide in him, if he seemed concerned that she didn't look too well? His thoughts ran on, until the throbbing in his head reminded him that too much thinking was bad for a bloke, and a hair of the dog was definitely what was needed.

It seemed as if the world and his wife was out in the city that day, he thought, scowling as he dodged the clattering wheels of a brewer's dray pulled by an enormous shire horse. You didn't want to get trampled under those hooves. They were very different from the sleek horses in the Melchoir stables. Fine looking beasts they were, probably Arabs and worth a bob or two, Brian thought, with his meagre knowledge of the animals he'd seen at travelling gypsy fairs. If ever the impossible happened and Cherry did get spliced to Lance Melchoir, he didn't think she'd see her brother left out in the cold. Which was why it was important that he kept in with her and didn't get her dander up the way he usually managed to do.

He vaguely remembered that he was due to have a meeting with his manager that night, but for now he intended to spend a few hours at the riverside pub, jawing with anybody who felt like sharing a yarn or two, and buying a pasty for his dinner from a stall. It wouldn't come up to Cook's standards, and God knew what kind of meat was inside it, but it filled his belly all the same. It also cleared his head a smidgen, and he finished off by taking a walk across the Downs so that Jake Gooding wouldn't think he had the shakes and would be good for nothing in the fight arena. That was the only drawback with having a bloody manager, he thought with another dark scowl. The bugger got you more money for your fights, but you weren't your own boss any more, and you had to obey his rules.

He pondered gloomily on the pros and cons of having Jake as his manager at all, and then his attention was caught by the sight of two young girls tripping across the Downs and giggling together. He could only see the back of them, but from the way they moved he could tell they were young and undoubtedly attractive. He liked the way the sunlight gleamed on the copper bob of the taller one, and the equally smart bobbed head of the other one. Brian flexed his muscles. A bit of banter was just what he needed to put his spirits back to rights. He crossed over the grass to where he could catch up with them, and felt the first doubts creep into his mind as he realized there was something familiar about them. When he came face to face with them, he knew the truth of it, and he gaped in astonishment.

'Christ Almighty, Cherry, what have you done to yourself?'

He saw her bristle, and remembered his intentions.

'What I mean to say is, you look a real bit of class, you and your friend. I wouldn't have known it was you. In fact, if you weren't my sister, I'd fancy you myself,' he added with a grin.

Cherry's first instinct to tell him to take a running jump was tempered by his apparently sincere admiration of her new look.

'It's nice of you to say so, Brian.'

'I mean it. You're a smashing-looking girl, Cherry, even if you are my sister, and so are you . . . uh . . . Paula. Are you going dancing tonight?'

'I don't think so,' Cherry said quickly, fending off any likelihood of her brother and any of his cronies being in the same place as herself. 'We thought of going to the flicks, didn't we, Paula?'

'That's right, the flicks,' Paula muttered.

'Enjoy it, then, and look after yourselves,' Brian said, and swaggered off, leaving Cherry frowning slightly.

'He's up to something. He didn't stay around long enough for me to work out what it is, but I don't trust him when he comes over all brotherly.'

'Oh well, at least he noticed our hair and was quite flattering about it, which was something.'

'You're too gullible, Paula, and I've known him too long to be taken in by any false flattery. No, he's planning something. I don't know what it is, but I know it's something.'

'Well, I'm more interested in what the rest of them are going to say about our new look, so don't let him put you off.'

It was worth the decision to have their hair cut and bobbed when they arrived back at the estate and walked into the kitchen. Gwen and Lucy, the two housemaids, were the first to see them, and they squealed with excitement, causing Cook to come bustling in to ask what all the fuss was about, and then her jaw dropped. It took a few seconds for her to compose herself and ask the inevitable question that was almost the same as Brian O'Neil's.

'My good God, what have you two maids been up to?'

'Don't you like it, Cook?' Cherry said, preening herself.

Cook considered, and then nodded. 'It's very nice if you want to put on airs and graces, and at least it makes you look neat and tidy, but don't go getting above yourselves. There's work to be done, and it's time you got on with it.'

Cherry and Paula laughed, knowing that they might have expected such a response, but they knew from the approval in Cook's eyes that she liked what she saw – even with the little barb that at least it gave them a neat and tidy appearance, which was intended to put them firmly in their place.

'We'll go and change into our working clothes,' Cherry assured her swiftly, 'and we'll be back here in a trice.'

Nothing could dampen her spirits now, and she couldn't help wondering what Lance Melchoir would think when he saw her again. Not for a moment was she going to admit to anyone that his opinion was what she craved the most, but it was true, all the same.

She might not have been so complacent had she known how her brother's devious mind was working now. Back in his lodgings that night, he thought of how classy his sister had looked that morning, with her hair newly bobbed and looking surprisingly good. With the right clothes she could almost pass as a lady. So that begged the question: was there some special reason for Cherry's changed appearance? He dismissed the fact that Paula had had her hair bobbed too. That she was a parrot of his sister was never in doubt.

No, there was definitely something behind it. And if he was devious, always out for what he could get, maybe his clever little sister was too. Maybe this new sophisticated look was a sprat to catch a mackerel, and in this case the mackerel was a certain Captain Lance Melchoir, heir to millions, if what he had learned in his kitchen forays with the talkative Cook was correct. And there was no better way to catch him than by Cherry getting herself up the spout.

His eyes gleamed, more sure than ever now that what he'd suspected was true. Of course she had to pretend to be terrified at the thought, in order to gain her gullible friend's sympathy, but he had to hand it to Cherry. They were more alike than he'd realized. As for Captain Lance, the poor sap probably didn't know it yet, but he was about to be caught in a trap, and before that happened, Brian 'Knuckles' O'Neil had every intention of helping himself to a little of the pot.

For a moment he contemplated going in league with his sister and working out a deal between them, but he dismissed it just as quickly. There had never been any love lost between them, and she would never agree to it. No, it was best to work alone. He'd give it a couple more weeks, so that by then there would be no turning back. He assumed that Cherry would also be working out how she was going to get around to letting the toff know he was going to be a daddy. But by then, Brian would have already given him the news, and threatened to expose him for the rat he was unless he paid over some cash to keep him quiet!

Six

True to their words, Cherry and Paula decided to go to the flicks that night. There was a weepie showing at the Gaumont, a film about a couple who had lost contact with one another years before, and had gone through plenty of traumatic moments and heart-searching, before they finally found one another again. It had them sobbing into their hankies along with most of the others in the cinema. By the time they all stood up for the strains of 'God save the King' there was plenty of hasty sniffling and swallowing all around. The girls had been so wrapped up in the film it was almost a surprise to see it was still daylight when they emerged outside, feeling a bit ridiculous, knowing they must have red eyes and blotched faces. Although it hardly mattered, since so did everybody else, and they walked quickly along the road to wait for the bus.

'Honestly, Paula, you are a nitwit. It's only make-believe,' Cherry finally said in exasperation when her friend was still bewailing how the hero had nearly drowned in a river before he was hauled out and delivered into the arms of his beloved. Any minute now she knew she'd be bawling too, but somebody had to be sensible.

'I know that,' said Paula, 'but they make it seem so real, and it was so lovely that they were going to be together at last.'

Cherry gave an impatient sigh. 'What you have to remember is that by the end of the picture, they'd both have gone back to their proper lives. Who knows what Valentino gets up to in his real life? He'd have gone off for a drink with his mates, or whatever they do in Hollywood, and she was hardly love's young dream, anyway. She would more than likely have gone home to a parcel of kids.'

Paula sniffed indignantly. 'For somebody who's so gone on Captain Lance, I sometimes think you don't have a romantic bone in your body, Cherry.'

'Yes, I have. I just prefer to know what's real and what isn't, that's all.'

Paula glanced at her as the bus came trundling along, and they climbed on board and found some seats in the general mêlée of passengers all trying to do the same thing.

'Talking about that, how are you?' she said meaningly. 'I know you told me to stop asking, but has anything happened down below yet?'

Cherry almost snapped her reply. 'Yes it has, if you must know. It was just before we came out, and we were in such a rush I didn't have the chance to mention it.'

'Well, that's a relief, isn't it? Though I must say you don't look exactly over the moon about it,' Paula said.

'That's because I've had the cramps all evening, and it didn't help to be sitting squashed-up in that fleapit all night. So now you know, and you can forget it.'

She tried to sound flippant, and of course she was relieved. It would have been disastrous if she really had been in the family way. She had hardly seen anything of Captain Lance lately, and she had the feeling he might be avoiding her. Which was totally absurd, because why should he think enough of her even to bother avoiding her? She was nothing to him and he was a very sociable person with plenty of friends in high places, while she was just a kitchen maid who had happened to be in the right place at the right time on one particular night.

Cherry had told herself over and over again that she had been foolish and irresponsible that night, and of course she was more than thankful that nothing bad had come of it. But deep inside, she also felt sad for something that might have been, even if it never was. The dragging feeling inside her now had nothing to do with the cramps, and more to do with a strange sense of loss. She admitted that there had been some little devil inside her that had wanted it to be true, no matter what the consequences – and *that* was madness, if you like. But to have had the prospect of holding her own precious baby in her arms, knowing that she and the man she loved had created it, had filled her with a sense of fulfilment she had never known before, and now it was all gone . . . and that was a secret she would never let on even to Paula.

Unwittingly, she had drooped in her seat on the crowded bus and she felt Paula's hand cover hers for a moment, mute with sympathy for the cramps. Her eyes prickled, wondering if her friend could have any idea of the turbulent feelings inside her. She felt a rush of affection for Paula, who was practically her shadow, and was still so innocently unaware of the passion inside Cherry, and never condemned her, no matter what.

'I'm all right,' she said, sitting up straighter. 'All that emotion in the pictures has made me tired, that's all. What with all that and the shock of seeing myself in the window of the bus every now and then, and wondering who the heck I am! Is that bleary-eyed dope with the fancy hairdo really me?'

She patted the new bob self-consciously, and Paula laughed, visibly relieved at her friend's self-mockery.

When they got back to the house, they found the kitchen staff all in a fluster.

'We're going to have the house to ourselves for the next couple of weeks, and it's to have a big spring-clean while the family is away,' Cook announced.

'What's happening, then? Where are they going?' Cherry exclaimed, not knowing what to make of this, and not liking the sound of it.

'It's going to take more than a couple of weeks to spring-clean the place from top to toe!' Paula gasped, clearly seeing the prospect of working even more hours than they did already.

'And we're not doing it all, neither!' Gwen put in, echoed by Lucy.

Mr Gerard took command. 'Now then, you girls, if you'll all stop your twittering and pestering us with questions you'll get the answers soon enough. Cook, I'll thank you for leaving it to me to explain.'

Cherry hid a smile as the woman backed down at once at the small reprimand. However much Cook reigned over the kitchen, she was still expected to know her place where the butler was concerned. Times may have moved on since the days of the Victorian kitchens, but not as far as Mr Gerard was concerned. But she was as surprised as the rest of them as they were told the news.

'Lord and Lady Melchoir and Captain Lance, together with a party of friends, are going to London to visit the Empire Exhibition at Wembley and to see some theatre performances. You'll have seen something about the exhibition in the newspapers and heard reports of it on the wireless. If you want to know anything more, I've got some pamphlets that one of my fellow butlers in one of the London houses has sent me, which you may borrow. Be sure to bring them back to me afterwards.'

It was hard to say which bit of news was more astonishing. The fact that the entire Melchoir family was going away, and to visit such an exciting and well-publicized exhibition that was drawing huge crowds of people, or the fact that Mr Gerard knew a fellow butler who worked in one of the London houses.

For Cherry and Paula the excitement of swooning over Rudolph Valentino at the pictures, and the continuing pleasure in their new appearances, were temporarily forgotten as the butler produced a small pile of pamphlets for them to read. As they all began chattering together, he held up his hand.

'I suggest you take several each and look at them in your rooms. And as for the spring-cleaning, Lady Melchoir has instructed me that a small firm of reliable and trustworthy outside cleaners will be engaged. I will oversee the work, as is proper in his Lordship's household, but we will also give them every assistance. Now, goodnight to you all.'

As he left the kitchen, the chattering began again, until Cook reminded them that it was late and that their voices carried, so they had better do as they were told and go to bed.

'Who does she think is going to hear us?' Paula grumbled as they went up the wooden staircase to their attic rooms. 'I'm sure their Lordships are well away in the land of nod by now, and Captain Lance is probably still at his club or wherever he goes of an evening. They won't be bothering about the likes of us, any more than they ever did!'

Cherry was hardly listening. All she could think of was that Lance was going away for two weeks. Even if she hardly saw him, the fact that he was here in the house brought him near in a strange way that would only make sense to people in love. Even if the love was one-sided. And the fact that the family was going with a party of friends did nothing to calm her, either. The Hetheringtons were old friends, and if Cynthia Hetherington was among the party, who knew what might come of this visit?

They might even come back to Bristol as an engaged couple, and if that happened they would have an elaborate engagement party, and then there would be a wedding . . .

The thought was enough to set her nerves on edge all over again, and she tried to concentrate her thoughts on the Empire Exhibition instead. Neither she nor Paula knew much about it. Cook had come over all patriotic with the newspaper publicity about it when it was first opened by the king and queen on St George's Day, but London was so far away, and since none of them had a snowball's chance in hell of ever seeing it, the interest had waned. But now Lance was going to see it, along with all his other toff friends, and probably in the company of Cynthia Hetherington too. If there was anything to make her realize even more how vastly different their lives were, this was it. And to her annoyance, she knew she was thinking about him all over again, when she was doing her best not to do so.

By the time she and Paula reached their room and shut their door she was firmly resolving to put any more ideas about Lance Melchoir out of her mind for good. And there was one very good way to do it. It was time she found a young man of her own, and one who was not so far out of her class.

'What are you thinking, Cherry? You've gone off into one of them trances. You're not sickening for something, are you?' she heard Paula say, and she realized the other girl was already sitting on her bed with some of the pamphlets scattered around her. Lord knew how Mr Gerard had acquired so many, but like most men of his ilk he was a keen follower of anything to do with royalty and tradition, and liked to air his knowledge of it all.

'I'm thinking it's all for show and a terrible waste of money, when there are still plenty of poor beggars on the streets trying to earn a crust selling matches and war souvenirs, that's what. The government never thinks about them, do they?' she snapped, still angry with herself for letting her own wild dreams carry her away.

Paula's eyes widened at this little outburst.

'Since when did you turn into such a do-gooder, for Gawd's sake?'

'I'm not. I just think it's a waste of good money when it could be put to far better use, that's all.'

'And you don't want to think of your precious Lance going off to London, especially if that other tart is in their party, so I'm guessing that's the real reason for your bad temper,' Paula said shrewdly.

'You talk too much. Give me some of those pamphlets and let's see what it's all about,' Cherry said, ignoring the obvious.

She undressed before she started to read them, all her pleasure in her new hairstyle, and the vague thought that Lance might even look at her differently now quickly evaporating. What was she thinking of? Because he was never going to see her as anything but a kitchen maid – and one who hadn't been averse to dropping her knickers, either. Her cheeks burned at the coarse thought. It had been thrilling and exciting at the time, and she had almost swooned with the thought that he had wanted her, but now she could see it for what it was – a cheap ending to a pleasant evening for him, and nothing more.

She tried to concentrate on the pamphlets again, and despite everything, her interest was caught by the details of the Empire Exhibition, which was intended to show Britain and her Empire in all its glory. There was even a replica building of the Taj Mahal in India, which could be seen across the lake. Cherry had never imagined what such a building could be like, and the printed sketch of it took her breath away, as did the brief history behind the monument. How sad that a man had built such a beautiful building for his dead wife, who had never even seen it.

She read on before she became too maudlin about a woman she had never known existed until now. So many countries were represented in the huge area, more than she had ever realized belonged to Britain, and it was anticipated that thousands of people would flock to see it, and all for their one shilling and sixpence entrance fee.

As Cherry read that little bit of information out loud, she also added cynically that this was where the government would get their money back.

'I daresay,' Paula said. 'Though I don't suppose the king and queen had to hand over their coppers, do you?'

'Shouldn't think so. Anyway, I've done enough reading for tonight and I'm going to sleep, or it'll be morning before we know it.'

But when they had turned out the light and settled down for the night, it was a long while before Cherry could sleep. In her mind's eye she imagined Lance at glittering society balls and fashionable theatres, accompanied by the lovely Cynthia Hetherington, or any one of a dozen other smart and sophisticated young ladies of the London set. The ladies would be dressed in silks and satins, ablaze with pearls and jewels. They would dance the night away in some elegant ballroom, and in the daytime they would gaze in wonder at the Empire exhibits, and with Lance's superior knowledge he would explain some of the finer points to every adoring companion. No matter how she tried, Cherry couldn't seem to stop torturing herself with these imaginary thoughts. He had never been hers, but now more than ever she knew she had lost him.

Brian O'Neil was still considering what words to use in the letter he was going to send to the Melchoir bugger. It would have to be forceful enough, and it needed to sound as if he was sure of his facts. It would seem as if his sister had gone to him in great distress about her condition and begged him to help her. She would have told him how she had been terrified and unable to fight off such a powerfully built young man. The threat would be that unless Captain Melchoir paid Brian what he asked for, he would go to the newspapers and expose him for the rat that he was in taking advantage of an innocent young girl in his employ.

That would be the gist of it, but O'Neil had never been a great letter-writer, and he knew it needed to be just right to put the bugger in a panic, thinking his family's good name was going to be smeared across the newspapers. He knew just how much these toffs fussed about their good name.

He felt briefly sorry for Cherry. He was fond enough of his sister, even though they had never been exactly close. If the worst came to it, though, he would try not to mention her name to the newspapers at all, unless some hack wormed it out of him. But then again, if the silly little bitch hadn't done the dirty with the Melchoir chap in the first place, this outcome would never have happened.

He consoled himself by thinking that if he was paid well for his silence, he'd see his sister right, and her name need never come into it. He chose not to think of what might happen if and when the blackguard himself confronted her, and the ugly scene that would follow, with her screaming and sobbing. If she had to leave her job, there were plenty of others, and toffs were always ready to employ a clean-looking girl to do their dirty work, especially one looking as smart as she did now. Anyway, he might even pay for her to get rid of the kid, and that would solve everything.

Armed with a pad of paper and a pencil Brian wrote half a dozen letters before he was finally satisfied with the result, and he set it aside for now until he decided on the best day to post it. In his eagerness to get some decent cash for himself, he had abandoned the idea of eyeing up his sister from time to time to see if her belly was showing the telltale signs.

By the time he posted his letter, he was mentally rubbing his hands at the prospect, unaware that it would be a while before it reached its recipient, who was even now driving the Rolls Royce to London and anticipating two weeks of pure pleasure with his family and friends.

Before leaving for London, Lance had instructed one of the grooms to be sure to exercise Noble every day as usual. The horse needed his regular gallops over the Downs to keep him in fine fettle. And since he was passing near the servants' quarters he couldn't resist a glance over at the kitchen gardens, where Cherry O'Neil was often to be seen cutting or pulling up vegetables or hanging out washing. He had avoided looking her way for days now, but he knew she would have heard about the family's departure for London, and he couldn't resist teasing her about going to London to visit the queen.

He couldn't see her at first. There was only a girl with short bobbed hair that shone coppery in the sunlight. She was bending over the vegetable patch, and Lance assumed that there had been more staff taken on below stairs for the annual spring-cleaning. It was only when she straightened up, as if some small move-ment had alerted her to someone's presence, that she turned around. Then he saw that it was Cherry O'Neil.

But what a different Cherry she was! She had been a lovely

and comely young woman before, but now she took his breath away. For a moment he simply couldn't believe what he was seeing, and if it hadn't been completely absurd for a gentleman to be dumbstruck at the sight of a kitchen maid, that's what he would have called himself. Gone was the long coppery hair that had hung below her shoulders when it wasn't neatly dressed for work, and instead was the sleek short bob and the heavy fringe of the flapper girl.

'Good morning!' he said, feeling as gauche as a newborn lamb for gaping at her so obviously, and completely flummoxed at finding anything more scintillating to say at that moment.

But she looked so different . . . despite her workaday clothes, there was an elegance about her that he had hardly registered before. It had something to do with the set of her shoulders and the way she carried herself . . . and he realized he was standing there like an idiot as he saw a smile curve around her lips.

'Well, aren't you going to ask me what I've done to myself?' Cherry said, more boldly than she felt, considering his scrutiny. 'Everybody asks the same question, so I suppose you're thinking the same . . . *sir*,' she added.

'I can see what you've done to yourself,' Lance said, quickly recovering himself. 'And if you're looking for compliments, I must say it suits you very well. I hardly recognized you.'

'Thank you,' said Cherry. She didn't know what else to say. It wasn't the done thing to stand here chit-chatting with the son of the house, and if Mr Gerard caught her, she'd be in the doghouse at once. Not that she had been the first to speak, she thought indignantly. She squared her shoulders still more and stared back at Lance defiantly and then said the only thing that came into her head.

'I hope you enjoy your London visit, Captain Lance. I hear it's all the rage now, and some of the exhibits are breathtaking from what I've been reading.'

'My, my, Cherry-Ripe,' Lance heard himself say softly. 'I didn't know you were so knowledgeable, nor did I expect you to be taking such an interest in what goes on in the rest of the country.'

He didn't intend to be patronizing. If anything, he admired her for having any knowledge of the exhibition at all. It surprised him too.

But Cherry, being Cherry, assumed that he was mocking her, and her eyes flashed. Unconsciously, her voice lost some of its local accent as she replied.

'I do read the newspapers, sir, and being a kitchen maid doesn't have to mean that a person is a dullard.'

'I never thought that for a moment,' Lance said, smiling at her huffiness, and amused by the effortless way she could put on a lady's voice when she chose to do so. 'In fact, it's a pity someone of your intelligence couldn't see such a spectacle for herself, isn't it? It's a pity we aren't taking servants along, or I might tuck you into my suitcase,' he added teasingly.

Cherry's bravado almost wilted at the sweet impossibility of such a thing, except that she was still seething at the way he seemed to be mocking her. 'I doubt that that would ever happen, and I'm far too big to go inside a suitcase! And if you'll excuse me, sir, I do have work to do.'

'Of course. And perhaps I'll tell you all about it on my return from the great metropolis. In fact I shall make a point of it.'

He turned and walked away before he was tempted to say anything even more ridiculous. He could just imagine his mother's face if he told her that as soon as they returned home he was going below stairs to tell Cherry O'Neil about all the marvels they had seen at the Empire Exhibition! For an even more fanciful moment he imagined himself taking her there and showing it all to her at first-hand. He imagined the look of wide-eyed wonder on her face, and the way she would be clinging to his arm in delight and awe.

And then later, as they danced the hours away to the latest hit tunes, she would be twirling and glowing in one of the latest flapper dresses, all fringes and beads and the luscious curves she couldn't quite hide, and with those gorgeous eyes alive with pleasure . . . and after that they would have the entire night ahead of them to know one another as intimately as on that one unforgettable occasion when he had taken her, the night that he couldn't quite get out of his mind, no matter how much he tried . . .

Good God, was he going completely mad? Lance asked himself furiously. He strode off towards the stables, where he had been going in the first place, knowing that a good gallop on Noble would help to clear his head of the preposterous notion that

Cherry O'Neil could ever pass herself off as a lady. But he knew
in his heart that it was far more than such a provocative charade
that kept her image in the forefront of his memory, and far more
often than was comfortable or appropriate.

As he rode hard across the Downs, he thought with dogged
determination that perhaps his mother was right after all. Perhaps
it was high time he got himself a suitable wife, one who would
grace the Melchoir table and honour the family name. So far he
hadn't found her, but perhaps this trip to London would get this
other romantic nonsense out of his head for good and let him
see where his future should lie. By the time he returned the
sweating horse to the stables, he had made his resolve.

Cherry found that her hands were shaking as she finished pulling
up the turnips in the kitchen garden. Why did he always have
this effect on her? she thought angrily. Was she such a simpleton
that she couldn't deal with a gentleman's polite conversation?

But just for a moment . . . just for one breathtaking moment
. . . she was sure she hadn't mistaken the look in his eyes, as if
he was imagining taking her to London too. As if he wanted her
as much as she wanted him. And that was *really* absurd. As if a
gentleman like him would ever want to introduce her to his
friends, those ladies with their white hands and pale complexions,
while her cheeks were ruddy and her hands rough and coarse
from pulling up turnips and potatoes and scrubbing floors.

Why would he ever think of her for a moment longer than
a passing thought? Except that for one blissful time they had lain
together in the hayloft, which she couldn't forget, even if he
could. If he had taken advantage of her, how much had she taken
advantage of him too? She hadn't objected, had she? She hadn't
cried rape or begged him to stop. She hadn't *wanted* him to stop.

Then, with a bizarre feeling that was almost akin to second
sight, she knew he hadn't forgotten it either. Whatever else
happened to the two of them, they would always have that.

A few minutes later, while she was still in dreamland, Paula
brought her down to earth by screeching at her from the kitchen
door that Cook was waiting for the blessed turnips and if she
didn't hurry up with them she'd box her ears. She hurried inside,
her face even redder than usual now as she was all too aware of

the strange urges filling her. Maybe she was turning into a wanton, she told herself in a mild panic, like one of those unfortunates down at the waterfront who sold themselves to men for pennies. But it wasn't like that. *She* wasn't like that. There was only one man she wanted, and it was the one man in all the world that she couldn't have.

Seven

That summer, London was so crowded it felt as though the whole country had converged on it for the Empire Exhibition. The Melchoir party, along with the Hetheringtons and several other families of their acquaintance, were now installed in one of the fashionable hotels in the heart of the city. Days were filled with social occasions and visits to the Exhibition and all its delights, and evenings were filled with glittering balls and soirées and theatre visits, both planned and spontaneous. It was an endless round of pleasure, meeting old friends and making new ones.

For a young man like Lance Melchoir, reluctantly on the lookout for a prospective bride, and egged on by both parents to do so, there was also an endless supply of eligible young ladies and debutantes to choose from, and plenty who made it plain they weren't averse to dancing with the tall, handsome captain. Some were highly intelligent and bored him silly with their attempts to impress him by discussing the finer points of government or the foreign situation – and there was always one – and others were simply airheads who giggled like sycophants at every word he said. There were those who thought themselves ultra-sophisticated and smoked Egyptian cigarettes in long holders, and some who were obvious predators on the chase for a husband at any price.

There wasn't one of them with whom Lance would care to share his life, and by the time the expedition was nearing its end, he had become resigned to the fact that looking for a suitable bride for the sake of perpetuating the family name in no way compensated for the simple act of falling in love. It was simple enough for other people, so why not him?

Every time the question arose in his mind, he knew the answer only too well. Shortly before their return to Bristol, he had still resolved nothing about his future. Perhaps taking up a post in a foreign country would satisfy his family honour, and deflect their obsession about providing grandchildren before they were too old to enjoy them! It was no more than a fleeting thought, and one that he had to admit didn't particularly enchant him, having seen enough of foreign fields to last a lifetime. But he also realized how aimless his life was becoming. It had no purpose in it, and it didn't suit him. It didn't suit him at all.

Their last full weekend in the capital was beautifully warm and sunny, and after the exertions of the night before, the obligatory restful morning and then a light lunch, the whole party decided to take a walk through the park during the afternoon to get some fresh air into their lungs. They spent a pleasant hour listening to one of the bands in the park, playing melodies of all kinds to appeal to the majority of visitors. When the performance was over, the younger members of the family groups went on their way at a slightly brisker pace, while the older ones strolled along behind.

Being old friends, Cynthia Hetherington found it perfectly natural to tuck her arm in the crook of Lance Melchoir's arm, well aware of what their families might be cooking up behind them.

'You know they'll be planning the wedding breakfast by now, don't you, Lance?' Cynthia said mischievously.

He laughed, too used to her banter to take it seriously. 'They'll be disappointed then, won't they?' he countered.

They walked on without saying anything for a few minutes, smiling at a group of children playing with hoops, and glimpsing several riders exercising their horses, which made Lance wish he was doing the same thing. In fact, apart from the undoubted wonders of the Exhibition, the constant round of pleasure and ineffectual conversation was really beginning to pall. London life was frenetic and exciting, but it wasn't for him. He had seen enough excitement during the last days of the war – if excitement was what you called it, he thought grimly. Unconsciously the muscles in his arm tightened, and Cynthia sensed it immediately.

'Where have you gone to, Lance?' she said softly. 'Wherever your thoughts are now, they're not really here with me, are they?'

'I'm sorry, my dear, and it's very ungallant of me to let them stray even for a moment from such a beautiful lady,' he began.

'Oh, fiddlesticks,' she broke in. 'Don't give me all that nonsense. We've known one another too long for all that false politeness.

So what is it? I could tell right from the beginning of this holiday that you've been wishing yourself somewhere else, and my guess is it's to do with *l'amour*. Am I right – and if so, who's the lucky lady?' she added.

Lance laughed. 'I didn't say there was anyone, and I don't know about her being so lucky, anyway.'

'So there *is* someone!' Cynthia said. 'And I'm just a blind to pull the wool over the parents' eyes, if that's not too many mixed metaphors. You'll have to tell me now, Lance, if you want me to keep your secret, otherwise I shall be speculating all kinds of things. So come on, who is it? One of the Crowther girls, perhaps? The older one's a bit of a horse, but the younger one's not too bad in a poor light. Or perhaps it's Julia Smythe-Robinson. She's blue-blooded enough to satisfy your dear Mama, isn't she?'

Lance laughed as she prattled on. 'Did anyone ever tell you that you talk too much, Cyn? And that you're a terrible snob?'

'Of course I'm a snob, darling. We all are! That's what makes us different from the rest of the world,' she said airily. 'So come on, tell your old pal who it is, and I promise I won't let on.'

It was tempting. By now Lance was prepared to admit to himself that he was head over heels in love – or lust, he wasn't sure which. And with the most unsuitable girl in the world as far as his family was concerned, which was why he had rejected the very idea for so long.

'I'll tell you just one thing,' he said at last. 'Her name's Cherry. And that's all you're going to hear from me.'

Cynthia was still smiling, trying to coax the secret out of him and clearly smelling some kind of intrigue, and then she fell out of step for a moment and looked up at him suspiciously.

'Well, there aren't many people I can think of with such a working-class name. In fact, there's only one that I seem to recall vaguely. Isn't there a girl who works in your kitchens who's called Cherry or Berry or something like it?' She laughed at the very idea. 'Or are you playing with me again? Is it a French *mam'selle* who's caught your eye? An actress perhaps, going by the glamorous name of *Cherie*?'

'No, it's not,' Lance said shortly. 'I told you, her name's Cherry.'

Before Cynthia's eyes had finished widening at his tone and she had grasped the truth of what he was saying, the rest of the party had caught up with them, declaring that they were feeling fatigued and that they were all going to a hotel on the nearby square for some much-needed refreshment.

'We'll join you, of course,' Lance said quickly. 'As usual, Cyn's been talking too much and I'm sure her throat is parched by now.'

His eyes dared her to say anything more, and the little squeeze of her fingers on his arm told him she wouldn't blab about his secret. He knew that already. If nothing else, he knew Cynthia Hetherington was the soul of discretion and would never betray his trust. He also knew she'd damn well have a lot more to say about it the minute she got the chance. But for now, he was saved from any more probing as they all repaired to the elegance of the nearest hotel and prepared to be waited on with tea and pastries while plans were discussed for the evening and the final days of their holiday.

And if Lance felt somehow relieved that another person knew of his infatuation for Cherry O'Neil, he also felt annoyed that the truth had been forced out of him. While it had been all in his head, it had been no more than a fantasy, but telling Cynthia had made it real – and even more impossible.

There were two more people who knew of Lance's brief liaison with Cherry. Lance guessed that she would have almost certainly confided in her friend Paula, since they always seemed to be as thick as thieves, but he had no idea of the machinations going on inside someone else's devious head.

Brian 'Knuckles' O'Neil had delivered his letter to the Melchoir house, giving Lance a time and place to meet him to hand over the money he had demanded. The letter had been full of threats as to what would happen if he didn't do so, and just to make his intention even clearer, in a burst of inspiration and self-preening, he had enclosed one of the small posters advertising his prowess as a bare-knuckle fighter. That should make the bugger aware that he meant what he said, if anything did, Brian reasoned smugly.

When the appointed date and time came and went with no sign of the man or his money, Brian began to see red. He was also uneasy that perhaps he had given away too much of his identity, and that any day now the constables might come knocking at his door and haul him away to the Bridewell. But he brushed such unwelcome thoughts aside in his keenness to continue with his scheme.

By now he wouldn't say he was exactly *stalking* his sister. Such an unsavoury word didn't come into his head. But he was fully aware that she still went dancing on most Saturday nights with that pale friend of hers, and a week after he had expected to meet Lance Melchoir and had gone to the bloody meeting place every day, he confronted his sister outside the dance hall on the next Saturday night.

Cherry jumped at the unexpected sight of him. 'Good Lord, Brian, what the heck do you think you're doing? You frightened us half to death jumping out of the shadows like that. If you're skint and looking for handouts, you can forget it because I'm not falling for it.'

It was nearly enough to make him laugh out loud. The pitiful handouts she could give him weren't what he was after when there were bigger fish to fry. He put on a pained face.

'Well, there's thanks for my brotherly concern over your welfare! I just wanted to ask how you are, that's all. Can't I be concerned about my sister now and then?'

He heard the other one giggle at his pious voice, and he glared at Paula the hanger-on, before he ignored her and turned his attention back to Cherry.

'So how are you keeping, sis?'

She looked at him suspiciously. 'I'm as well as I look, thank you. And if that's all you were worried about, get out of our way and leave us to reach the bus stop before we miss our ride back.'

'If I had a posh car like the nobs I'd drive you there myself,' Brian said expansively, 'but maybe some day soon my ship will come in, eh?'

He swaggered off, laughing, leaving Cherry watching him impatiently.

'What a fool he's turned out to be, always sponging off other people. His ship will never come in unless he finds himself a decent job, and you could hardly call bare-knuckle fighting that, could you?' she said.

'Forget him, Cherry. He's a wrong 'un and you shouldn't let him upset you,' Paula told her.

'I know, but I can't help it. He's my brother after all. I know he's no good and all that, but he's all I've got.'

'Besides me,' Paula reminded her.

Cherry agreed wholeheartedly. Whatever else happened, she always had her best friend, but no matter what, she couldn't help a sense of sadness that her brother had turned into such a waster. They walked on towards the bus stop arm in arm, unaware that Brian was still watching them, his eyes narrowed at the way his sister seemed to be taking her problem mightily easily. Or perhaps she was playing a little game of her own as well. Perhaps by the time she started showing, she was going to go to her bosses, all tearful and dewy-eyed, and demand that the son of the house did right by her.

The crafty little bitch, he thought, with more than a grudging admiration. But if that was the case, she was leaving it a bit late, since Brian had already set the wheels in motion for his own benefit.

By the time the Melchoir party were due to arrive back in Bristol after the holiday that had extended into nearly a month, the house had had a full spring-cleaning, and practically sparkled in the sunlight. Aided by the household staff, the professional team had done splendid work, and Paula had been invited out to tea by a personable young man whose job had been to reach the high ceilings and paint the fancy sconces. His name was Harold, and he'd had his eye on Paula from the start, according to the other maids.

'You should go,' Cherry had encouraged her when Paula dithered as usual. 'It's only to a Joe Lyons, for heaven's sake, and no harm can come to you there. It's time you had a bit of romance in your life.'

'Don't be daft,' Paula said, going pink. 'Anyway, afternoon tea's not exactly being invited home to meet his mother!'

'Would you go, if it was?'

'I don't know. Perhaps.'

Cherry laughed. 'Oh, go on, you know you were taken with him. Enjoy it, Paula! God knows we don't get many chances working all hours the way we do.'

'Are you still thinking of Captain Lance?' Paula asked.

Cherry shrugged. 'Who said I was ever thinking of him – at least, not in the way you mean! No, it was just something that happened, and is best forgotten.'

It was easy enough to say but not so easy to put into practice. The hell of it was that since he had been away, she thought about him more and more. She missed catching sight of him astride his horse in the mornings. She missed the unexpected times he seemed suddenly to turn up when she was outside in the garden, giving her palpitations. She missed the little chats they had together, even if it meant nothing to him, and meant everything to her. She had even toyed with the idea of leaving Melchoir House and looking for a different post, just to avoid seeing him and torturing herself. If it hadn't been for the thought of leaving Paula, she might even have absconded while Lance was away, leaving no forwarding address . . . But she couldn't have done that to her friend.

Things might be different now, of course. Paula had a young man who was interested in her, and who knew what might come of it? There had to come a time when one or other of them was going to leave the employ of the toffs and hopefully find love and happiness of their own. It was what every young girl hoped for, no matter what their status in life. Guiltily, Cherry knew they had always assumed that she would be the one, being the more confident and prettier of the two girls. But it was Paula who had the rugged Harold asking her out for afternoon tea, and it was Cherry who couldn't forget one night of bliss with a man who was far beyond a kitchen maid's expectations.

But now the family was coming home, and for all her good intentions to try to put it all behind her, she was all of a flutter at the thought of seeing him again. How would he look? Would these few weeks have changed him? Would he have become engaged to the elegant Cynthia Hetherington, or even to some other girl he had just met and had a whirlwind romance with? She couldn't blame any girl for falling for him. She just didn't want to know about it.

It was always the same to come home after an absence, Lance was thinking. Everything looked different – and this time it *was* somewhat different, of course, after the annual spring-cleaning.

He had felt the same sense of strangeness when he had come home for a few weeks' leave after the war, and then gone away again to rejoin his regiment before he finally resigned his commission. The house was the same, and yet different. But there was always a solidity about it, and a welcoming familiarity that came from occupation by several generations of the Melchoirs. It was a family home, and as such his parents had every right to expect him to carry on the family name.

There was a large pile of correspondence to be attended to that would be mostly for his father, but his own could wait, Lance decided. As soon as he could, he went out to the stables to get his expected welcome from Noble and to take a walk around the gardens and shrubbery. He was a nature lover at heart, and after the stuffiness of the city, it was easy on the eyes to see the gardens now full of spectacular summer colour, thanks to the attentions of the gardeners. It was definitely a team effort, Lance thought, appreciative for all that they did to make the estate run smoothly. Without them – and the stable lads, the cook and butler and the housemaids – life would be very different for the family. He wasn't often given to so much intro-spection, but the shallowness of some of the people he had met during the London visit was certainly making him value his home more.

After an hour or so he reluctantly went indoors again. The faintly lingering smell of paint was far less attractive than the fresh scent of roses and honeysuckle, but he couldn't remain outside for ever, and when he went inside the house his father called to him from his study.

'I've brought the post in here to sort out, Lance. I'm leaving the least important-looking ones until tomorrow when my head is clearer after the journey, but there are some letters here for you if you want to collect them.'

'I've already decided there's no rush and I'll look at them later too,' Lance agreed. He picked up the small pile and retired to his own rooms to glance through the usual motley collection of advertisements and requests for charity donations and letters from people he knew. One envelope carried a distinct whiff of violets, and he groaned as he saw the sender's name and address scrawled on the back of the envelope, recognizing it as one of the fawning young women who had been most eager for his attentions at the society balls.

There was also a letter written in a bold hand that he didn't recognize at all. It didn't seem like an educated hand, since all the words were written in capital letters. Lance frowned. It would probably be a begging letter of sorts, and he was almost tempted to throw it in the waste-paper bin without opening it, but it just might be a genuine one, and he simply couldn't ignore it. He picked up his letter-opener to slit the envelope when there was a knock on his door.

'Pardon me for intruding, Captain Lance, and welcome home,' he heard the butler say when he had called out to him to enter. 'Cook wants to know if you will be home for dinner this evening, or, since it is a Saturday, if you will be dining at your club.'

'Good God no, Gerard,' Lance said with a smile. 'I've had enough restaurant and hotel meals to last me for a while, and some of Cook's home-made cooking will be just what the doctor ordered.'

'I'll tell her, sir,' the man said. 'And I trust you had a good holiday? I hear from some of my London acquaintances that the Empire Exhibition has been a great success.'

'That it was. But despite all the wonders and tremendously exciting exhibits, there's really no place like home, is there?'

Lance hid a smile as the butler agreed and went away. The man was as big a snob as anyone, he thought with a smile, never missing a trick of mentioning his London acquaintances, but he had a good heart for all that.

He looked again at the envelope with the capital letters and gave an impatient sigh. Whatever it was, he couldn't be bothered to open it now, and it could wait. It couldn't be anything important since there was no sender's name and address on the back, and it was obviously not from anyone he knew personally. He put it aside and dealt with more pressing correspondence until it was time to join his family for dinner.

It was late evening before he went to bed and by then he found it difficult to sleep. Even though he was glad to be home, the normal country noises that he was used to were by now in such contrast to the raucous city traffic sounds and the distant rumble of the underground trains that he actually found himself missing them!

Finally, he threw on his dressing gown and went into his adjoining study. Perhaps a good dose of medicinal whisky, he thought with a smile, would send him into the Land of Nod. He poured himself a good glassful from his decanter and sat by the window, watching the low hills in the distance, made softly blue by evening, and wondering if there was ever such a peaceful county as Somerset, even though some diehards preferred to call Bristol a city and county all of its own. Whatever the name, it was preferable to London and the sometimes very dubious smells wafting up from the River Thames. The Avon was bad enough, but the Thames was so much worse . . .

He listened to himself, comparing such inconsequential things in the middle of the night, and wondered what the hell was wrong with him. Almost angrily he turned on the light above his desk and saw the unfamiliar writing on the last envelope to be opened, the words looking up at him almost accusingly now, wanting to be read. *Demanding* to be read . . .

He tore it open without bothering to use his letter-opener, and the first thing that fell out was an advertising sheet, as he had half-expected. Someone wanting his support, no doubt. He frowned. He knew all about bare-knuckle fighting, and disapproved strongly of the fellows who did it. Boxing according to the rules was a noble sport and he had done his share of it in the Army, but bare-knuckle fighting was nothing short of brutality. He was about to toss the advert and the whole thing away when something else caught his attention. The fact that the fellow's name was Knuckles said it all, as far as Lance was concerned, but it was the surname that was familiar. It was O'Neil. Knuckles O'Neil.

It was the same surname as Cherry's, and even though the possibility of a connection was remote it was enough to bring her image instantly to his mind's eye. As if it had ever been very far away! And as if he hadn't been doing his best to push her out of his mind . . . Angrily, he opened the folded letter to see what this fellow wanted, and as he did so, his face blanched.

The stark words Knuckles had used were written in the same capital letters as those on the envelope, and were no less intimidating.

MEET ME AT THE SMUGGLER'S INN ON THE
WATERFRONT ON FRIDAY AT 8 O'CLOCK
WITH FIVE HUNDRED POUNDS UNLESS
YOU WANT ME TO TELL YOUR FATHER
HOW YOU GOT YOUR KITCHEN MAID IN THE
FAMILY WAY. DON'T TELL THE ROZZERS IF
YOU KNOW WHAT'S GOOD FOR YOU. IF YOU
DON'T DO AS I SAY THE NEWSPAPERS MIGHT
BE GLAD TO HEAR ABOUT IT AS WELL. AND
REMEMBER THAT I AIN'T CALLED KNUCKLES
FOR NOTHING.

His heart pounding now, Lance grabbed the envelope that he
had thrown into the waste-paper basket and saw that there was
a smudged date on the postmark. When he managed to decipher
it, he saw that it was right after he had left for London. His mind
was in a whirl. There was no way he would ever pay a blackmailer, and he considered himself fit enough to deal with any
ruffian. But it was the implications of the letter that were rushing
into his brain now. The fellow's name on the small advertising
poster was O'Neil. And so was Cherry's. His Cherry-Ripe.

For a few seconds his senses went into a black rage. How well
did he know the girl after all? Was she some kind of con-artist
who had persuaded this fellow with the same name to extort
money out of him? And if that were so, had she wormed her
way into Lance's affection that night in the hayloft with her full,
luscious body and her glorious eyes that had so entranced him?
Had she coerced with this blackguard to get the money out of
him? Was her name even O'Neil at all? And what the bloody
hell did that matter . . .?

And then his brain cleared. He wouldn't believe it. He had
been the one to seduce her, and he had been certain that he
had been the first. She had been as virginal as the first winter
snow, and he was the one who had taken advantage of her. Never
mind that she had seemed to enjoy it, and had not been averse
to the few exhilarating times they had spoken since. He had been
the one to make the move on the sweetest girl he had ever
known.

But then the dark thoughts began to intrude again. Since that night she had given no hint that she was in trouble. Surely she might have said something by now? Or had she and this fellow cooked up the whole thing – and what was the connection between them, if any? It was nearly a month since the letter was written and there had been no follow-up. There could have been no mention of any wrongdoing in any newspaper or he would surely have heard of it. Perhaps the fellow had simply got cold feet since Lance hadn't met him at the Smuggler's Inn on the waterfront. His head throbbed with all the speculation whirling around in it now. He still didn't know Cherry's part in all this, or if she was completely innocent of what the rogue had planned, but there was only one way to find out. He would have to confront her as soon as possible and demand to know the truth. And if she really was pregnant . . . At that point his senses deserted him and he refused to think that far ahead until he knew for sure.

Eight

To the city's underclasses, word of mouth usually filtered through about what any influential nobs were doing. Brian had eventually learned that the Melchoirs had gone away for a few weeks, and he had resigned himself to not hearing from the bugger until he got back. But he was impatient, and when the days went on and he had got tired of his nightly visits to the Smuggler's with no sign of Lance Melchoir, he decided it wouldn't hurt to send the daddy a little note as well.

It would be a nice little wake-up message awaiting them all on their return from London, and if anything would stir the family into action, it would be the threat of scandal to their good name. If the son wouldn't come up with the cash, Brian had no doubt that Melchoir senior would. The letter was among the pile of correspondence on the silver salver that the butler had placed for Lord Melchoir to collect, and which had been put to the bottom of the pile as being unlikely to be of any consequence.

On Sunday morning, after a sleepless night when he tossed and turned as he waited for morning to come, Lance planned to go below stairs as soon as he could to seek out Cherry O'Neil. His parents would be going to church, but he had already told them at breakfast that he had a sore head and wouldn't be joining them. He waited with barely concealed impatience for them to leave the house before he went downstairs and into the servants' domain.

Cook looked up in astonishment as he entered. It was rare for any of the toffs to enter her kitchen, especially the young master of the house, and looking more dishevelled than usual, she observed. Mr Gerard hastily donned his jacket and put down his Sunday newspaper as he saw their visitor.

'Can I help you with anything, sir?' the butler asked quickly.

'I wish to speak with your kitchen maid. The one called Cherry,' Lance said in a clipped tone, realizing what an unusual request this was, and one that could only draw speculation and excitement among the rest of them.

But so be it. If they thought Cherry was guilty of some misdemeanour it was far better than having them suspect there had been any connection between himself and a servant. He hated himself for the unworthy thought, knowing he'd had his fill of her, but he kept his eyes steely as he waited for one of the other maids to go scurrying into the pantry to fetch Cherry.

She came into the big kitchen, her face flushing immediately as she saw him standing there, his hands rigidly at his sides. Whatever he wanted to say to her, she knew it wasn't going to be good news. The only thing she could think of was that someone had snitched on her for chatting to him now and then, and that she was about to be sent packing for her boldness.

But she had never been the one to make the first move, and he had seemed to enjoy their little chats as much as she had. She stuck her chin in the air and gazed back at him unblinkingly.

'You wish to speak to me, sir?' she said, speaking as calmly as she could, considering how her heart was pounding.

'Please come outside.'

He turned on his heel and went out of the kitchen, unable to bear the sight of everybody's eyes watching him like a hawk – watching them both, and no doubt about to start inventing all kinds of reasons as to why the son of the house should seek out a servant in such a way.

Cherry hurried after him and shut the door firmly behind her. Instead of pausing in the kitchen garden as she had expected, Lance strode on towards the seclusion of the shrubbery, well away from the house, and she had no option but to follow him.

Then he stopped walking so abruptly that she almost crashed into him, and she stepped back hastily, crimson with embarrassment. He looked so tense and angry she was sure it must be something dire that had brought this meeting about. She wished he would get on with it, since it was obvious this was not going to be anything good.

'I've no idea what I've done wrong,' she blurted out. 'But if you're about to give me the sack, let's get it over with.'

He didn't speak at first. He just stood and looked at her, her hair gleaming like burnished copper in the morning sunlight, her green eyes blazing like emeralds, and despite all that he was about to do, he thought he had never seen anything lovelier. Her body was as tense as his own feelings, her breasts taut against the roughness of her servant's dress, and he swallowed several times before he dragged out the letter from his pocket. The incriminating letter that was going to finish whatever there was between them.

For one last moment, he wished he had simply thrown it away and never had to confront her with it. But he couldn't do that. Not if the most vital fact of what the uncouth devil had told him was true.

'I know you can read,' he said in a clipped voice. 'So read this.'

He thrust the piece of paper at her, leaving Cherry still in the dark until she took in the briefly worded letter. She could hardly concentrate on it at first, but it quickly fell into place as she recognized the threat of blackmail.

'I don't know what to say,' she began in a choked voice.

'Perhaps this will help you,' Lance went on, still in that icy tone that was a world away from any hint of feeling for her. He handed her the advertising poster that Brian had included with the letter, and Cherry felt an acute sense of shame sweep over her that her brother could have done this.

'Are you going to deny that you know the fellow?' Lance demanded. 'He has the same name as yours, so there must be some connection.'

'He's my brother,' she whispered. 'But I had no idea he would do this – that he would stoop so low.'

Lance continued to stare at her as if trying to look into her very soul. The connection between Cherry and the rogue had hit him harder than he had expected. *Her brother . . .* Then it was even more obvious that this had been a devious plan between them!

'So how did he know of any possible connection between you and myself if you didn't tell him?' he went on, not yet willing to ask the one vital question that was going to complicate everything.

'I don't know. I certainly never told him!' she said indignantly. 'I keep as far away from him as possible. Paula will vouch for that!'

'I don't think we need to bring anyone else into this. So are you telling me that if I had paid him what he demanded, you and he weren't about to share the spoils of your evil little plan?'

'Of course not! I had nothing to do with it!'

Cherry was furious that he could even think such a thing. But why wouldn't he? It was what the toffs thought of the lower classes – always out for what they could get, and finding any despicable way to get it. She had thought she loved him, but right now she hated him for the way he was looking at her, as if she were lower than a slug.

'And what about this other thing?' he finally felt obliged to ask. 'Or was this some ruse on the fellow's part to make me pay up?'

Cherry's eyes flashed again. He obviously couldn't bring himself to mention the word *pregnant*. It was just *this other thing*. For one wild moment she almost wished it *was* true. Not for the impossible dreams she'd had before – the dream about how wonderful it would be if circumstances were different, and that she and man she loved were expecting a much-wanted child of their own – but so that she could fling the truth at him and demand to know just what he was prepared to do about it . . .

'Well? Is it so hard to answer a simple question now?' Lance said, becoming unnerved by her silence, and by the undoubtedly bewildered way she was reacting. 'Are you expecting a child or not?'

She was so enraged she felt like slapping him. In those other fanciful circumstances this should have been a beautiful moment, when he would take her in his arms and tell her everything was going to be all right. She couldn't think beyond that. But his arms were tightly folded now, and he looked every inch the hard Army Captain, used to having his every word obeyed. He was the impossible one, and it was as though some hateful little devil inside her was urging her to let him suffer just a while longer. What harm would it do?

She let her head droop and she would no longer look at him. 'I'm sorry,' she mumbled.

It was giving away nothing, but she knew it was as good as confirming a condition that didn't exist.

At her words, his explosive expletive shocked her, and she flinched visibly. She knew very well she had done something terrible in letting him believe she was expecting. She also knew she had to say something to put things right, but he was frightening her now, and the words wouldn't come. And while she was still floundering he turned and stalked away, leaving her stunned at what she had done.

By the time she went back to the kitchen she was still shaking, but she had composed herself as best she could, and thought up a story that she hoped would convince the rest of the kitchen staff as she found them still twittering over what could have happened.

'Before you ask, it was something and nothing,' she said. 'There was a small china vase that had been broken in the drawing room that had been swept out of sight and Captain Lance wanted to know if any of us had had anything to do with it. I assured him it had nothing to do with us, and must have been one of the cleaning company.'

'That's all very well, but why did he ask you?' Cook demanded, full of suspicion. 'Kitchen maids don't go cleaning in the drawing room. Why didn't he ask Gwen or Lucy?'

'We all did our bit while the family was away, Cook,' Paula put in when it seemed as if Cherry had lost her tongue, 'and Captain Lance did sometimes have a few words with Cherry in the garden, so he probably just remembered her name and nobody else's. I daresay he wanted to keep it as private as possible.'

To Cherry it seemed more of a feeble explanation than her own, and if it hadn't been that they were all going to be kept busy for the usual Sunday meals, she was sure it would have been probed further. As it was, Mr Gerard clapped his hands and told them all to stop gossiping and get on with some work instead of idling the day away over a trivial matter.

As soon as Cherry was sent out to the garden to pull up vegetables as usual, Paula followed her, demanding to know what had really happened.

'I think I've done something terrible,' she said shakily.

'*What*, for heaven's sake? You can't fool me, Cherry. I knew it wasn't anything simple as soon as I saw your face. All that talk about a broken vase was make-believe, wasn't it?'

'I wish that was the only thing that was make-believe. But it's all my bloody brother's fault,' she blazed now. 'If he'd kept his nose out of things it would never have happened. And how did he get to hear of it, I'd like to know!'

Paula grasped her arm. 'You're talking in riddles now. What did your brother have to do with anything?'

Cherry took a deep breath. 'He sent a letter to Lance asking for money, or else he was going to tell his father that he'd got me in the family way. I can hardly believe that even Brian would do such a thing, but Lance showed me the letter so I know it's true.'

Paula's mouth had fallen open by now. 'But how could he have known anything about it? We certainly never told him. Unless he was prowling around the kitchen the way he sometimes does, currying favour with Cook, and if so he must have overheard us talking. It had to be something like that, Cherry.'

'I suppose it must have been,' Cherry said, seeing the sense in what her friend was saying. 'But how could he have done such a thing to his own sister? We both know what a low-life rat he is, but giving it away and demanding money from Lance was too much, even for him.'

'Well, at least you could put him right on one thing. You did tell Captain Lance you're not in the family way, didn't you?'

After a moment Cherry said uneasily, 'Well, not exactly.'

'For God's sake, Cherry, what do you mean by "not exactly"?' Paula squeaked. 'You don't mean you let the poor sap believe that you're really up the duff, do you? He'll think you and Brian were in league together now.'

'No he won't. I told him I had nothing to do with blackmail.'

'But you didn't tell him there'd be no little pitter-patter of tiny feet in six months or so! How stupid was that? Next thing you know he'll be ordering you off the estate or fixing you up with some reliable doctor to get rid of the kid.'

Cherry had never seen her friend so angry or so aggressive. In minutes their usual roles seemed to have been reversed. Paula was normally the timid one, but she was now taking control, while Cherry was shaking at the enormity of the stupid lie she had perpetuated. She retaliated in the only way she could.

'My God, this sudden affair with Harold the painter seems to have turned you into some kind of monster,' she said angrily.

'It's not an affair, so you can leave Harold out of it, and you're not answering the question.'

'What question was that then? Am I in the dock now? And what gives you the right to question me about anything anyway? You're not my keeper!'

They glared at one another, and Cherry realized it was the first row they had ever had in all the years they had known one another. They had had plenty of minor tiffs, yes, but never anything as serious as this promised to be. And she didn't want it to be like this. Of all people, she wanted and needed the support of her best friend, and her eyes prickled with unshed tears.

'Paula, please don't let's fall out over this,' she said desperately. 'I know what I did was stupid and wrong, but I couldn't seem to stop myself. What with seeing Brian's letter and then hearing Lance's accusation that I was a partner in it all just shook me so much that I didn't know what to say.'

'So you let him think that what Brian said was true. Don't you think that makes you as bad as him, or don't you have a conscience any more?'

'Bloody hell, Paula, since when did you turn into some kind of saint?'

'You're only getting angry because you know I'm right. The best thing you can do – in fact, the only thing you can do – is to go straight to Captain Lance and tell him you made a mistake.'

'Oh yes, and how would that look? Am I supposed to say that in some miraculous way everything had returned to normal in the short time since we spoke? For God's sake, Paula, it's been well over two months since . . . since it happened. And we both know it did happen, even though you were out of it at the time. You do believe me about that, don't you?'

The memory of the encounter in the hayloft, which had been so ecstatic, was quickly turning into something of a sordid nightmare now. And to cap it all, Cherry had a sick feeling in her stomach as she could see her friendship with Paula disintegrating by the second, to say nothing of the job that she loved slipping away from her. Although, if she ever thought about it seriously, she didn't love it that much! Skivvying for rich folk was simply the only job she had ever known, and it would never have been the same without Paula to laugh and joke with. She felt her bravado wilting and she clutched her friend's hand as Paula answered huskily.

'Of course I believe you.'

'I know I have to do the right thing,' Cherry mumbled. 'I just don't know how to do it, or how he'll take it now.'

'I should think he'll take it a damn sight better than thinking he'd got you up the duff and ruining the family name,' Paula said smartly, not prepared to let her off the hook that easily.

But then she wilted too, and the next minute they were hugging one another, eyes damp with tears and apologizing for all the hurtful things they had said. A voice from the kitchen door made them spring apart.

'What the dickens are you two doing out there?' Gwen yelled out. 'Cook's asking where you've got to, Paula, and she's waiting for them veggies, so get on with it. It don't take two of you, anyway, so God knows what you're playing at.'

Lance Melchoir had a lot of thinking to do, but right now his head was in such turmoil he wondered if he was ever going to get things straight. The fact that Cherry O'Neil hadn't denied what the fellow had written in the letter had shocked him, and he knew he had been desperately hoping that she would have denied everything, especially knowing the rogue. But she hadn't. She had gone even further, admitting that he was her brother. And that was the family his Cherry-Ripe was a part of, he thought bitterly. So much for letting any romantic notions cloud his normally astute judgement of people.

He resorted to his usual method of trying to clear his head, that of saddling up Noble and galloping him hard across the Downs while he tried to think. Eventually he had to slow the horse down, both for its own safety and that of other people out and about on this fine Sunday morning. Some distance ahead of him he recognized the elegant shape of Cynthia Hetherington exercising her dogs. He made to turn Noble away, but before he could do so she had caught sight of him and waved. There was no way he could avoid her without appearing impolite, and so he cantered towards her and slid off Noble's back as he joined her with a false smile.

'Good morning, Cyn,' he said, as calmly as possible.

She nodded, her eyes narrowing. 'Good morning yourself. I've been watching you, Lance. If you'd raced that horse for very much longer, the poor thing would have expired before you got him home again. What's happened to get you both in such a lather?'

'Nothing's happened. Noble just needs his exercise, that's all.'

'And I'm the Duchess of Devonshire,' Cynthia said dryly. 'Come on, there's a park bench over there. Let's sit awhile and you can tell me your news.'

It was the last thing he wanted or intended to do. But the Hetherington girl had a knack of getting people to do what she wanted, and he grudgingly joined her on the bench, leaving Noble cooling off nearby.

'Is it something to do with your mysterious *Cherie*?' she said teasingly.

'Of course not. And it's not Cherie. It's Cherry,' Lance said, falling straight into the trap. He gave a heavy sigh as she said nothing, which was more provocative than if she'd demanded a thousand answers. But of all the people in his world, he knew he could trust her with anything he told her.

'I've had a letter,' he said abruptly.

'From her?' Cynthia enquired.

'From her brother, except that I didn't know he was her brother until she told me.' He couldn't hide the bitterness in his voice now, nor the sense of betrayal he felt at Cherry's part in all this. A man in his position was used to the falseness of some girls, but regardless of their social positions in life, he'd genuinely thought Cherry was different.

'If you want to tell me more I'm willing to listen,' she said softly. 'It's clearly something that's very upsetting, and it seems to have spoiled the excitement of this last month we've all had away from home.'

The pleasure of the London visit had practically disappeared from Lance's mind already. How quickly everything could change, and how difficult it was going to be to put things right. It was still an impossible equation in his mind.

'You'd better read it for yourself,' he said now. 'I know you're not easily shocked, Cyn, but be prepared.'

She tried to lighten the moment. 'Well, unless you've actually murdered somebody, it will take a great deal to shock me, darling.'

He took the letter out of his pocket and handed it to her silently. She read the stark words quickly, and he heard her sharp intake of breath. She gazed at him unblinkingly.

'Is it true? Is the girl this Cherry you've spoken of? And is she . . .?'

He nodded, looking away from her. 'Correct on all counts. I've spoken with her and she doesn't deny it. So now I have to think what to do about it.'

'But who is she, Lance? You haven't told me that yet. I thought she may have been an actress,' she said, her voice falling away at the tortured look on his face now.

'I think if it ever came to my father's ears, God forbid, then we might just have been able to cope with my dallying with an actress. But not with one of our kitchen maids.'

She gasped. 'So that's why the name was vaguely familiar. I must have heard it mentioned somewhere. But, Lance, how could you? And more to the point, *when* did you?' she added delicately.

'It doesn't matter,' he said roughly. 'The real point is, I don't know what the hell I'm going to do about it now that this fellow knows.'

The only sounds to be heard then were the distant laughter of children playing across the Downs, the crying of seabirds as they swooped and dived over the Clifton suspension bridge as the river far below filled at high tide, and the contented snuffling of the dogs. That, and the rapid beating of his heart.

'Any man in your position would know what has to be done, Lance, and that would be to send the girl packing, and get the police on to her duplicitous brother. But I suspect there's another complication to all this.'

'Oh? And what would that be, Sherlock Holmes?'

'*L'amour.*'

'Don't be ridiculous, Cyn. That doesn't come into it.'

'No? When we were in London I seem to remember you confessed you had certain feelings for a young lady called Cherry.'

'I confessed to no such thing. I may have implied that she was fairly presentable, but that's all.'

'And now I think the gentleman doth protest too much! It won't be the first time a gentleman has had feelings for a servant. Good heavens, in Victorian times it was practically a national sport, providing the gent didn't get carried away with the outcome. I think you know what I mean. You've always been an honourable man, but you have to remember your family, Lance. How would your dear mama and papa react if they knew their first grand-child was the result of a liaison with a kitchen maid? That's the question you need to ask yourself, Lance, and you have to sort it out. In the end, it just won't do, darling.'

'For pity's sake, I wasn't thinking of marrying the girl!'

'I'm glad to hear it. So send her off to some discreet quack and put it down to experience,' she said bluntly.

'My God, I never thought you could be so callous.'

She put a soft hand on his arm. 'It's not being callous, Lance darling. It's just saving your honour – and saving the girl from being ruined too.' She gave him a sympathetic look. 'Whatever you decide, you can count on my support.'

She got up to go and the dogs scampered around her. Lance stood up as well, too polite to let a lady stand while he was still seated. He squeezed her hand and thanked her for listening. But by the time he remounted Noble and let him have his head before turning for home, he knew that any decision over how to handle the situation was as far away as ever.

A day after the return from London, Lord Melchoir was in no hurry to finish opening his correspondence. As a wealthy man of some stature in the city, he was patron to various charities, and there were always requests for more of his patronage as well as invitations to open this or that. A gentleman could spend his days on such a circuit if he wished, and when he was younger he had had no objection to being seen at the forefront of it all, nor to having his name endorsed on letter-headings.

But now he was older and such things no longer had the power to add to any prestige he might once have felt. In fact, he admitted he was beginning to feel his years, and never more so than now, when the endless round of pleasure in London was finally over. Now at last he could relax within his own four walls and grounds, extensive as they were. He could take pleasure in his gardens and his favourite hothouses. The exotic and unusual plants that flourished there were his delight and joy – and in pottering among them he was also provided with a frequent and welcome respite from his wife's voice.

On that particular Sunday afternoon, while Lady Elspeth took a nap after church and a cold-cuts lunch – to which his son hadn't even bothered to turn up from God knew where he had gone – Francis Melchoir took the remaining pile of correspondence to the conservatory to read or discard. The intention to throw out most of it was high in his mind and he had done just that quite cheerfully when he came across a cheap envelope with his name and address written in bold capital letters.

It was undoubtedly a begging letter from some unsavoury source, and he was about to toss it out with the others when his better nature came to the fore. It just might be genuine, and he was feeling expansive on this lovely summer's afternoon, so it wouldn't hurt to spare a few minutes to see what it was all about. He slit open the envelope, and took out the folded piece of paper inside it.

Nine

Once he had taken Noble back to the stables and given him a good rub down Lance decided to get away from the house and spend the rest of the day at his club, which catered for its select clients every day of the week. He could get an evening meal there, and he wouldn't have to answer to anybody. With the mood he was in, he didn't bother to tell the kitchen staff or his family. The farther away he could get from the house and its occupants right now, the better for everyone, he thought grimly.

He drove into the city and entered the stuffy, elegant confines of the club, sure of a discreet welcome by the staff and the few other members who chose to visit it on a Sunday, plus the opportunity to be left strictly alone if it was what he wanted. And he did want it. Plus a good stiff drink to settle his nerves. In fact, right now he wished himself as far away from Bristol and anyone who knew him as it was possible to be. For one reckless moment, he wondered if taking up his old commission in the Army and applying to be sent to one of the far-flung posts of the Empire might not be the best thing to do. To India . . . or beyond . . .

Even as he thought it, he knew it wasn't the answer and that he would never do such a thing. He had never been a coward, and it would be the coward's way out of a difficult situation. The difficult situation that was not only the devil's own servant, Knuckles O'Neil, but Cherry. He drew a deep breath and took a large swallow of the double brandy that seemed to have mysteriously appeared at his side. He couldn't really remember ordering it, or the second one that followed, but it soothed his fury somewhat as the fiery liquid coursed down his throat, and he tried to think less emotionally.

Cherry was the person most affected by all this, and he couldn't ignore it, no matter how much he might want to do so. Nor could he overlook the fact that whatever condition she was in, he had been responsible for it. No matter whether or not she and that brother of hers had cooked up this whole blackmail scheme between them, the girl was in the family way, and the child was his. He had no doubt about that.

He stared into space, seeing none of the fine and costly surroundings of the central members' lounge in which he sat, enveloped in the soft, dark green leather of an armchair that had seated hundreds of illustrious personages over the years. But now, for the first time he felt stirrings of a different kind, replacing the anger and revulsion he had felt at being so duped by two tricksters.

Oh yes, the child was undoubtedly his and he never questioned it. And Cherry would surely have been feeling frantic all these weeks, not knowing what to do about it, wondering what was to become of her. Although he couldn't say that she had given him that impression on the occasions when they had bantered together in the kitchen garden. But you never knew with some people. She would be as adept at hiding her true feelings as any girl in her position needed to be. But just what had she intended to do about it? The brief softening he had felt a few minutes ago, just as quickly vanished. He couldn't risk letting himself have any more tender feelings towards her until he himself had decided what to do.

He took another long draught of brandy from the glass that never seemed to be empty, as the memory of his earlier conversation with Cynthia Hetherington came sharply into his head.

'*Any man in your position would know what has to be done, Lance, and that would be to send the girl packing, and get the police on to her duplicitous brother. But I suspect there's another complication to all this.*'

'*Oh? And what would that be, Sherlock Holmes?*'

'*L'amour.*'

'*Don't be ridiculous, Cyn. That doesn't come into it.*'

'*No? When we were in London I seem to remember you confessed you had certain feelings for a young lady called Cherry.*'

'*I confessed to no such thing. I may have implied that she was fairly presentable, but that's all.*'

His hand wavered slightly as he motioned for the flunkey to bring him more brandy, just as eager now for the spirit to dull his senses so that he didn't have to think at all, but it was as if Cynthia's practical words had no intention of leaving him alone.

'*And now I think the gentleman doth protest too much! It won't be the first time a gentleman has had feelings for a servant. Good heavens, in Victorian times it was practically a national sport, providing the gent didn't get carried away with the outcome. I think you know what I mean. You've always been an honourable man, but you have to remember your family, Lance. How would your dear mama and papa react if they knew their first grandchild was the result of a liaison with a kitchen maid? That's the question you need to ask yourself, Lance, and you have to sort it out. In the end, it just won't do, darling.'*

'For pity's sake, I wasn't thinking of marrying the girl!'

His arm jerked against the pungent leather arm of his chair, and already half-dazed by too much brandy and the overwhelming events of the day, it was as if his brain relaxed for a moment, letting in the sweet impossibility of such a thing. Of course marrying the girl was never an option . . . But just supposing it was . . . just imagine the beautiful green-eyed Cherry O'Neil with the glorious copper-coloured hair, wearing a satiny white wedding gown, walking up the aisle to join him in the cool interior of their local old church, and vowing to love him for ever, in sickness and in health, for richer or poorer . . .

His hand jerked again, waking him properly from the brief stupor into which he seemed to have fallen. Because of course it would be for richer as far as the scheming little trollop was concerned, he thought angrily, and she would be egged on by her bastard of a brother. That was the whole purpose of it all, and that was what he would do well to remember, without getting diverted by any mad thoughts of an unsuitable marriage.

'Are you quite well, Captain Melchoir?' he heard the club's white-haired flunkey say in a concerned voice, and he saw the man hovering beside him as if he was seeing him through a mist.

'I'm not at my best today, Pinkers,' he croaked. 'If there's a room available, I think I shall go and have a lie down.'

'Of course, sir. That will probably be wise. Allow me to accompany you.'

At any other time Lance might have thought it comical to think of the doddery old chap, whom he had always thought looked about a hundred years old if he was day, helping a strapping young ex-army officer upstairs to one of the discreet little rooms set aside for members who wished to stay for an hour, a night, or longer.

It wasn't amusing to him now. In fact, he felt too damn groggy to find anything amusing, and to his humiliation, before they even reached the first landing he was obliged to go into one of the bathrooms and discharge the contents of his stomach.

'Better out than in, I always say, sir,' old Pinkers said when he emerged, his face slightly greener than before. 'It was something you ate, I daresay.'

Lance smiled weakly. 'When you die, Pinkers, they should put a plaque on your gravestone saying, "He was discreet until the end."'

'That would be nice, sir,' the man said, seeing nothing odd about it.

Once they reached the bedroom and Lance sank down on the bed, he felt he should give the man a small explanation, even though it wasn't necessary, and Pinkers certainly wouldn't have been expecting it. Lance had long suspected that the information gleaned by discreet gentlemen such as Pinkers would fill a volume if ever one of them were to disclose it. But such a thought was farthest from his mind now.

'Nasty business, puking up like that, Pinkers. It must have been the fish I ate last night. I thought there was something strange about the taste, and then I foolishly skipped breakfast this morning,' he said, his voice sounding false and strangely high-pitched.

'As you say, sir. I'm sure that would have the case, and I daresay the brandy reacted with it too.'

In other words, you silly young bugger – and pardon the language, sir – you drank too much on an empty stomach.

Lance lay down on the bed, praying that he had only imagined the reply, and that the spinning sensation in his head would go away. Next thing, he vaguely realized that the man was pulling off his boots. This was way beyond the call of duty, he registered, and he waved him away.

'You're a good old boy, Pinkers, and if I sleep too long, perhaps you'd give me a call in time for supper. I suppose there'll be something to eat tonight?'

'I shall see to it personally, sir. Perhaps something light and easy on the stomach would be in order?'

Lance smiled faintly. 'Whatever you say, Pinkers.'

He knew nothing more. He didn't hear the man leave the

room, nor some while later the sound of the telephone in the
hall below. He had no idea that an irate Lord Melchoir had called
his club and several other places, trying to track down his son's
movements. Nor was he aware that the loyal Pinkers gave no
indication that he had seen Captain Lance at all since he had
returned from London.

'I really don't know what's the matter with you tonight,' Lady
Elspeth said irritably, when her husband flung down his knife
and roared for someone to come and take his tough piece of
meat away. 'There's absolutely nothing wrong with the beef,
and Cook has roasted it to perfection. You'll have her giving
in her notice and looking for a better-tempered employer if
you don't stop your nonsense. And what was wrong with the
soup, may I ask?'

'It was cold,' Lord Melchoir snapped. 'If food is meant to be
served hot, then it should be served hot, and not taste as if it
came out of a cold store.'

'It was not cold, Francis. There's either something wrong with
your taste buds, or else you're having trouble with your digestion.
I think perhaps you should see Doctor Davey and see if there's
something wrong with you, because I can't abide this vulgar side
of you.'

'There's nothing wrong with me, woman,' he roared. 'And
where the devil is Lance this evening? I need to have words with
him, and it won't wait.'

'Well, it will have to wait, since he isn't here,' Elspeth said
crisply, irritating him even more. 'I can't say I blame him with
the foul mood you've been in since we got back from church
this morning. I thought our jaunt to London might have improved
your temper, but it's obvious it has not. And please stop shouting,'
she added. 'We don't want the servants to hear you ranting and
raving. It's not seemly.'

For no reason that Elspeth could perceive, her logical words
seemed to incense him even more.

'The bloody servants are the least of my problems! Or maybe
not . . .'

With a muttered oath, he flung down his napkin, scraped back
his chair and stomped out of the dining room, leaving his wife

staring after him crossly at such lack of manners at the dinner table. Among their associates it was no secret that she was the more autocratic of the two, and her own distinguished family went back generations. In fact, secretly, Elspeth had always modelled herself on their dear Queen Mary, with her starched and rigid demeanour and haughty manners. That was how a lady should conduct herself, in Elspeth's opinion, and a gentleman should applaud and respect such decorum. He should also provide a proper accompaniment for his wife, not this shouting banshee that Francis seemed to have become this evening.

And why he should be so bothered about where Lance had got to, she couldn't begin to guess. A young man was entitled to go about his own pursuits without having to sit with his parents every evening. She gave an impatient sigh, finished her dinner and retired to her own sitting room to listen to some relaxing Schubert melodies on her gramophone, glad of some peace away from her irascible husband and his imaginary ills.

Lance awoke with a hangover of volcanic proportions. He wasn't aware that he'd had too much to drink, but he knew he must have done, because it had knocked him right out. He could see that it was still daylight outside, and he registered that he certainly wasn't in his own bed. By the time it dawned on him that he was lying fully clothed except for his shoes on a bed in one of the pristine and quiet upper rooms of his club, he was also aware of someone knocking on the door. The next moment the man Pinkers entered the room.

'If you're feeling quite refreshed, Captain Melchoir, a light supper is being served in the dining room in half an hour.'

'Thank you, Pinkers,' he said huskily, his mouth as dry as if it was filled with sand. 'How long have I been asleep?'

'About four hours. I've also brought you a jug of water and some aspirin, should you need them,' the man added. 'Oh, and your father telephoned earlier, enquiring if you were here. I thought it best in the circumstances to say you were not. I hope I did right, sir.'

Lance nodded, and then wished he hadn't when his head throbbed anew.

'You did, Pinkers, and if you're ever looking for a new job as a gentleman's gentleman, please come to me first.'

He smiled politely. 'Thank you, sir, but at my age, I think I'm quite settled here. In the dining room in half an hour then.'

Despite his age, he was as regimented as any soldier and a stickler for order, and Lance knew that he had better report to the dining room in the said half an hour, or there'd be frowns and silent accusations. He would much prefer to have something sent up, but on a Sunday it was the one night that such considerations weren't given, even to their most respected members.

He quickly sluiced his face and hands in the small washstand basin, and swallowed two aspirins with water from the jug. Why the hell he should feel so bad he couldn't yet recall, nor why he had drunk so much in the middle of a Sunday afternoon. Nor even why he was here . . . Until the memory of all that had happened rushed back at him so fast he almost reeled backwards.

Paula hated the feeling that she had to tiptoe around Cherry for fear of upsetting her. Her usually sensible friend had been a right nitwit in letting Captain Lance think she was up the duff, and she only had herself to blame for whatever came of it. She had made things a hundred times worse now, of course. She would have to tell him the truth, and that was the end of it. She couldn't let the lie continue to fester. Besides, in a few months' time, it would be obvious that there was no baby growing inside her. If Paula had always thought Cherry was the bright one, she considered her as dim as a burnt-out light bulb this time.

Paula dearly wished she could have confided in Harold, but they didn't know one another well enough for such confidences yet, and besides, it wasn't her secret to tell. She couldn't deny that her nerves tingled deliciously every time she thought of him, and she hadn't told Cherry yet that she was spending her Sunday evening off with him. They were going over the Downs to watch the world go by, and maybe stay out late enough to watch the sunset over the river.

On her next afternoon off he was going to take her to Temple Meads railway station to watch some of the trains come puffing and snorting into the station from London and other faraway places. It might not be everybody's idea of entertainment, but by now she knew that Harold didn't intend to be painting other people's houses for ever, and that he really wanted to work on the railways. He dazzled her with his big ideas. He had ambitions, and Paula admired him for that. She wished she'd never confided them to Cherry, though, who pooh-poohed them at once.

'I don't think that's much of an ambition,' she'd said that morning. 'What's so wonderful about working on the railways? Trains are nasty, smelly things and you're always in danger of getting smuts in your eyes. You want to watch yourself, Paula, if that's how you're going to spend your time off!'

'Well I think it's a lovely idea, and I'm looking forward to going down to the station to watch the trains come in. I bet you didn't know they've all got names on them, did you?'

'I didn't know and didn't care, unless you think they've named one after you. You can tell me about it tonight if you think I'll be interested,' she added with a mock yawn.

'I can't. Me and Harold are going out walking. He sent a note up to say that he'll meet me outside the gates once we've cleared up here.'

Cherry stared at her. They always spent Sunday evenings together. If either of them had expected to be taken out walking with a young man, it would have been Cherry who was the first . . . She felt a strange sense of loss, which was perfectly ridiculous, because it was only one evening, and she was sure Harold whoever-he-was would soon get tired of simpering little Paula. But even as the unworthy thought entered her head, she realized how Paula had bloomed since knowing him. She had never noticed it before, but Paula had a certain glow about her now, and that came from only one thing. She had fallen for him already – and Cherry felt suddenly protective towards her because of it. She replied as lightly as she could.

'Well, I hope you enjoy yourselves – and don't do anything I wouldn't do.'

The minute she had uttered the trite words, Cherry bit her lip, knowing the irony of such a statement. It wasn't Paula who had been seduced so easily and willingly, and who was now facing the appalling consequences of that one reckless night. Nothing had come if it, but she had let the lie go on that it had, and ruined whatever chances she might have had with Captain Lance.

Even if she had dared to dream about such a thing, she knew bitterly that it was all over now.

Paula was looking at her uneasily, and she knew her feelings must have shown on her face. 'Look, if you'd rather I didn't go, I could see Harold and tell him you're not well and that I feel I should stay in with you,' she began.

Cherry took a deep breath and shook her head. 'Don't be so daft. I wouldn't hear of such a thing. Just because my head's in a muddle, there's no reason for you to suffer, and in any case, I wouldn't be fit company for you, Paula. I shall be far better left on my own this evening.'

'Will you try to see him?' Paula went on meaningly, determined not to let her welsh on doing what was right.

'I might. Or it might just be best to let things stew a while longer. He was in such a rage earlier that I might get the back of his hand if he thought I'd been lying. I'm thinking it might be best to leave it a few days, or longer, then tell him that nature's finally taken its course. He'd have to believe that, wouldn't he?'

'Make him suffer first, you mean. It's a weird way to treat something you're supposed to have fallen for, if you ask me.'

Cherry felt her heart twist. It wasn't what she wanted at all. It just seemed the only way out of this mess, other than proving herself an out and out liar. And she couldn't bear it for Lance to think so ill of her – not any more than he did already, and that was bad enough.

'I have to do this my way, Paula. I know you think I'm wrong, but I will tell him the truth eventually, I promise.'

Just when that was going to be, she had no real idea.

'You won't say any of this to Harold, will you?' she went on.

'Of course not,' Paula said indignantly. She gave a sudden giggle, making her eyes sparkle. 'Anyway, we'll have plenty of other things to talk about. You're not our main topic of conversation, Cherry, and nor are you the only one with a secret.'

Strictly speaking, having a beau wasn't exactly a secret, since all the kitchen staff were aware of the sudden infatuation between Paula and the house painter. She had been a little mouse for so long that they all thought it sweet to see how she had suddenly blossomed, and it struck Cherry that the other girls were treating Paula as a bit of a pet now, teasing her and asking when they were going to hear wedding bells. It wasn't likely to happen for ages and ages yet, Paula would tell them airily, but as if she could see into the future, Cherry had a funny feeling that it wasn't going to be Paula who was trailing along at the radiant bride's heels, it was more likely to be *her*.

She tried to stop feeling sorry for herself. She had got into this mess, and now she had to deal with it. One thing was for sure. As soon as she got the chance, she was going to tell her brother exactly what she thought of him. Although, knowing now what a terrible thing he had done in trying to blackmail Lance, how she was going to face him without wanting to kill him, she really didn't know.

As it happened, Knuckles O'Neil was not going to be in the vicinity for a few days, having been engaged for several fights in venues out of the city by his agent, Jake Gooding. In such a dubious line of work, just above the law, it was to his advantage to keep moving about, and in one way it also suited Brian very well. He needed the money to pay the rent on his lodgings, and a chap needed to eat. But in another way he was still keyed up to see how the Melchoir buggers were going to respond to his letters. The fact that the young one had never turned up with the black-mail money at the Smuggler's Inn did nothing to lessen his resolve to see this through, especially once he'd learned that the whole lot of them had gone off to the fleshpots of London. But it wasn't over yet. By now he had no compunction any more for landing his sister in it. If the silly little bitch hadn't opened her legs for the toff she would never have got herself in this state in the first place. He was biding his time, deciding when to make his next move.

That Sunday evening he'd been larking about with some low companions near the waterfront and taking a stroll over the Downs to clear his head of drinking some illegal moonshine, when he saw his sister's soppy friend traipsing over the grass with some chap. He gave a sardonic grimace. So she'd found herself a bloke at last, had she? He wouldn't mind betting that Cherry wouldn't be so pleased that her little puppet friend had somebody in tow at last. He decided to brighten up his evening with a bit of fun, and seeing the two of them engrossed in conversation and laughing together, he suddenly leapt out of the bushes in front of them.

Paula squealed with fright, clinging on to Harold's arm as if it was some kind of apparition. And then she recognized who it was, and snapped at him.

'For goodness' sake, Brian, what do you think you're doing, jumping out and scaring folk like that?'

'Do you know this fellow?' Harold said at once, taking charge.

'I only know who he is because he's Cherry's brother,' she replied, feeling more and more shaky now, remembering the situation that was occurring with her friend. 'I don't want to get into conversation with him, Harold,' she said in a lower voice. 'Let's get away from him, please.'

Harold stood his ground. 'I don't know that I want to, seeing that he gave you such a scare. He's been drinking too, from the smell of him.'

As Paula saw Brian's eyes flash at his scathing words, she started to feel panic. Harold was a brawny enough chap, but she was sure he would be no match for a bare-knuckle fighter, and she couldn't bear to see him caught up in a brawl with the lout.

'If you don't leave us alone, I shall call the constables,' she said, loudly enough for several other couples out for a stroll to glance their way and stop walking. 'They're always patrolling the Downs on a Sunday evening, and it would only take one scream to get them to come running.'

It might not do much for Harold's self-esteem for her to take the lead like this, but it was the only thing Paula could think of doing. The last thing she wanted was for him to start crowing about how he was trapping his sister, and as several gentlemen began walking their way, Brian backed down, sneering at Harold as he left.

'Be glad you've got your girl's skirts to hide behind this time, Nancy,' he said as he swaggered away.

'You shouldn't have done that, Paula. You should have left it to me,' Harold said at once, rounding on her. 'Scum of the earth like him shouldn't be allowed to accost young women in broad daylight.'

'I didn't mean to say anything, but you don't know him! And I do. Only too well!' To her horror she burst into tears, and his arms went round her at once.

'Now I've upset you as well, but we're not going to let the

likes of him spoil our evening, sweetheart. We'll go and sit down under that tree until you've recovered,' he said, 'and then I think you'd better tell me just what you know about him and why he scared you so much.'

Helplessly, knowing he only wanted to be her champion, and still slightly bemused at the fact he had called her sweetheart, Paula followed him to the bench beneath the shady oak tree, wondering just how much or how little she could get away with telling him about the hideous Brian O'Neil, without betraying Cherry's confidence.

Ten

Lance toyed with the idea of staying the night at his club, but finally decided against it. It was well past one o'clock in the morning when he drove back to the house, the car's engine making little sound as he parked it and let himself quietly indoors. He still felt groggy, but sleeping it off in his own bed would be far preferable to waking up in bed at the club and having to go through the motions of appearing at home the next morning in the clothes he had worn the night before. Everyone would be asleep by now, and he hoped that a couple more aspirins should see his head all right by daybreak. Then, with a clearer brain, he would have to think seriously about what to do about Cherry O'Neil.

He walked carefully up the darkened stairs, and into the sanctuary of his bedroom, breathing a sigh of relief that he hadn't disturbed anyone. Servants seemed to be awake at all hours of the day and night and the last thing he wanted was to encounter any of them and cause more gossip below stairs. Not that it would be any of their damn business, he thought, in a burst of annoyance. As he made to close the door behind him, a voice roared out from the direction of his father's sitting-room along the corridor.

'Lance, get your sorry backside in here this minute!'

It was so unexpected, especially shouted in such terms, that Lance felt his flesh crawl. So much for his own careful creeping into the house unobserved and unheard. Any second now and the whole damn household would be awake and wondering what was going on. He sped along the corridor to where his father awaited him and shut the door firmly behind him.

It was obvious to anyone that Lord Melchoir was far from pleased. His face was puce with rage, and the long hours in which he had tried to contact Lance without success had only incensed him more. He leapt to his feet as soon as his son walked into the room, his hands clenched so tightly he could feel his nails biting into his palms. But none of that mattered. Right now all he could see was a dissolute son swaying slightly on his feet, and bringing disgrace to an honourable family.

'What's wrong, Father? Are you ill?' Lance said at once. 'Do you want me to fetch someone, or send for the doctor?'

'I want no bloody doctor,' Francis shouted. 'You and your mother seem to think that's the answer to everything, but it's not the answer this time, you stupid young buck.'

Oh God, he knows, thought Lance at once.

'Father, please sit down and calm yourself, and tell me what's happened.'

As if he didn't already know . . . but he still had to hear it from his father's lips. He still needed to know how far this whole fiasco had gone . . .

Francis strode across to the small desk where he dealt with personal matters, and drew out an envelope. The minute he saw it, Lance's heart began to pound. So the bastard had sent his father a missive too, had he?

'Read this, and tell me what you intend to do about it,' Francis snapped.

Lance took the envelope and took out the letter, written on the same cheap notepaper as the one he had received. He scanned it quickly. It was much shorter than the letter he had received, but it was just as damning.

ASK YOUR SON ABOUT THE £500 HE OWES ME TO KEEP QUIET ABOUT THE KITCHEN MAID AND HER BRAT. I WON'T WAIT MUCH LONGER. HE KNOWS WHAT TO DO AND WHERE TO DELIVER.

Beneath the stark words were a crudely drawn skull and cross-bones. Lance ran his tongue around lips that suddenly felt too big for his mouth. They were already dry from drinking too much brandy earlier, but now he felt as if his throat had completely dried up.

'*Well?*' his father barked.

'Father . . . I . . . I don't know what to say . . .'

'Well, you'd better bloody well think of something!' Francis

was practically dancing with rage now. 'I'm waiting for an explanation as to why some layabout thinks to send me something of
this kind, and if it has anything to do with the reason you've
conveniently kept out of the way for the entire day. *Well?* Is there
any truth in what it says?'

Before Lance could get any more words out, the door was
flung open and Lady Melchoir appeared, a voluminous velvet
dressing-robe covering her nightgown, her hair swathed in a net.
Her eyes flashed furiously at the two men, facing one another
now like warring gladiators.

'I don't know what's going on in here, but have you two any
idea what time it is, and what a spectacle you're making of yourself, Francis? You've woken me up, and I'm sure I'm not the only
one. Your booming voice can be heard all over the house, and
heaven knows what the servants will make of it.'

'For Christ's sake, woman, there are more important matters
to be dealt with here than the feelings of the bloody servants,'
Francis grated, turning on her at once.

'Please don't use that tone with me, and please don't resort to
swearing like one of the lower classes,' she replied at once. 'It's
most unseemly.'

If anything was set to arouse her husband's ire still more, that
was it. He strode across the room, and before either of the others
could guess what he was about, he caught his wife's hand and
pulled her over to the small desk. Gasping with shock at such
treatment, Elspeth was forced to go with him, while Lance tried
to remonstrate with his father.

'There's no need to involve Mother in all this, Father,' he said
angrily. 'Let her go back to bed and leave things to us.'

'It's too late for that! She's always considered me of a lower
class than herself, and it will do her good to see how some of
that uncouthness has rubbed off on her precious son, and the
type of person he chooses to consort with.'

'What are you saying, Francis?' Elspeth said, clearly unnerved
now.

'Mother, go back to bed,' Lance intervened, trying to pull her
away. 'It's very late and all this can be sorted out in the morning.
I'll go down to the kitchen and bring you up some warm milk
to help you sleep.'

It was the worst thing he could have said. Francis let go of her hand so fast she almost stumbled, and then he was shouting at the top of his voice again.

'That's the last place you're going to, my lad. How many more times have you sneaked off in the middle of the night to carry on with your philandering in the kitchen, eh? A well-brought-up young woman like the Hetherington girl not good enough for your tastes, I suppose. You prefer one with the smell of cabbage and floor polish to tickle your appetite, do you?'

Elspeth was near to fainting now. She clutched at her chest and looked at them both with frightened eyes. 'Will somebody please tell me what's going on?' she whispered, the words almost dragged out of her.

As Francis thrust the incriminating letter towards her Lance tried to grab it away, and his father lashed out at him with the back of his hand, splitting his cheek. He felt the warm trickle of blood run down his face, and wiped it away angrily, more concerned with his mother's reaction than any hurt to himself.

'I'll never forgive you for this,' he snapped to his father.

'And you think I'll forgive you for what you've done to this family, if all this is proved to be true?' Francis retorted.

By now Elspeth was holding the letter with the tips of her fingers, her eyes dilating as she took in the meaning of the words. She looked from one to the other of her menfolk, but whatever she might have said was lost as she sank to the floor in a dead faint.

'Fetch some water for her, Father,' Lance said, taking charge. 'And then help me get her back to bed. You've done enough damage for one night, and she's in no fit state to hear any more.'

Neither of them was sure who was censuring who any more, but it was concern for Elspeth that galvanized both of them into action now. She was a heavily built woman, but between them they managed to rouse her sufficiently with some sips of water on her lips, and then half-carried her along to her own room and lay her on her bed where she lay with her eyes closed. Lance put a coverlet over her, and the two men waited a while until they were sure she was breathing easily, then Lance kissed her ashen cheeks before going back to his father's sitting room where two glass of brandy were already being poured out.

'I hope you realize what damage you've done to Mother with your theatricals. This could have been discussed in a civilized manner between two gentlemen,' he told Francis coldly, the cut on his cheek starting to sting. He had to take the initiative, though, or risk appearing as a snivelling and guilty party to it all. Which he knew damn well he was . . .

'I hardly think you've behaved as a gentleman,' Francis said, just as coldly, but clearly shaken at how Elspeth had reacted. 'So, is the allegation true? And is this fellow demanding money from you?'

Lance took a deep breath and another long draught of brandy. They said the hair of the dog was the best thing to take after going on a bender, so why not?

'You've seen for yourself that the fellow's demanding money from me. If you mean have I consorted with a kitchen maid, I'm afraid it's true, and she hasn't denied that she's expecting a child.'

'One of *our* kitchen maids?' Francis went on ruthlessly.

'Does it make any difference? But . . . yes.'

It was Francis's turn to take a long drink of brandy and pour himself another one.

'Good God, man, we all know what attractions these girls can have, actresses and servants and the like, and God knows a man needs to sow his wild oats, but didn't you have any more sense than to keep your trousers buttoned up while at home? And how the devil did this blackguard come to know about it?'

'He's her brother. And a bare-knuckle fighter at that.'

'Oh well, this just gets better and better, doesn't it?' Francis almost exploded now. 'I suppose the two of them are in cahoots to extort money out of us, is that it? Well, it won't do, Lance. There's no question that we'll descend to paying blackmail money. The girl will have to get rid of it, and naturally she'll be sent packing as well.'

'I know,' Lance said.

Something in his voice made his father look at him sharply.

'You're not suggesting that you have any feelings for this girl, are you?'

Of course not. It's only that she's the most beautiful, wonderful, spirited girl I've ever met . . .

'Of course not.'

'You don't sound convincing. How often have you been seeing her?'

'I see her all the time when she's going about her chores. If you mean how often have I . . . you know . . . it was only once.'

'Once is enough,' Francis snapped.

By now Lance was becoming increasingly resentful at being made to feel like a naughty schoolboy, caught out in some misdemeanour.

'Look, Father, why don't you leave it to me to sort out? It's my mess, and I'll deal with it.'

'How? By trying to have it out with some bare-knuckle fighter who wouldn't abide by the first rule of boxing? I don't think so.'

'I'm no slouch with my fists, but that's not what I meant. I'll see Cherry and talk some sense into her, because I'm sure she won't want to keep the child.'

'And what if she does?'

'She can't.'

'So it's Cherry, is it? Is that the one with bright-coloured hair your mother always says looks more like some cheap music-hall vamp?'

Lance ignored the barb. 'What have you got against actresses? You and Mother always enjoy going to the theatre, don't you?'

'Yes, but we don't bring it home with us,' Francis said dryly.

But gradually, now that Francis had let off steam, the tension in the room had inevitably lessened. Nothing had been resolved, and nor could it be done easily, but at least it was out in the open now. All this in the short time since they had come home from London, which seemed like eons ago to both of them now.

'Am I permitted to go to bed yet?' Lance said finally, when the conversation seemed to have dried up for the moment.

Francis drained his glass. 'I think it's the best place for both of us. I shall look in on your mother to make sure she's all right, and we'll discuss this again in the morning.'

'Good night, Father.'

He left the room quickly, wishing his mother had never had to be involved at all, and praying that she wouldn't expect to be present at whatever was to be done next. The thought of hauling Cherry upstairs to face the two of them was something that made his heart quail. She didn't deserve such an inquisition. It wasn't her fault for being so very desirable that no healthy, red-blooded man could fail to be aroused by her.

By now he was utterly exhausted, and he fell asleep almost at once, but his dreams were full of Cherry and her luscious red lips that echoed her name, and her inviting young body, and of himself taking his delightful fill of her. His own Cherry-Ripe . . . He awoke several times, needing drinks of water for his parched throat, but he gladly drifted back to sleep in the knowledge that the dreams would come again. And if dreams were the only way he could have her now, he intended to make the most of them.

While the rumpus had been going on in Lord Melchoir's small sitting room, none of them had heard the quiet footsteps of the butler on the landing outside. His room was nearer to the Melchoirs' rooms than those of the other servants. Ever alert to his duties, his ears were finely tuned to any disturbance in the house. Gerard was ready to be attentive at any hour of the day and night, and he had assumed there must be something wrong with one of his employers, and was prepared to send for the doctor if need be. He had hovered outside the room for a while, not wanting to intrude unless he was called, and what he heard almost knocked him sideways. It needed serious thinking about, that was for sure.

It wasn't illness that was causing the fuss, but the fact that the young master was being blackmailed. For what reason Gerard hadn't been able to ascertain before Lady Melchoir came bustling along the corridor, and he had melted into the shadows, awaiting instructions if there were any. When none seemed to be forth-coming, and he was unable to hear anything more, he went back to his own room to think things over. It had to be some gambling debt, he decided. The young Captain had probably got in above his head, and now his debts were being called in by some heinous blackmailer. No wonder Lord Melchoir was incensed at this affront to the family honour.

Like all good servants, Gerard was fiercely loyal to his employers and would always defend them to the best of his ability. But like all servants, too, he was not above a bit of gossip, especially when he was the one with the titbits of news when the rest of them awoke early the following morning.

'I'm surprised none of you heard his lordship raising his voice to the Captain,' he declared when they were all agog at what he had to say. 'I thought he was going to explode, the rage he was in, and before you ask me what it was about, all I can tell you is that it was something to do with blackmail. My guess is that it's a gambling debt and the Captain hasn't paid up.'

'It's a nasty business, blackmail,' Cook commented. 'Here, hold on, where do you think you're going, Miss?' she exclaimed as a small whirlwind rushed past her and out into the kitchen garden.

Cherry gasped out something in reply, leaving the rest of them to fathom it out for themselves.

'I think she's got the squits, Cook,' Paula said quickly. 'She was moaning something horrible in the night.'

'Well, you'd better go and see if she's all right. And don't go blaming it on any of my cooking, neither,' she added.

Paula rushed out of doors to do as she was told, to find Cherry as white as a sheet, bending over and looking about ready to bring up her innards.

'I know what you're thinking, but it's got nothing to do with you,' Paula hissed. 'It's probably like Mr Gerard said, and Lord Melchoir was going on at his son for gambling.'

'If you believe that you'll believe anything,' Cherry said in a shrill voice. 'Of course it was to do with me, and more likely to do with my brother. You heard what he said. It was to do with blackmail, and we both know that's down to Brian, don't we?'

Paula looked at her silently. 'Well, if I was you I'd lie low for a bit then, and keep out of everybody's way.'

'That's just what I intend to do, and I'm starting right now.'

'What do you mean?'

'I'm not staying here to have them come down on me like a ton of bricks. I've got to get away, Paula.'

'You can't do that. Where would you go?' Paula said in a panic.

'I don't know. I've just got to keep out of sight until the fuss dies down. Brian's started all this, so I'm going to find him first and tell him what a rat he is. Don't worry, I won't desert you for ever. Anyway, you've got lover-boy Harold to keep you company now.'

Paula remembered uneasily that she had told Harold a little too much about what had been going on, but she trusted him, and it wouldn't do any good to let Cherry know she had been a bit indiscreet.

'Look, I'm going right now,' Cherry continued hastily, as they heard sounds coming from the kitchen. 'I'll keep in touch somehow, and it'll probably only be for a day or so but I need time to think, and I can't do it here.'

Before Paula could argue any more she had gone like the wind, unable to face any more questions and suspicious looks, and panicking to get away before anyone from upstairs came seeking her out with accusations. She would go to Brian's digs and confront him with what he had done, and try to get him to take it all back, however hopeless a task it seemed. But there seemed no other way. If she had to stay there for a couple of days, then she would — not that she relished being in the same vicinity as him, nor even in the same country any more, she thought, enraged, knowing he had brought all this trouble on her. She mentally disowned him as her brother, but the least he could do was give her a roof over her head while she thought about what to do next.

It was very early in the day, and the city was still only just waking up, the sky still a lingering pre-dawn shade of blue with the sun just dappling the river with pearly pink and gold. On any other day Cherry would have registered how beautiful it all looked without the hurly-burly of traffic and street vendors to break the mood. But this was not like any other day, and her breath was coming too fast as she raced across the dew-fresh Downs towards the city, and by the time she reached Brian's lodgings, she had a severe stitch in her side. She hammered on the door several times before there was any answer. When it came, it was from a window high above, and a man's harsh voice yelled down at her.

'He ain't there. He said summat about going away for a few days on a job, but I don't know if he's gone yet.' He frowned, recognizing her from the few times she had been here before. 'You're the sister, ain't you?'

Cherry felt her heart sink. She looked up at the man, whom she vaguely remembered as the landlord. She thought quickly.

'Yes. I'm not sure where he's going, either, but can you let me in, please? I said I'd tidy up the place while he's away,' she said, as coolly as possible.

Reluctantly he let her in to the lodgings, and she had to pinch her nose at once at the foul smells coming from various quarters. She had been brought up to respect herself and her surroundings, and so had her brother, but obviously none of it had rubbed off on him. From years of habit, Cherry automatically began picking up clothes and magazines, and then set about clearing the mountain of dirty cups and plates littered about, and after scouring the filthy sink, she washed them all up and stacked them away. At least it kept her hands and mind busy, and by the time she heard her brother come lurching into the house some time later, she was ready for him.

'Bloody hell, what's been going on here?' he slurred, still thick in the head from last night's moonshine as his bleary eyes looked around the tidied room.

'That's what I want to know,' Cherry snapped. 'What do you think you've been doing, Brian?'

After a puzzled moment he growled a reply. 'Well, last night I think I slept rough on somebody's floor, or it could have been on a park bench.'

She resisted the urge to hit him, seeing that he was in no fit state to be sensible. 'That's not what I mean and you know it! You've been sending some horrible letters to my employers, trying to blackmail them and saying wicked things about me.'

His eyes narrowed. 'Well, if you hadn't had a fling with your fancy man I wouldn't have needed to, would I? We all have to live, sis.'

She seethed at his manner. If she was still letting Lance go on thinking she was pregnant for a little while longer, maybe she should let her brother believe it too . . . But she couldn't do it.

'I'm not having a baby!' she yelled. 'You've got it all wrong.'

'Tell that to the fairies,' he jeered. 'I know what I heard and your bloke will pay up in the end. His sort always do.'

Cherry glared at him, seeing him sway and guessing he might fall over at any moment. If that happened, she couldn't bear to be here to see it. She pushed past him to get to the door and into some fresh air, and he grabbed her arm with unexpected firmness, twisting her soft flesh.

'I'll get my money one way or another, girl. You can count on it.'

She wrenched away from him and out of the door, running away from the place as fast as she could. The lodgings were in a seedy part of the city that had come to life now, and she brushed against pimps and prostitutes, sobbing as she ran, back to the only place she knew where there was safety. Back to Lance.

When she reached the Melchoir house, she opened the kitchen door cautiously, praying that she would get inside without anyone noticing her, but it was a futile hope. The rest of the staff looked at her in astonishment, and Cook stood with her arms folded, eyes full of condemnation.

'Well, Miss, what do you have to say for yourself?'

'What do you mean?' Cherry stammered.

Surely Paula hadn't betrayed her . . . Or had someone from upstairs already been down here demanding her presence – or, worse still, sending her packing?

Cook was in full flow now. 'Paula said you had the squits, and if that was the case you've taken a blooming long time getting over it. Not that I believed a word of it, mind. From the look of you, all red-eyed and flustered, I'd say you've been meeting a young man, same as young Paula here. Whoever he is, you'd do best to be rid of him if he's the type to be knocking you about. Go and clean yourself up and then come back and get on with your work. You're not paid to go gallivanting with young feller-me-lads.'

Following her glance, Cherry saw that her sore arm was starting to bruise now. Her feet were still damp from the early morning dew, and she realized what a sight she must appear to be. Paula gave her a sympathetic look, but suddenly feeling as though she was about to throw up, Cherry bolted for the back stairs and up to their room before she disgraced herself completely.

What a nightmare it all was, she thought, splashing cold water on to her face and dabbing a cold flannel on her arm to try to reduce the bruising. The thought that one brief encounter with the man of her dreams could end like this was something she could never have imagined.

By the time she had composed herself reasonably well, she went back downstairs, her legs still shaking as she begged Cook for some toast and tea.

'There's plenty of work to be getting on with, but I suppose you'd better have it if you've got rid of everything in your stomach one way or another,' she said, 'otherwise we'll get nothing more out of you for the rest of the day.'

'Thank you, Cook,' Cherry muttered.

'Anyway, you're wanted upstairs this afternoon, along with the rest of you young ones,' she went on, shattering Cherry's brief moment of complacency. 'Lord only knows what they want with you all, but it's as good as a royal command, so you'd better do your best to hide those bruises, my girl, or they'll wonder what kind of person they're hiring these days.'

At her words, Cherry felt numb. Cook might not know why the younger members of the kitchen staff were wanted upstairs, but she did, and so did Paula. As soon as the two of them could snatch some time alone in the kitchen garden, she couldn't control her emotions a second longer, and she burst into noisy tears.

'For goodness' sake, stop it, or they'll hear you,' Paula said. 'It's a good job you came back. I was starting to run out of ideas about you. Did you find your brother?'

'Yes, and much good it did me,' Cherry said bitterly. 'I told him the truth, but he didn't believe me. He still thinks I'm in the club, and he's still going to blackmail Lance. Do you think he's told his father? Is that why they want to see us all, to find out which one of us it is before they sack me?'

'Lord knows. But if you go, I shall go too. It won't be much fun here without you.'

'Oh, no, you mustn't do that! As well as losing my job, I'll be the cause of you losing yours as well. Don't make me feel even worse, Paula.'

The other girl shrugged. 'Well, why don't we wait and see what it's all about before we think of doing anything rash? It might not be anything to do with your little problem at all,' she added delicately.

Her little problem! Cherry gave a weak smile at the irony of it. But Paula was right in one thing. Until they knew exactly what they were wanted for, they just had to get on with doing their job — while they still had one.

Eleven

Lady Melchoir was having nothing to do with the meeting that afternoon. It was up to the gentlemen to sort out this sordid mess. She completely blocked from her mind the thought that any servant girl could be having her son's child. For one thing, it was not like Lance to be so stupid. Some might call him feckless and a rich playboy nowadays, but both she and Francis knew of his exploits during the final days of the war, and how responsible a young man he had been in charge of his regiment.

It hadn't been an easy choice for him to give it all up, but he had done it for the sake of his family, and she wouldn't hear a word said against him. A gentleman had standards and should also have control over any wanton feelings. She had said as much to Francis many times, and he usually returned the barb by telling her that she was wearing blinkers as far as her hot-blooded son was concerned. A remark that made her instantly assume her stiffest face and retire to her own rooms in annoyance at such vulgarity.

But now this dreadful thing had happened, and if there was any truth in it at all, naturally she blamed the girl in question. But what were they going to achieve by calling all the young girls from below stairs to account? If one of them was guilty of loose living, then either all the others would rally round her in a sense of misplaced loyalty, or more likely, they would be just as ready to condemn one of their number in order to get themselves out of the firing line. As far as Lady Melchoir was concerned, they were all tarred with the same brush. They had their place in a decent household and, providing they did their jobs well and unobtrusively, that was all that was required of them. She was under no illusion that her husband thought her the biggest snob in Christendom, but that was because Francis had no real class to speak of. Not compared with her own.

Still in a spirit of resentment at the way her entire day was being spoiled, to say nothing of the harmony of the whole house, she decided to speak with her son that morning to remonstrate with him, and to demand to know the truth. Unpalatable it might be, but without being armed with the facts, nothing could be resolved. As she had half expected, Lance was nowhere to be found in the house. She eventually tracked him down in the stables, grooming his horse with unnecessary vigour, and doing the job that belonged to the stable boys.

'Really, Lance, I don't know why we pay these people when you come here and do the work yourself,' she began at once.

'I do it because it suits me to do it, Mother. There's a bond between a man and his horse that you probably don't understand.'

She bit back the retort that he obviously had more of a bond with his horse than with his mother.

'I want to talk to you, and I'd be glad if you would leave that alone and take a walk with me.'

He gave a heavy sigh. 'Whatever you've got to say to me, I think you made your feelings clear last night. It's best if we leave it until this afternoon and let Father and me sort things out.'

'I don't think you and your father are in the right frame of mind to do what has to be done.'

Lance paused in his grooming. 'Oh really? And what frame of mind do you think we are in? I assure you this is no picnic for me, and neither do I take kindly to being blackmailed!'

Elspeth wouldn't be dissuaded now from saying what had been simmering in the back of her mind ever since the events of last night.

'Don't be obtuse, Lance. Unfortunately any man is capable of having his head turned by a pretty and persuasive young trollop, but I thought you had more sense and decorum.'

Her face flushed a deep pink at having to say such words. But there had been times in the past when she had even wondered if Francis had strayed off the rails a little. It wasn't something a lady ever cared to ask, or even chose to know, but that didn't prevent a tiny frisson of doubt at times.

'Well, Mother, I can assure you that I did not have my head turned by a pretty and persuasive young trollop, so at least you can set your mind at rest about that. I have never lied to you, and I'm not lying now.'

He flung down the grooming brush and she flinched at his

harsh words. And then he said what had been uppermost in his mind.

'Look, this meeting that Father insists on is a farce. Only one of them is involved, and she's the only one we need to see — if that's what you both want.'

'I would much prefer to see none of them,' Lady Melchoir snapped. 'But I can see that it's a problem that won't go away on its own. I'm sure you'll let me know what you decide in due course.'

She turned and walked away, and if he'd never seen it before, Lance could see exactly why she thought herself cast in the same mould as Queen Mary — and she was just as stern and unforgiving, he thought. His stomach churned, but he had made up his mind, and a moment later he left the stables and strode off towards the kitchens.

With the doors open to let in some air, he could hear the noisy chatter long before he got there. There was much gossip and surmise among the staff as the reasons for the summons upstairs became wilder and wilder. With her inner knowledge of what it was all about, and the need to preserve her part in it as secret as possible, Cherry had become almost hysterical with her own pretence at guessing. Perhaps a valuable piece of china really *had* been smashed and the evidence only just discovered. Perhaps one of them had been trying on one of Lady Melchoir's gowns and torn the hem. Perhaps someone had overheard her mimicking her ladyship's voice and let it slip to those upstairs.

Cherry was speaking out loud now, in a perfect copy of the lady's haughtiest tones, to the accompaniment of giggles from the others.

'I wouldn't put it past any of those young gels to be at fault. It may be necessary to stop their wages for a week or two, to let them see the error of their ways, don't-ya-know!'

While Paula and the others were still giggling, and Cook was chiding them while wiping the tears from her eyes at such antics, they heard the slow handclap coming from the open doorway. Then Captain Lance walked into the room, and where seconds before the room had been full of animation, now it seemed like a frozen tableau.

'That was an excellent rendition, Cherry,' Lance said coldly. 'Would you please come outside for a few moments? I wish to speak with you.'

Her heart pounding, and aware of the stares of everyone else in the room, Cherry wiped her hands on her apron and went outside. He walked quickly away from the house, and she had no option but to follow him until they reached the shrubbery. Whatever he was going to say to her, she knew it could be nothing good. Her brother had seen to that. He finally stopped and faced her, standing with his arms folded and saying nothing for a moment, which unnerved her even more.

'Whatever you've got to say, can't we get on with it?' she stuttered.

'Good advice. Well then, we've got ourselves into a fine pickle, haven't we, Cherry-Ripe?'

His use of the silly pet-name took her off-guard, but he was far less aggressive than she had expected. He was almost allying himself with her in all this – and so he should, she thought indignantly. She hadn't been the one to seduce him – although that was far too harsh a word to use for that mutual ecstasy which had seemed so perfect at the time . . .

'What do you mean?' she asked, husky now with remembering.

'I mean I think you should be the only one to be at the meeting this afternoon. There's no reason to involve anybody else, is there?'

'So it is all about the letter my brother sent you,' she said, as though it could possibly be about anything else.

'And the one he sent to my father.'

Cherry felt her mouth drop open. This was the first time she had heard anything about a second letter. So Brian had sent another one to Lord Melchoir. She wanted to die of shame at that moment, knowing that her own brother could have betrayed her like this.

'I can't believe it,' she said shakily.

'Well, you'd better believe it,' Lance said, more grimly now. 'Your charming brother is not merely demanding money for his silence now. He was sure to let him know that there's a child involved.'

Hearing his bitter words, as if he was condemning her, Cherry knew exactly what it meant about wishing the ground would open up and swallow her. But it took two . . . even if she wasn't in the condition he thought she was. And now was the time to tell him. She *had* to stop this farce right now. It wasn't fair on anybody to let the pretence go on. She opened her mouth, but somehow the words wouldn't come.

He grabbed hold of both her hands, and then he noticed the large purple bruise on her upper arm. It had been half-hidden by her sleeve, but it was fully exposed now.

'Did he do that?'

She nodded, unable to speak.

'For God's sake, don't look at me like that, Cherry,' he said, in a lower voice now. 'I know you – and he – must hate me now, and I'd do anything to turn the clock back. Except that a part of me never wants to do that, because if that happened, I would never have known your sweetness.'

'You shouldn't say such things to me,' she whispered.

She wasn't really sure what he was saying. Did he mean that he remembered that closeness with the same feelings as she did?

Even while the bewildering thoughts swirled around her mind, she hardly knew how she came to be enfolded in his arms, or how she came to be leaning her bright head against him, feeling the beat of his heart against her own.

'My sweet girl, what I should do and what I want to do are two different things. But of one thing I'm sure. We're both responsible for what's happened, and we're going to see it through together. You'll come upstairs to the drawing room at three o'clock this afternoon, and we'll sort things out between us.'

'Just me? Without the others?' she said in a fright.

She struggled out of his embrace now. It had been a daunting prospect before, but if she was to be the only one on the carpet, there could be no denying that she was to blame for what happened. She would share in her brother's guilt, and no matter how Lance might be softening towards her, the clever Melchoirs would twist things whichever way it suited them.

'Just you, Cherry. I hardly think either of us would relish the thought of my father asking the kitchen staff, one by one, if they had had carnal relations with me,' Lance said.

'Is that what it was?' she asked.

'It's a biblical term.'

'I know very well what it means. I'm not stupid.' And all the tenderness of moments before had vanished in that one ugly term. She lifted her head high.

'Then will you please see to it that the others are informed that I'm the only one to be summoned this afternoon? Clearly I'm the only one at fault here, but the new arrangement should come from my betters.'

She used the word deliberately, more hurt than she could have imagined by the way the tone of this conversation had changed so quickly.

'Of course. I'll see to it,' Lance said, but before he could say anything more, she had turned away from him and was running back to the kitchen where she belonged, and to the people she knew best.

Cook immediately said what they were obviously all thinking. 'Come and have a nice cup of tea, Cherry. I can see you're upset. Did you get a good telling-off from the captain for aping her ladyship like that?'

'Well, I think it's a shame,' Gwen put in. 'We were only having a lark, and I thought he might have seen the funny side of it.'

'He wasn't too bad, but I'd rather forget it,' Cherry said, letting them think what they liked, which was preferable to the reality of it all.

A short while later the butler informed them that the afternoon arrangements had changed, and that it was now only Cherry who was summoned upstairs.

'I knew it,' Cook said indignantly. 'They're going to censure you for acting the way you did. Don't you let them walk all over you, Cherry. You've got to know your place, but it would serve them all right if you went up there and answered them back in exactly her ladyship's voice, and see what they make of that. Who's to say that a skivvy can't act the part of a lady when she chooses?'

'I'd never dare to do that!' Cherry said, thankful at least that they had no idea of the real nature of the summons and were all ready to take her side, whatever the cause.

'Why don't you do as Cook said?' Paula said to her a while later. 'It would be a lark, Cherry, and if they're going to give you the push, you might as well go out in style!'

Cherry shivered. 'You don't know the half of it. Lord Melchoir's had a letter as well as Lance, and Brian told him about the baby.'

'You mean the baby that never was.'

'Well, you know that, and I know it, and Brian knows it now too, but nobody else does.'

'You mean you still haven't told Lance yet?' Paula squeaked. 'I never thought you were a fool, Cherry, nor so devious. You're not being fair to him.'

'I never got the chance!'

But of course she had. She had had every chance, and she still didn't know why she hadn't come clean. But maybe this afternoon would be the best time, when she could be dignified, and tell his parents that she wasn't the wanton they clearly believed her to be. She would tell them all.

At three o'clock that afternoon, she presented herself at the drawing-room door. She had changed into a clean dress, brushed her hair until it shone, and defiantly, she had applied some lipstick and powdered her cheeks, trying to subdue the nervous redness in them. But when she entered the room, her nerve almost failed her at the sight of the three people awaiting her. Lady Melchoir was sitting stiffly, while the gentlemen were standing behind her. When Cherry appeared, Lance motioned her inside, and she stood in front of the trio, as terrified as if she was about to face the guillotine.

'Don't be frightened, Cherry,' Lance said at once, immediately stilled by his father's hand.

'You know why you're here, don't you?' Lord Melchoir said.

His wife stared straight ahead, as if she wasn't part of this little gathering at all, as if she wasn't really seeing the girl in front of her. Her eyes seemed to go right through Cherry, and it was as insulting as if she was a fly on the wall. That was what made Cherry act the way she did. She took a deep breath and looked directly at Lord Melchoir.

'I have a fair idea of why I'm here, Lord Melchoir, since Captain Lance has informed me a little. But until this morning I had no idea that you too had received an incriminating letter, supposedly sent by my brother. Before I can defend myself in any way, I would appreciate seeing both letters before we proceed.'

It was hard to say who was the more astonished by this little speech – not least Cherry herself, who had not intended to say anything of the kind and certainly not in the clear, crisp voice of a lady until the words seemed to spill out of her mouth all by themselves.

'*Good God Almighty!*' exclaimed Lord Melchoir.

It wasn't so much his startled reaction, nor the glimmer of laughter in Lance's eyes that caught Cherry's attention now. It was Lady Melchoir, whose hand had gone at once to her chest; her mouth had opened, and her eyes had become firmly fixed on Cherry. If she had ever wanted to catch the lady's attention, she couldn't have found a better way of doing it.

'I think the condemned person has a right to see what she's being accused of, Father,' Lance said, barely able to conceal his amusement now. He strode across to Cherry, the two pieces of paper in his hand. She had no idea where he had produced them from, but it gave her a moment's respite to gather her wits.

'Well done,' Lance breathed, so that only she could hear.

And suddenly they were two conspirators in this together. If it was a totally false assumption, for the moment it gave her a sense of bravado, of recklessness, of 'us against them', and that together they could achieve anything.

She let the crazy notions simmer while she looked at the first incriminating pieces of paper she held now, the letter sent to Lance. It was undoubtedly Brian's clumsy work, she thought scornfully, but the ridiculous amount of money he was demanding made her gasp.

'Five hundred pounds is an awful lot of money,' she burst out. 'I can see why you would have wanted nothing to do with it, and I wouldn't have blamed you if you had handed this straight over to the police.'

Putting her brother behind bars where he could do nobody any harm might have solved everything, she thought seethingly.

'This arrived while we were away from home, before any suggestion of complying with his demand could be put into place, and then my father had a second letter waiting for him on our return from London.' Lance went on, 'The writer was obviously becoming impatient for his blackmail money.'

He was still standing beside her as if there were only the two of them in the room. She scanned the second letter quickly, and her face flamed as she saw what Brian had informed Lord Melchoir, but even worse was the hateful way he had described her and the imaginary child.

'I see,' she murmured, her heart beginning to beat uncomfortably fast now.

She handed the pieces of paper back to him as if they were red hot, but to his parents her flushed face apparently told their own story.

'Is this disgraceful allegation true?' Lady Melchoir finally found her voice.

Now was the moment. With her next few words she could deny everything and let Lance off the hook. He had suffered enough, and she felt ashamed of letting him continue to think she was pregnant when she wasn't. Cherry tried to gather up strength and her last shreds of dignity to say the words of denial, and as she did so the room seem to spin in front of her. There was a roaring in her ears, and the next moment her legs gave way beneath her and the last thing she remembered was of being caught in Lance's arms, seconds before she fell to the carpet in a dead faint.

The next thing she knew was hearing Lord Melchoir's voice, and she was aware of the pungent smell of *sal volatile* beneath her nose.

'She's coming round. Give the girl some air,' Lord Melchoir was saying.

Cherry struggled to sit up and was pushed gently back on the chaise longue where someone had carried her. She registered that she was still in the drawing room of Melchoir House, and then the memory of what had been happening rushed back at her. She tried to speak, knowing there was something vital that she had to say, something she had to put right, but Lance put his hand gently on her arm.

'Lay still for a few more moments until we see that you're all right. Mother wants to send for the doctor.'

'*No*. It's not necessary,' she said jerkily. 'I must get back to work, but I really need to say something, and I'm sorry to have caused such a fuss.'

'Never mind all that, as long as you're all right,' Lord Melchoir said, brisk now. 'I suggest you go back to your room and recover before you resume your duties. My son will see you out and then we'll consider what's to be done.'

He was curt, where moments before he had seemed so concerned. Truth to tell, he was out of his depth now. If the girl was pregnant she had to see a doctor who could be trusted to deal with the situation, and she also had to be dismissed. But he couldn't fail to notice the way his son had tended to her when she fainted. If he had any real feelings for her, then that too must be nipped in the bud. He waited for Lance to return to the drawing room, meaning to have things out with him properly, since Elspeth had simply washed her hands of the whole affair and retired to her own room. From long experience, Francis knew she was best left alone until she decided to face him again.

By the time he realized that Lance was probably not coming back, he was starting to get his dander up again. Surely the young devil wasn't spending time with the girl in the servants' quarters. Whatever else he got up to, this was beyond the pale. He rang for the butler, meaning to find out what was going on, but he was forestalled by an anxious Gerard asking if everything was all right, and the hope that Cherry O'Neil hadn't committed any crime.

'Nothing that can't be put right,' Francis said testily. 'If you haven't seen her, then it's probably because she was unwell when she left the drawing room. It was simply a misunderstanding, but the small problem has been dealt with and, before any gossip begins, please leave it at that.'

Anything was better than to start unwanted speculation among the servants. Gerard nodded, hopefully reassured, thought Francis.

'By the by, have you seen my son recently?' he asked casually.

'I believe I saw him making for the stables a short while ago, my Lord, and he was in something of a hurry,' he added with a slight smile.

'Thank you, Gerard.' He dismissed him with a wave of his hand and lit a Havana cigar before drawing deeply on it and letting the fragrant aroma waft around him, soothing his frazzled senses. He was relieved to hear that Lance had gone riding, as he often did when he needed to think. Hopefully it would clear his head of any such nonsense as making an honest woman of the O'Neil girl – if that was what he was starting to think. His strong mouth twisted at his own thoughts, since honesty hardly came into what he could only think of as a low-class scheme to extort money from the Melchoir family. For all any of them really knew, she may not even be pregnant at all, and it would need a doctor to determine the truth of that. He resolved there and then that nothing else was going to be decided until that happened.

Lance's escape from the house had nothing to do with thinking things through. He had done enough of that and it had got him nowhere. He regretted having to submit Noble to yet more hard riding, but he knew exactly where he was going now, and he intended to wait there until Brian O'Neil turned up. Once at the waterfront, which was busy with old sea salts and ripe with smells of indiscriminate origin, he tethered Noble to a post near the Smuggler's Inn and strode along the river's edge. Knowing he stuck out like a spare part in his elegant clothes, he ignored some of the catcalls that followed him.

'Have any of you seen Knuckles O'Neil?' he asked around, using the name that he assumed would be most likely to be recognized here.

'Who wants to know?' was the usual retort.

'I need to speak with him,' he would snap back.

'Well, if he's in any kind of trouble with the law, you won't find a squealer around here,' others would jeer.

It was a similar story for the couple of hours he spent in these unsavoury surroundings, although he would spend all night here if need be, he thought grimly. The bastard had to learn that he couldn't mess with the aristocracy and get away with it.

Finally, he heard a shuffling in the vicinity of the Smuggler's Inn and the brawny looking man stood squarely in front of him.

'I hear you've been looking for me. Have you brought the necessary?' Brian drawled.

'I have not, and you're getting no such amount from me.'

Brian laughed, his eyes gleaming as he scented a battle of wills.

'You know what will happen if you don't. Can your hoity-toity family afford a scandal?'

Lance was not demurred by his mocking tone. He hated this

whole seedy affair, but he was prepared to be reasonable. 'Look here, man, purely out of respect for your sister I'm prepared to give you fifty pounds because of the upset you've caused her, and that will be the end of it.'

Brian laughed louder. 'Fifty pounds! What good's a pittance like that when it's your reputation that'll suffer if you don't pay up? As for my sister, she'll get over it. I daresay you weren't the first.'

Lance wasted no more time. While Brian was still speaking, his fist had shot out and smashed into the lout's face. His nose immediately spurted blood, and almost before Lance knew what was happening, a small crowd had gathered around the two of them, scenting a fight. Most of them were shrieking for Brian to kill the bastard, but others were supporting the well-dressed bloke who had the audacity to think he could get the better of a bare-knuckle fighter.

Lance was no slouch when it came to boxing, and thanks to his army training and his prowess at horse-riding, he was physically very fit, but even so, he was no match for a man who earned his living by his fists and was always prepared to play dirty at every opportunity.

Despite the leering crowd that seemed to have surrounded them from nowhere he might have held his own for a while longer had not Brian's fist smashed into his face, splitting open his wounded cheek still more, and causing him to stagger backwards. Even as the crowd hastily parted, Lance fell, winded for a moment, and as he did so his head made contact with a small stone pillar and he slumped unconscious to the ground. Everybody began shouting at once.

'You've killed the bugger,' someone yelled in Brian's ear.

'Does anybody know who he is?'

'Don't matter. Send for an ambulance and let the doctors deal with him.'

'He ain't dead, only winded,' someone else bellowed. 'Best get him out of here, though, and then disappear. What ain't witnessed can't be told.'

Brian knew it was good advice. The last thing he needed was to be hauled before the magistrates on an assault charge when he was due at his new fight venues later that week. In the general confusion of shouting and various instructions on all sides, he helped himself to the contents of Lance's pockets and chose his moment to melt away. As an afterthought he whipped away the horse's tether and whacked him on the rump, causing him to whinny in protest and then gallop away in a fright, scattering folk as he went.

Twelve

Lance was bemused by the way the ground seemed to be moving beneath him in such an alarming manner. Then he gradually became aware that he must be in a swaying vehicle. His head felt as if a hundred angry bees were buzzing away inside it, made worse by every bump in the road that the vehicle covered. He had already tried to open his eyes, but everything had swirled in front of them in a nauseating way and he had closed them quickly again. But now he could sense that someone was bending over him, and he forced open his eyes a fraction to see a man wearing dark glasses peering down at him. He groaned inwardly, wondering if this was the angel of death spiriting him away, but he hardly cared because of the pain in his head and the abominable stinging in his cheek.

'Hold on there, mate,' a voice said. 'We'll be getting you to the hospital as fast as we can and they'll soon put you right.'

Hospital. Was that where they were taking him? If so, he wasn't dead. Not yet, anyway. He couldn't remember how or why he had got here, and the thought filled him with panic, jerking away at his consciousness until another rut in the road made the ambulance lurch, and the man beside him cursed angrily. Lance turned his head with an involuntary movement, and the searing pain it caused made him pass right out again.

The next thing he knew he was waking up in a hospital bed with the curtains drawn around him. He supposed he must be very ill, but still without much concern. His head still hurt like hell but he felt as though he was floating somewhere above it, and when he put a shaking hand to his cheek without thinking he felt a heavy bandage covering it and around his head. This was definitely how they laid people out, he registered numbly. He had seen enough of such scenes during some other part of his life that he couldn't rightly recall. Some bad part . . . They bandaged the head of the deceased from the chin upwards so that the jaw didn't sag open. Next thing, there would be pennies on his eyes. He tried to blink them open, wondering if the pennies were already there, then knew with a semblance of logic that of course they weren't, or he wouldn't have noticed the bed curtains. His thoughts were so random and muddled he could hardly sustain them for more than a few seconds, and he wondered if he was also going mad. If so, death would be preferable to this half-world . . .

The curtains were suddenly whisked open and a white-coated doctor and a nurse came inside. So now it was truth time. He saw that the doctor was smiling, and it was the false smile of a man who was about to deliver terrible news. He had seen that smile before. It was meant to persuade you to keep your pecker up, no matter what. He had even smiled that smile during that other missing part of his life, when he had been the one to deliver the news . . .

'Tell me the worst,' he croaked.

The doctor kept on smiling. 'Now then, cheer up, young man. You've had a nasty crack on the head and you're suffering from concussion, but it's nothing that a few days' bed rest can't put right. The gash on your cheek will need some stitches, and you'll be going down to theatre in a little while to sort that out. Meanwhile, just lie still and rest.'

The relief that he wasn't dying or going mad was short-lived. Lance felt his blood boil at the man's cheerfulness, even though he guessed that such a reaction wasn't doing him a lot of good.

'Just a minute! Where the hell am I?' he said angrily, wincing as the movement of his jaw made his cheek sting still more. Then he felt as if his stomach threatened to erupt as another vital question rushed into his mind.

'And, more to the point, *who* the hell am I?'

The doctor seemed to have disappeared behind the curtain now, and the nurse held his wrist and tried to soothe him.

'Don't be alarmed. A person's memory often plays tricks when they're concussed. It will all come back to you very soon. Can you remember anything at all? You name is always a good start, of course,' she added, with an attempt at whimsy, 'but anything will do to trigger your memory.'

He hated her complacency. How could she possibly know what it felt like to be so helpless and so full of panic at not even knowing his own identity?

'Noble,' he said, as obediently as if he was reciting a child's nursery rhyme. He didn't know where the word came from, or what it meant.

'Well done, Mr Noble, that's a wonderful start,' the nurse said. 'Now then, I'm just going to give you a little injection to make you woozy, and we'll be getting you down to theatre very soon to stitch up your cheek.'

He wanted to snap at her that he didn't need any injection to make him woozy. His head was already going round in circles and he was seeing stars with the effort of trying to think at all, but then he felt the sharp prick of a needle in his arm, and he knew no more.

'You do realize the implications of all this, don't you, Elspeth?' Lord Melchoir asked her when he finally decided to retire for the night and leave anything more until tomorrow when he felt less wound-up.

'I don't want to talk about it.' He heard the mumbled words from the other side of the bed.

Francis contemplated the pile of bedclothes. Apart from her head, swathed in its usual sleep net, he could see nothing more of his wife. Not that that was anything unusual. Francis hadn't seen his wife properly undressed for years, and when he did, it was to see her in a neck-to-toe nightgown that did nothing to invite intimacy. Perhaps it was one reason why he felt a small sense of sympathy for his son. The love of a good and passionate woman was something that every man desired and needed – and damn well deserved.

He cleared his throat. 'My dear, this is something that won't go away on its own.'

'I know that.' She turned her head a fraction to face him. 'Which is why we must get something done about it quickly. You know what I mean, Francis, so don't pretend that you don't.'

'For such a God-fearing woman, Elspeth, I'm surprised that you would even think for a moment of destroying a life.'

She turned around completely now, her face a deep red at even having to discuss such a thing.

'Nor would I, except for the good of our family reputation. You know that. It's not something I consider lightly, but a child conceived out of wedlock is something I cannot hold with. And with such a girl!'

'And what if the girl wants the child? What if Lance wants it?'

'Don't be ridiculous. Her opinions don't count, and of course he doesn't want it! How could he?'

'He wanted *her*,' Francis reminded her. 'And I think he still does.'

Elspeth sat bolt upright in the bed now. 'Have you completely taken leave of your senses? I don't know how you can possibly think such a thing. Go to bed, Francis, and clear your mind of such nonsense.'

She was so implacable that he found himself becoming angrier.

'Well, you've been egging him on to find a wife, and it's obvious that the Hetherington girl didn't come up to scratch and she's a presentable enough wench. In fact, there have been times when he's shilly-shallied for so long, I'd begun to wonder if he was batting on the other side of the fence.'

'How dare you say such a thing!' Elspeth spluttered.

He shrugged. 'It happens, my dear, even in the best of families, but now at least we know he's got normal male desires, and I saw the way he was looking at the girl. I tell you, there was more going on there than just a hasty roll-about.'

'Sometimes you disgust me,' his wife said icily, 'and if you can't talk about something less objectionable then perhaps you should sleep in your dressing room.'

'Then that's what I shall do. But I'll leave you with one more thing to ponder over, Elspeth. We want grandchildren, and since Lance is not too keen to tie the knot with anybody, this may be the best that we can do,' he said, and he strode off, leaving her to her prejudices and the shock of his last remarks.

He couldn't have said what woke him by the time dawn was breaking, or if he had even been asleep. He was certainly wishing he hadn't put his theories into words at all. Not about Lance being on the queer side, of course. He'd never seriously thought that, but it was this business with the girl. What he said was true, and the more he thought about it, the truer it became. The child would be his and Elspeth's grandchild, and as such deserved a place in their life.

It wouldn't be the grandchild Elspeth had always wished for, of course. She would want it to be the child of some titled young lady, who would bring added prestige to the family. In her wildest nightmares she would not have wanted it to be the child of a kitchen maid. But it was their grandchild nonetheless, he thought doggedly, and in the end it wasn't up to them to make the final decision. Lance and the girl were the two people most closely involved, and somehow the matter of the two scabrous letters they had received were of less importance in his own mind now, than trying to do what was right.

As dawn broke, he was still wrestling with all the implications that lay ahead when he heard the sounds of shouting outside, and then what seemed to be a horse's hooves quite near to the house, coupled by the shrill sound of an animal in distress. What in God's name was going on now? While he was still trying to think, he heard someone knocking rapidly on his door, and he sprang out of bed to find the butler standing outside.

'Sorry to disturb you, my Lord, but it's Captain Lance's horse that's come back on its own, all lathered up and sweating and wild-eyed, and looking as if it's been running around all night and done a marathon,' the man gasped. 'The stable lads are just calming it down now and taking it back to its stall, and as I can't rouse the captain in his room, I thought I'd better come and let you know.'

Francis was already tying his dressing robe around him and brushing the butler aside. If Lance couldn't be roused, and Noble had come back on his own, then where the hell was Lance? Had he even gone out riding on him at all? The stable lads would know that, and he had better find out everything that he could before he raised the alarm. He followed the butler down the main staircase, out into the cool night air and around to the stables.

'Did anyone see my son take the horse out?' he demanded.

One of the lads nodded, his eyes big and scared in the lantern light of the stables. 'He went out hours ago, sir, and when he never brought the horse back we assumed he was staying at a friend's house for the night as he's sometimes done before. It didn't seem nothing unusual, sir,' he added anxiously.

It wouldn't be unusual at any other time. But remembering the mood Lance was in when his father last saw him, and now the return of the horse without him, Francis felt a sharp stab of alarm.

'See that the horse is cared for,' he said unnecessarily to the stable lads, and he went quickly back to the house with Gerard at his heels.

'Is there anything I should do, my Lord?' the butler said.

'Thank you no. I shall attend to this myself, so please don't disturb yourself, Gerard,' Francis said. 'I'm sure there's a simple explanation.'

He doubted it very much, but the last thing that was needed was for the kitchen staff to start more speculation. By now his heart was thumping uncomfortably fast. Images in his mind of the horse being spooked and throwing Lance to the ground were large in his mind, as was the thought of him being attacked and robbed, but since he rarely carried large amounts of money with him, it seemed unlikely. Then again, how was a potential robber supposed to know that? That the earlier events of the night could have had anything to do with his son's disappearance was something he was reluctant to consider, but he knew it could have done. Lance might have foolishly gone out to try to confront the blackmailer, and who knew what the result might have been . . .

He was not normally a very imaginative man, and after all, they had faced worse eventualities while Lance was overseas with his regiment. Even so, his blood felt chilled for a moment, and all he could think of was the appalling possibility that if the worst had happened to Lance – or if it ever did in the future – then the kitchen maid's child would be all that they had left of him.

He went back inside the house and into his study, refusing to let himself get over-emotional about this. He was a rational and hard-headed man, and it was not his normal style to get flummoxed until he knew all the facts, but even so, his hands were shaking as he reached for the telephone book and the number of the local police station.

'My God, there were some goings-on earlier this morning,' Gerard informed the kitchen staff when they assembled to their duties. 'Lord knows what's going on, but if you ask me, it seems as if Captain Lance has done a bunk.'

'*What?*'

Everyone started talking at once, wondering what was going on, and what could have caused him to do such a thing, and trying to find out exactly what made Gerard come out with such a statement.

'If you'll all let me get a word in edgeways and stop twittering like a lot of excited hens I'll tell you,' he said loudly. 'I don't know what was going on upstairs yesterday, either, but apparently Captain Lance went off on his horse in a bit of a state, and never came back last night. The first thing anybody knew about him going missing was when his horse turned up on its own, looking fit to drop.'

In the general mêlée Paula had clutched Cherry's hand. Her face had gone white, and she was the only one not saying anything. But Paula could see that she was in danger of giving the blessed game away. Right now, only the two of them knew about it, now that Paula had heard the whole tearful story from her friend when she went to bed. But her very silence had caught the attention of the butler and he looked at her sharply.

'Do you know anything about this, miss?'

Cherry flinched. 'Why should I know anything about it, any more than the rest of you do?'

'Only that you were the one hauled upstairs yesterday afternoon, so you might have sensed what was going on.'

'I told you the reason for that, and I hardly think it could have anything to do with Captain Lance going off on his horse,' she replied, trying to keep her voice under control since everyone was looking at her now.

Gwen giggled. 'Well, we all know you've got a soft spot for the captain. I'd say you were quite smitten.'

'And I'd say you were quite wrong,' Cherry snapped.

It was nothing as simple as being smitten, but they were never going to know it. Even so, she felt more than a touch alarmed if Lance really had disappeared. She knew better than most of them where he might have gone, and also what her brother was capable of.

She swallowed the dryness in her throat as the others lost interest in her and tried to imagine what could have happened. If only she had the nerve to go to Lord Melchoir and ask him what he knew . . . but it wasn't her place, and she knew she wouldn't dare to do such a thing. She could only fret and wait, like everyone else, until there was any definite news.

'I'm sure he'll be all right,' Paula told her when they had a moment alone.

'You know that, do you?' Cherry said, her eyes bright with tears she dare not shed. 'Are you a clairvoyant now? Or is this your new-found confidence coming out since you've been seeing your painter friend?'

'Perhaps it is,' Paula said defiantly. 'But for goodness' sake, the man was a captain in the army, and he knows how to defend himself.'

'You do think he's been attacked then? And you also think you know who did it, I suppose,' Cherry returned.

'Don't you?' Paula said.

Cherry wilted. Of course she knew who had done it – if anybody had done anything, and they didn't even know that yet. But even if Lance hadn't been attacked, she was sure he must have gone off in a fury because of the afternoon's events, and his father would undoubtedly be thinking the same. She wished she could see into Lord Melchoir's head and know what was going on in there, but if there was anything more likely to damn her and her brother in his eyes, she couldn't think of it.

Paula was doing her best to be practical as usual.

'Look, Cherry, we've got to go down to the shops this morning. I know where Harold's working and it's on our way. Do you want me to ask him to sniff around and see if he can find out anything?'

'I don't know. I suppose we could just say we're curious, but I don't want him to know I'm involved in any way, mind.'

The minute she said it Paula's expression told her that it was too late.

'He doesn't know the whole story, Cherry, only that you thought the captain took a bit of a fancy to you and he's chatted to you a few times, and that's all, truly it is,' she defended herself.

As far as Cherry was concerned, that was enough, but there was nothing she could do about it now. In any case she was glad to get away from the house with Cook's list of supplies that were needed, and just hope that by the time they got back Lance would have returned too. Harold didn't look too concerned when he heard what all the fuss was about. He was just glad to see Paula, and it was obvious they were besotted with one another. Lucky Paula, thought Cherry, to have found someone of her own class whose family wouldn't look down on her for daring to fall in love with their son.

'How old is your boy, sir? The voice at the other end of the telephone enquired.

Lord Melchoir smothered an oath. 'For God's sake, man, what does it matter? I tell you he's missing, and all you're interested in is how old he is.'

'It's important in these matters, sir. For instance, if the boy is a minor then the case takes on an entirely different meaning. The younger the child is, the more serious an offence may have been committed.'

'And does this affect your interest in finding him?' Lord Melchoir snapped. 'Is this what we pay our police force for nowadays, to waste time in asking stupid questions and doing unnecessary paperwork?'

The sergeant at the other end of the line put his hand over the telephone receiver and commented to his colleague in an aside.

'We've got a right toffee-nosed one here. Lost his kid and thinks the world's coming to an end because he can't find him.'

He returned to the conversation with Lord Melchoir in a mild tone that infuriated him even more.

'If we could have your son's name and personal details, sir, I assure you the matter will be given every priority,' he said, giving his colleague a sly wink.

Francis took a deep breath. Having by now been nagged remorselessly to do this by his wife who was as near to hysteria as gentility allowed, he was in no mood to be patronized.

'Then please listen carefully. My name is Lord Francis Melchoir, and my son is Captain Lance Melchoir.'

'Here, hang on a minute. You say the boy is a captain?'

'Late of His Majesty's forces, who served his country well,' Francis snapped. 'He went out yesterday and hasn't been seen since. His horse returned without him in a hell of a state and looking fit to drop, so obviously something must have happened to the boy.'

The sergeant tried hard to hold on to his patience. 'I would say your son sounds more than capable of looking after himself, sir. But before you do anything else, I suggest you try the local hospitals, to see if he's turned up there. Now that we have your details, if we hear anything we'll be sure to contact you, so leave it with us.'

He hung up the phone before he could hear any response, and rounded explosively on his colleague.

'Bloody toffs. He's lost an army captain, would you believe, and thinks all we've got to do is run around looking for him.'

'Calm down, Sarge,' the other man replied with a grin. 'The chap's probably off on the razzle, but you know what these loaded daddies are like. They can't bear to think their precious offspring might have come in contact with any roughnecks. I'd say forget him.'

'Good advice. All the same, take down the details and if you hear anything, let me know.'

Francis was thinking he had been given good advice, albeit in an offhand way that incensed him. He was reluctant to phone any hospitals, fearing what he might hear, and even though he knew it would be the logical thing to do. He put himself in his son's place, imagining how he would feel if he knew his father was acting in such a frantic way. Good God, it was only a few hours, and Lance might very well have stayed the night at his club. There were liveries nearby where he could have tethered Noble for the night, and the beast might just as easily have got free. Francis was sure Lance must have sent Noble home alone, and there had to be some sensible explanation for it.

If he was burying his head in the sand, so be it, he thought grimly. It was better than thinking the worst, and he reckoned he had already made a fool of himself by phoning the police. So there had to be some reason for it. His head went round and round, trying to think what to do for the best, but on an impulse he went back to the stables again.

'Are you sure the horse is all right?' he said abruptly, when the lad seemed incapable of answering a simple question after seeing him so unexpectedly for a second time.

'He seems so, my Lord,' the boy gulped. 'He's had a good rub down and he's much calmer now. He's none the worse for his experience.'

'And he wasn't injured in any way?' He hardly knew why he asked, but it would be important to Lance to know it.

'Not at all as far as I could see, sir. He just seems to have been running wild until he found his way back here.'

'Well, thank God he did,' Francis said.

He was about to go back to the house when he saw two female figures carrying bags of shopping approaching, despite the early hour. One of them was the kitchen maid he recognized all too well now. She was a fine-looking young woman, he registered, despite himself. She had that glorious hair that shone in the sunlight, and an upright bearing, and he could understand any young buck falling for her. He angrily quelled such wayward thoughts as they approached.

'I'll go on inside,' Paula whispered. 'Have a word with him, Cherry.'

'I can't!' Her heart had begun to beat faster as soon as she saw him, and she all but dropped her own bags of groceries as she got nearer to him and realized he wasn't turning away.

And then some little devil inside her told her not to be so stupid. Why should she be afraid of him? Any time now she was going to be dismissed, so she might as well find out what she could.

'Is there any news, sir?' she asked huskily. 'We heard what happened.'

'None,' he said briefly.

'Sir, I pray that my brother had nothing to do with this,' she ventured to say, her voice trembling, 'and I'm so sorry if he has.'

Francis held up his hand, cutting her off. 'Since I know all the staff will be anxious, naturally Mr Gerard will be informed if we hear anything, and he will pass any news on to the rest of you.'

'Thank you, sir.'

Well, what else had she expected? That he would welcome her as someone who had more than a vested interest in his son? That he would confide in her because of the fiasco and the lies that she had let him believe?

She hurried past him, humiliated, her face hot and flushed as

she realized that with his words he had put her firmly in her
place. The butler would be told if and when there was any news,
and he would pass it on to the rest of the staff. It was the proper
order of things. Cherry O'Neil was nobody important, just
someone well down the list of people to be told.

If she had known of Lord Melchoir's thoughts right then, she
would have felt slightly better. He was struck by the anxiety in
the girl's face, which she couldn't hide. It was as if she genuinely
cared for his son. He had heard the tremble in her voice and
knew it wasn't fake. He had known enough sycophants in his
life to recognize a fake when he saw one. For one unbelievable
moment as he saw her hand slip on the heavy bag of groceries
she was carrying, he had almost been tempted to carry it for her.
And how would that have looked, with his Lordship carrying a
bag of groceries for a kitchen maid?

The moment seemed to emphasize the enormity of the situation that Lance had got himself into with the girl and her thug
of a brother. It was enough to curdle his guts with anger, but the
fact was that his son was still missing, and right now the worry
over his safety overrode any feeling of anger. Nothing was more
important than being assured that he was safe and well. Lance
had got himself into a hell of a mess, but all the same, if the silly
young fool really had spent the night elsewhere without bothering to tell him, Francis would have more than words with him
when he returned.

Thirteen

Elspeth was sitting at her dressing table in her bedroom, fully clothed, without a hair out of place and looking as though nothing ever worried her. Francis felt as thought he could read her mind perfectly. She had decided what must be done with the kitchen maid: others would deal with it, and life would go on as before. With such ability to blot out any unpleasantness, he wondered, not for the first time, if she ever seriously thought about anyone but herself.

'What was all that rumpus about earlier?' she said at once. 'I could hear people shouting from here. Has something happened?'

He took her cold hands in his. 'My dear, don't be alarmed, but Lance didn't come home last night.'

She gave a short laugh. 'Well, can you blame him? I should think he'd do well to keep away from the house and that girl until all the fuss has died down.'

Francis tried to keep his temper. 'Lance didn't come home, but his horse did, in quite a distressed state.'

She swivelled round on her velvet-covered chair and stared at him. 'What do you mean, Francis? What's happened?' she repeated.

'I've told you all I know. Lance didn't come home last night and his horse did. Draw your own conclusions, and if you've got any brilliant ideas about why that was, then you'd better tell me,' he added sarcastically.

'Then I'd say he obviously stayed at his club or with friends,' Elspeth snapped. 'I refuse to get in a state over such a silly thing – and why are you still wandering about in your dressing gown?'

He looked down at himself, hardly realizing that this was the case. When Gerard had brought him the news, it had seemed far too important to bother about getting properly dressed, but he might have known that Elspeth would be disapproving and totally insensitive to the real issue here.

'I was worried,' he said harshly. 'And since you're his mother, I thought you might have been worried too. I phoned the police station earlier to report that he was missing, but they couldn't give me any news.'

Her face was almost comical in its outrage now.

'You did *what*? How could you have been so foolish? Don't you know that they have those dreadful newspaper people sniffing around for any stories they can print in their scandal rags? How will it look if one of them gets wind of this? How will Lance feel when he comes home from a perfectly inno-cent night away from home and finds himself the centre of a front-page sensation?'

'Elspeth, for heaven's sake, don't be so ridiculous,' he snapped back as her voice rose more than usual. 'For your information they didn't take me seriously. In fact they probably thought I was some time-waster playing a joke. Now I'm going to get dressed, since my appearance is obviously offending your sense of propriety.'

He slammed out of her bedroom, wondering how she had ever changed from the once loving girl he had married into this harridan of a shrew for whom outward show was all. The hell of it was, for all her haughtiness, he still loved her, and he could see the sense of her words, damn it.

He could even admire her for her capacity in putting the events of yesterday behind her in the ostrich-like certainty that everything would come right in the end. Presumably, in her mind, at any time now Lance would come walking in and all his father's anxiety would have been for nothing. Despite all his misgivings, he decided to try to believe that too. For now, they would do nothing but wait.

'I should have told them the truth yesterday.' Cherry's voice was still shaking as she and Paula put away the groceries in the pantry. 'I was so stupid to let it go on and they'll hate me even more when the truth does come out.'

'Well, I won't say I told you so, even though I did. But if you ask me, the best thing you can do now is to let them think you've had a miscarriage,' Paula said.

'Tell them another lie, you mean.'

'Have you got any better ideas?'

'I can't even think about that now until I know that Lance is all right. I could kill my brother for what he's done. And before you ask, I just know he's had something to do with it.'

It helped to keep the anger against Brian simmering. It helped to stop her thinking quite so much. Then she heard the sound of the butler's voice talking to Cook in the kitchen and it made her pause for a moment.

'Her ladyship's sent down a message asking me to drive her to her charity meeting later this morning. I daresay nothing has to stand in the way of her doing her good works, not even worrying over her son.'

'She was always a cold fish,' Cook replied. 'I always thought charity was meant to start in the home, but the upper classes have different ideas from the rest of us.'

'That's because they don't need charity,' Gerard reminded her. 'Anyway, I'll be off to get the motor ready now, so if anybody needs me I'll be back in a little while.'

His voice drifted away and Paula sniffed. 'Cook's right about Lady Melchoir being a cold fish, not that I'd dare to say so out loud. Imagine having to listen to her jawing about her charities all day.'

'I'd rather not, thanks.'

'Well, if Captain Lance was to make an honest woman of you, you'd have to,' Paula said, giggling at the thought of it.

'You do talk some daft stuff, Paula! A toff like him would never marry the likes of us, so it wouldn't ever happen! And a good thing too,' she said ferociously.

'Yes, but what if he ever did ask you? What would you say if he did?'

For a moment Cherry let the dreams into her head. But only for a moment. She almost smashed the packets of sugar and flour on to the pantry shelves, threatening to split them open.

'I'd say no, of course. Who in their right mind would want her ladyship for a mother-in-law?'

'What do you think's happened to your captain then?' Paula said, going off at a tangent.

'He's not *my* captain, and how the hell do I know?' She paused. 'Still, there's one way I might be able to find out something.'

Before Paula could ask what she meant, she had gone back to the kitchen and begged Cook to let her have a couple of hours off, promising to make up the hours whenever Cook asked.

'What do you want time off for?' Cook said suspiciously.

'I've got some personal errands to do for my brother,' she invented quickly, knowing that Cook had always had a soft spot for Brian, for reasons that Cherry could never fathom.

'All right then, but don't be any longer than you've got to.'

Paula followed her to the stairs.

'What are you going to do?' she hissed.

'I'm going to find out what happened to Lance, and I know the best place for it. Don't worry, I know what I'm doing.'

Cherry sped back upstairs to her room and changed out of her work clothes into a more presentable dress. Her heart was beating fast at what she was about to do, but there was no way she was going to the disreputable Smuggler's Inn looking like a kitchen maid and having the dregs of the waterfront sniffing around her. She was going to act like a lady, and if she had ever needed to play the part, she needed it now.

She caused a bit of surprise when she reappeared in the kitchen, knowing she didn't have the nerve to go out by the front door of the house, but she didn't stop for any questions. She had a definite purpose in mind now, and the sooner she put it into operation the better.

The early morning mist that so often covered the Downs and spangled bushes and trees in gossamer, cobwebby threads, had long dispersed, and there was the promise of a lovely summer's day to come. Cherry noticed none of it as she sped away from the house, across the grass and down into the city to the waterfront that was already bustling with life. She was aware of catcalls and whistles and raucous comments as she walked, but she ignored them all and carried on with her head held high. That she was going to attract attention she had had no doubt, but it was the last thing on her mind. She needed to find out just what had been going on here last night.

Outside the Smuggler's Inn a motley collection of men sat or sprawled on wooden benches, chattering idly. They perked up when they saw Cherry approach and she told herself they were not going to harm her providing she kept her cool and didn't let on how very unnerved she really was.

Act the part of a lady, she reminded herself.

'I'm enquiring after something that may have occurred here last evening,' she said in the imperious tones she did so well.

'Oh yeah, and what may that have been?' someone jeered.

'That's what I'm asking you. My . . . my friend's horse seems to have been badly distracted by something and arrived back at the stables without its rider. Do any of you know how such a thing could have happened? Could my friend have been unseated, for instance?'

Dear God, it sounded lame, even to her . . . Referring to Lance as her friend was stretching it a bit too, but anything was better than giving away his real identity . . .

'None of us saw any horse on the loose around here,' another of the old salts drawled, to which the rest of them loudly agreed.

'Well then, do any of you know a person referred to as Knuckles O'Neil?' she said in desperation.

'Blimey, it looks as if the old turd's found himself a rich bitch,' she heard one of the men give a lewd chuckle.

Cherry turned on him. 'Was he here last night? Did he have a fight with anyone? Please tell me if you know anything.'

Without warning, her eyes filled with tears, and one of the older men cleared his throat noisily.

'Come on, you buggers, give the young lady a chance. Yes, Knuckles was here and there was a bit of a scuffle with some toff.'

'Was he hurt?' Cherry asked, finding it hard to keep her composure now.

The men glanced at once another and then shuffled away, and it was obvious they weren't going to get involved. The older one finally replied again, but Cherry could tell he was being guarded now.

'The bloke had a bit of a bang on the head. 'Tweren't nothing much but the landlord sent for an ambulance and everybody scattered, and we never saw nothing of Knuckles after that so I can't tell you no more.'

'Thank you,' Cherry gasped.

Her thoughts whirled. If there had been an ambulance then it would have taken Lance to hospital and the nearest one was the Infirmary.

She raced away from the waterfront, unheeding of the pain in her chest from her shallow breathing. She had to know for sure how serious Lance's injury was, and if it took all day to be away from her duties, then it hardly mattered, since she was only there on borrowed time now. Pregnant or not, she knew she would never be allowed to stay there now. The unbending Lady Melchoir would see to that.

She reached the hospital and rushed inside where the antiseptic smells assaulted her nose immediately. She grabbed the hand of the nearest person in a brown duty coat and gasped out her request.

'Please, I'm looking for someone who was admitted by ambulance some time last night. His name's Captain Lance Melchoir, and I've been told he had a blow to his head.'

'I'm only a porter here, miss. You'll have to ask for information at the desk,' the man said, shaking her off. 'It's through there.'

She followed his direction and presented herself at the desk. She babbled out her request again, wondering if everyone in the world was destined to be so obstructive today. The woman behind the desk looked through a list of admittances. Could there be so many in one night? Cherry fumed.

'There's nobody of that name down here, love. There were a few drunks and others brought in, and some who didn't want to give their names anyway, but no captains.'

'Please look again. He was a young gentleman and he was very well dressed, and I know he was brought here,' she pleaded, even though she didn't really know anything of the sort.

'No,' the woman said after another brief search. 'There was one good-looking young chap brought in, though he wasn't looking so clever with blood all down his cheek. I'm told he gave his name as Mr Noble.'

After a few seconds trying to take in what this meant, Cherry gasped. 'That's him! Where can I find him?'

'Just a minute, miss,' she was told, before she picked up a phone and spoke quietly to someone before turning back to Cherry.

'A nurse will be here soon and she'll take you to Mr Noble's room.'

It was like something out of a play, thought Cherry dazedly, having no choice but to wait for the nurse to arrive. Here she was, putting on airs and graces in the belief that it would have

got some action quickly, and referring to Lance as Mr Noble . . .
As she thought it, she wondered just why he had given a false
name, but thank heavens he had used Noble's name, or she would
never have recognized it. Then she thought no more of it as a
nurse appeared and told her to follow her through the maze of
the hospital before they entered a small ward with curtains drawn
around a bed.

Cherry's throat felt choked as the curtains were pulled back,
and she gasped to see Lance lying very still with his eyes closed
and his cheek heavily bandaged.

'How bad is he?' she whispered.

'You'll have to ask the doctor that, miss,' the nurse said. 'He'll
be round to see Mr Noble shortly, if you want to wait.'

'Yes, of course I do. But in the meantime is it possible for me
to use a telephone? I have to tell somebody that he's here.'

The nurse looked dubious, but Cherry's tone of voice seemed
to reassure her. 'I'll ask Sister,' she said.

As she went away, Cherry moved forward to look down at
Lance. He looked so vulnerable, and she wished desperately that
she dared to hold his hand, to kiss him and weep over him, but
it wouldn't be proper to do such a thing. In any case, the nurse
came back very shortly, and said she could go into the Sister's
room. Following her, Cherry realized she didn't have the faintest
idea how to make the call. Summoning up her dignity, she asked
the Sister to do it for her, feigning shock at finding her friend
in such a state.

'Very well, my dear. What is the number?'

How *stupid* she was, Cherry thought! She didn't know any
telephone numbers, but she thought quickly.

'I'm afraid I don't know, but I need to speak to Lord Francis
Melchior. The operator will know the number,' she said, mentally
crossing her fingers.

It must have been her false air of sophistication that made the
Sister do as she asked. Either that, or she was anxious to get the
young woman out of her room and return to her duties. Whatever
it was, after a few seemingly endless moments, the woman handed
the receiver to Cherry.

'Your gentleman is on the line, miss. I'll leave you for a few
moments to speak with him.'

'Thank you,' Cherry gasped, taking the instrument from her and gripping it as if her life depended on it.

Lord Melchoir was in the middle of sorting through some household accounts, simply in order to keep busy, when the telephone sounded. He snatched it up and tried to make sense of the tearful-sounding voice at the other end.

'Who is this?' he said testily. 'I can't make out a thing you're saying. If you're wanting a donation for something or other, this is not the best time.'

He was about to put down the phone when the voice sounded louder and slightly more familiar, and then his heart stopped for a moment as he realized what she was saying.

'Lord Melchoir, it's me, Cherry. Please listen to me. I've found Captain Lance. He's in the Infirmary, and he's been slightly hurt.'

When she didn't get an immediate response, she swallowed hard. Surely he didn't think this was some kind of hoax and that she was involved in it? He surely couldn't believe she would do anything so cruel.

'Lord Melchoir, please believe me. I'm here at the Infirmary and for some reason Captain Lance seems to have told the doctors his name is Mr Noble.'

The name seemed to do the trick. There was a kind of choking sound at the other end and she waited anxiously for him to speak, praying that the shock hadn't given him some kind of seizure. He finally spoke again.

'Tell my son I'll be at the Infirmary as soon as possible.'

The line went dead, and Cherry replaced the receiver with shaking hands. She had done all she could, but she wasn't going to leave Lance now. She had to give him his father's message, anyway. She went back to his bedside and sat down beside it, preparing to wait all day if need be.

Francis went ranting through the house, calling for his wife. She should surely would have come back from her wretched charity meeting by now. He was in a foul mood when he should have been elated to know that at least his son was in safe hands. Truth to tell, he was less than pleased that the little chit of a kitchen maid had been the one to track him down, when it should have been himself. His brief softer feelings towards her vanished in an instant as he fumed and fretted that the car wasn't here when he needed it. It was another half-hour before he saw it cruising towards the house, and he was already at the front door to meet it.

'Don't get out of the car, Elspeth. We're going to see Lance,' he said curtly, and he turned to the butler. 'Gerard, I shall drive myself and Lady Melchoir, but you may tell the staff that all is well.'

'Very well, my Lord,' Gerard said smoothly, but knowing damn well from the look of his lordship's eyes that all was not as well as he claimed.

'He looked fair crazy,' he declared to Cook and the other kitchen staff. 'There's something going on there and no mistake about it.'

'You don't think he's eloped with that Hetherington young lady, do you?' Gwen said excitedly. 'It would put her ladyship's nose right out of joint if she was denied a big society wedding for her precious son.'

'Of course he hasn't eloped with Cynthia Hetherington, Gwen. Don't be so daft!' Paula said forcefully before she could stop herself.

They all looked at her, and Cook said what they were all thinking.

'And how would you know that, miss? What do you know that the rest of us don't? And where's that young Cherry got to, I'd like to know? She should have been back here an hour ago.'

Cherry was sitting at Lance's bedside and willing him to wake up. All she wanted was for him to open his eyes and look at her, and to know from his expression that she was the one person he wanted to see. A doctor had come and gone, and told her that he was still getting over the anaesthetic from the surgery on his cheek, but that once he had recovered from the concussion and the little lapses in his memory, he would almost certainly fully recover.

It was that word *almost* that Cherry didn't like. It held no guarantees, and until she saw the recognition in Lance's eyes for herself, she wouldn't stop worrying. What if he had lost his memory for ever? What if he never came round at all? She shuddered at the thought. But at least while he was asleep she could do what she would never dare to do while he was awake. She cradled his hand in hers now, and once, she had even dared to bring it to her lips. But she was beginning to feel exhausted after all that happened yesterday and then the trauma of today. For a few moments she closed her own eyes too, and just listened to the gentle rhythm of his breathing.

'Cherry-Ripe?' she heard a thin, husky voice say when she was almost drifting off to sleep.

Her eyes flew open and she saw that his were open too. They were clear and knowing, and she was overwhelmed with relief.

'Oh, Lance, I was so worried,' she said, forgetting where she was and who she was, and just so thankful that he had come back to her.

'How did I get here? I remember a fight. Your brother.'

'I know, and I'm sorry,' she said, shame rushing over her.

'You don't have anything to be sorry for,' he said thickly, his hand squeezing hers. He tried to smile, but the numbness in his cheek was wearing off and at the stabbing pain he winced instead.

'But I do,' Cherry said in a low voice. 'I have so much to be sorry for.'

Was this the best time to tell him, giving him something else to think about when he was obviously still in pain? Would it relieve him, or make him so angry that in his present condition the telling would do him more harm than good?

She had no chance to decide either way because there was a sudden fluster at the door as Lord and Lady Melchoir arrived, and Cherry blanched at the sight of them. She should have got out of here before they arrived, she thought frantically. They would only think the worst of her, sitting here and leaning over their son, with her hand held in his.

'My dear boy,' Lady Melchoir said, moving forward and brushing Cherry aside as though she didn't exist. 'What on earth has happened to you?'

'I'm all right, Mother,' he said weakly. 'Or at least, I will be.'

His mother spoke decisively. 'When I've seen a doctor we'll arrange to have you moved at once. If you're not fit to come home for a few days we'll get you into a private nursing home.'

'There's no need for all that,' he protested. 'It's only a scratch on the cheek and a bit of concussion, plus a few bruises here and there.'

'I suppose that wretched horse threw you,' Elspeth went on as if he hadn't spoken. 'I always said you were far too reckless, riding him the way you did.'

'It was something like that,' he said, his eyes still on Cherry, who had moved away from the bed and was talking with his father near the door now.

'So how did you find him? And don't think we're not grateful,' Francis was saying, even though his cold eyes said something very different.

'I simply asked some people who I thought might be able to help and they directed me here,' she told him shakily.

'Well, we shall reimburse you in some way for your trouble, and now I must have words with my son.'

She was dismissed. Just like that, they wanted nothing more to do with her. She couldn't even bear to glance back at Lance and see the way his mother was fawning over him, making plans that would never include her. She knew that so well, just as she had always known it. She didn't figure in the lives of such as the Melchoirs, except to do their bidding and see that their house ran smoothly. They would certainly never forgive her once Lance told them it was her brother who was responsible for his injuries. She smothered a sob and slipped away as quickly as she could, leaving them to their reunion and wondering now how long she could bear to remain in their household at all.

There was a reception committee waiting to greet her when she returned to the house, all wanting to know what was going on. It was late in the afternoon by then, and she had been gone far longer than she had intended, so she had expected a barrage of anger from Cook. Surprisingly, she didn't get it, since they were too concerned over what news there was of Captain Lance.

'I had to tell them something,' Paula said shamefaced. 'I said we'd heard a few rumours when we went shopping this morning, and that you, being so curious, were going to find out if there was any truth in it.'

'And with you having a fancy for the captain too,' Lucy put in with a grin.

She was too weary to deny it. She shrugged and accepted the cup of tea and piece of seed cake that seemed to have come from nowhere. She hadn't had any food all day and her stomach was rumbling, and she hungrily bit into a large piece of cake and took a slurp of tea before she said anything.

'I went to ask around at the waterfront,' she said, knowing that much at least was true. 'They said there had been a fight and Captain Lance had been taken to hospital, so I tried to find out where it was. All they could tell me was that a Mr Noble had been admitted yesterday.'

'He named himself after his blooming horse?' Gwen said incredulously. 'I thought the toffs were supposed to have some sense.'

Cherry's eyes flashed. 'He had concussion and he couldn't remember anything, not even his name. For some reason when he said the word Noble, they thought he meant he was Mr Noble. I guessed what it was, and sure enough it was him. So I telephoned Lord Melchoir, and his parents are with him now.'

'Blimey, you telephoned Lord Melchoir?' Gwen squeaked now. 'Seems to me you fancy yourself as well!'

'Be quiet, Gwen,' Gerard said. 'I think you did very well, my dear, and I'm sure his Lordship will show his gratitude that you showed such initiative.'

'Yes, well, I don't care if he does or he doesn't. I'll go and change into my work clothes now, Cook, and thanks for the tea and cake.'

'You take a few minutes to calm down as well, my girl. You've had quite a day yourself.'

They didn't know the half of it. They didn't know that when she left the hospital, she had marched straight down to Brian's lodgings and that the landlord had allowed her inside again. They didn't know that she had written a letter to her brother, telling him exactly what she thought of him and what had happened to Lance, and that if he ever contacted either of them or the Melchoirs again in any way, she would report him to the police at once. She said she would have no hesitation in doing so, nor of informing them of several of his other little schemes that she knew about in the past.

She told him she had not the slightest feeling of loyalty towards him, and that she never wanted to see him again. She had left the letter propped up on his bed, where he couldn't fail to see it when he returned from his latest jaunt. And if it gave her a sad little pang to think she was obliged to be saying these things to her brother, the wickedness of what he had done only hardened her resolve.

Fourteen

Lance found himself with plenty of time to consider things. Some might think he had led an indolent life after his army days, but this was a different kind of indolence and one that he didn't relish at all. Besides, there were others in this hospital who were far more needful of attention than himself. He hated being dependent on other people, but the hospital staff were adamant that until they were sure there was no infection in his cheek and that the concussion had left no lasting damage, he wasn't going anywhere.

He had smiled to himself, imagining the clash of wills between the buxom, no-nonsense Sister and his mother. The thought of a private nursing home didn't inspire him, either. It made him think of well-heeled old men being sent there to be pampered for their last days. But he had decided to indulge his mother for the time being, since he had been thinking more and more about the future, and if she knew of the vague ideas that were going around in his head he knew there could only be ructions ahead.

At least he wasn't confined to bed like some of the poor devils whose moans he could hear from time to time. But even sitting here in an armchair in the day room, the sights and sounds and smells of a hospital reminded him all too clearly of his army days, of other times and other places when the screams of the wounded had been almost too much to bear. He shut the memories out of his head, just as he tried to ignore the stabbing headaches that still assaulted him now and then, reminding him that he was in here for a reason, and that reason was the bastard brother of Cherry O'Neil.

By now he had discovered that the hospital staff hadn't been able to check on his identity because his pockets were empty when he was brought here, and he put that down to Knuckles O'Neil as well. The worst thing in the world, as far as he was concerned right now, was that the two of them were linked in any way. He would never believe that Cherry, his Cherry-Ripe, was involved in any scheme to fleece him, but the fact was that they were brother and sister, and if blood was thicker than water, then she would never be truly free of him. It posed more problems than his head was capable of dealing with now, and he closed his eyes and let his current allocation of painkillers do their work.

Cherry was feeling completely deflated after the last traumatic few days. Even when Paula tried to persuade her to go dancing on their next Saturday night off, she couldn't raise any enthusiasm. She felt as though she was living on a knife-edge, wondering what was going to happen next. One thing she was sure about, though: the Melchoirs were hardly going to give her the push immediately, since she had been the one to trace their son. If they did, with the kitchen staff not knowing all the facts and treating her as a bit of a heroine, it would raise anarchy below stairs. It was one small grain of comfort.

When Lance didn't return home straight away, they had learned through Mr Gerard that the hospital had insisted on keeping him a couple more nights until they were sure he was suffering no ill effects from the blow to his head. Then he had agreed to his mother's wishes to go to a private nursing home for a week or so until his wounds healed properly.

'I daresay he'd agree to anything to stop her going on at him,' Cook said with a sniff when she heard about the private nursing home. 'The toffs probably don't call it nagging, same as us, but that's what it is, all the same.'

Cherry hardly cared whether he was here or elsewhere. The fact was she was getting increasingly nervous at what she knew she had to do to put things right. She would never have dared to try to visit him in hospital again, and now she didn't know where he was, so her confession had to wait. She could have gone straight to Lord Melchoir and told him there was no baby, of course, but that wasn't right, either. It was Lance who had to hear the truth from her, not his father, and certainly not his mother. She shivered at the very thought of those cold, accusing eyes, sure that in Lady Melchoir's mind, she had been the one to seduce her son.

'So are we going dancing or not?' Paula said impatiently, when Cherry sprawled out listlessly on her bed at the end of their

Saturday shift. 'You're not doing anybody any good by moping about here, are you? And you're not likely to run into your brother if he's out of town if that's what you're worried about.'

Cherry's eyes flashed. 'I don't ever want to run into him again, and he knows that. Besides, aren't you seeing Harold tonight?'

Paula blushed. 'He did say he might be at the dance hall,' she said with studied carelessness, 'but this afternoon he was going to see a man about that job I told you about, on the railways. He really wants to do it, Cherry, and it's more money too which will give him a bit of security. He says there's a big future in the railways.'

Her voice had gathered momentum as she spoke about Harold's ambitions and Cherry gave a small smile.

'Good for him.' She wasn't all that interested in Harold's plans, until she took in what Paula was really saying. She sat up and looked at her sharply. 'So does this mean that you two are getting serious about one another? Does this railway job mean a nice little house and a garden and living happily ever after?'

'It might. Why? Do you think it's too soon?' She was defensive now, and Cherry felt a rush of affection towards her, as she had always done. And she had to be truthful now.

'I don't think it's too soon at all,' she said. 'You might not have known each other more than five minutes, but I think that when you meet your one and only, and you know darned well that he's the one, nothing on heaven and earth should keep you apart.'

'Amen to that, and it's something you should remember too,' Paula said meaningfully. 'So are we going to get our glad rags on or not?'

'Of course we are,' Cherry said, scrambling off her bed.

What was the point in staying indoors, crying over something that could never happen in a million years? She was sure that when Lance did hear the truth, he was never going to forgive her for her deception. She could try to say that she'd had a miscarriage, as Paula had suggested, but she had a horrible feeling that when it came to the point, she just wouldn't be able to do it. If you loved somebody, then the first and most important thing was always to be honest with them. And she did love Lance. She was never more sure of anything now, especially when she had seen him looking so helpless and vulnerable in that hospital bed.

And then, when he had opened his eyes and called her Cherry-Ripe, she could have fainted with the surge of love that flowed through her.

'Come on then, slowcoach,' Paula urged her.

She jerked herself into action. 'Are you sure Harold won't mind you going dancing if he's not going to be there?' she asked.

''Course not,' Paula replied. 'It's more likely to be us girls who are dancing together these days, and besides, he trusts me. He knows I'm not interested in anybody else.'

That seemed to say it all, thought Cherry. She gave up worrying about anything, and after attending to her ablutions she put on her favourite blue dress with the fringes at the hem, added her long string of glittery blue beads, brushed out her bob until it gleamed, and once she had donned her white stockings and shoes, she twirled around for Paula to see.

'So will I do?'

Paula snorted. 'You don't have to ask me that. It's a certain somebody else who would say that you look like a million dollars.'

'Yes, well, he's not here for me to ask him, so you'll have to do.'

She tried to be brittle and uncaring, but she still didn't have much heart to go dancing. She did it for Paula's sake, but that was a laugh, because it wasn't Paula who needed cheering up. She had Harold, and a promising future that beckoned. It might be what some would call a whirlwind romance, but Cherry firmly believed what she had said. Once you found your one and only, nothing on heaven and earth should keep you apart.

But as the evening wore on, she realized she was enjoying herself. She danced with Paula, and with several of the young chaps who took a fancy to the lovely-looking girl in the blue dress with the glorious hair. She threw herself into it, and was practically the life and soul of the party by the time Harold appeared a couple of hours later. By then, both girls were glad to sit out and hear what he had to say while some of the chaps brought them something to drink. It didn't seem to bother Harold that they had their temporary escorts, which said a lot for the security of their relationship, and he seized Paula's hands eagerly.

'I've got the job, sweetheart. I'll be able to pack in the house painting and cleaning jobs and I start on the railways on

Monday week. It's more money and there might be a little house going for rent sometime soon.'

'All you'll need then is somebody to cook and clean it for you,' Cherry said cheekily.

He didn't seem to notice any mockery in her words. He was too taken up with gazing into Paula's shining eyes, and it was bitter-sweet for Cherry to see the feelings they had for one another displayed so blatantly for all to see. They had no need to hide from disapproving families.

'It's wonderful, Harold. I'm so pleased for you,' Paula finally breathed.

'For *us*,' he said meaningly, giving her hands an extra squeeze. He didn't quite dare to kiss her in public, but he might as well have done, thought Cherry, swallowing the lump in her throat. Lucky, lucky Paula, to have found her heart's desire while she was so unlikely ever to realize hers.

The young chaps bringing the drinks realized something was going on, and it all ended up with them drinking a toast to Harold's new job, which only thinly disguised the fact that they were also toasting Harold and Paula.

They started to go home that night as a threesome, with Harold escorting both girls on to the bus before the final walk across the Downs, and loudly proclaiming that he must be the luckiest bloke in Bristol to have two such good-lookers to take home.

'Better than blooming film stars you look tonight,' he said expansively, making Paula giggle and Cherry wince. She spoke lightly.

'Give over, Harold, we all know there's only one angel in your life, and quite right too. Look, I'll leave you two now and walk the rest of it on my own.'

'You don't need to do that, Cherry,' Paula protested at once.

'Yes, I do,' she replied, giving her shoulder a squeeze. 'You've got things to talk about that are private, so I'll see you back at the house, Paula.'

She walked on ahead, annoyed to find her eyes prickling as she imagined the excited conversation that might be going on between the other two now. They would be making wonderful, tentative plans that may or may not come to fruition, but were exciting enough in themselves to dream about. Plans that could never be the same for Lance and herself.

As his name entered her head as it so often did, she wondered what he was doing right now. She looked up at the moonlit sky and the myriad stars above, and she wondered if he too was looking out of some hospital or nursing-home window and thinking of her. A sob caught in her throat, because of course he wasn't. Not unless it was with hate that he had been foolish enough to get caught up with her in the first place. She couldn't expect anything else, and he would hate her still more when she confessed the truth.

She had been in bed for some time when Paula returned, but even though she feigned sleep she knew very well Paula would be too excited to let her be.

'Cherry, are you awake?' she heard her say urgently.

'If I wasn't before, I am now,' she said. 'So are you engaged?'

Paula laughed. 'I suppose I am! Not that I've got a ring yet, and that will have to wait until Harold gets his first pay packet from his new job. I've told him it doesn't matter if I get a ring or not, but he says of course I must, so I said all right, but I only want a modest one, since we'll have to save our money now. He's got such great plans, Cherry, and it's so thrilling to think I'm going to be a part of them.'

'Good Lord, you'll expire in a minute if you don't stop,' Cherry said when she paused for breath with a gulp. 'So when's the wedding?'

'Oh, we haven't got around to thinking about that yet, not for months and months anyway, and even longer. But we know there are railway houses for some of the workers to rent, so he's going to see about getting one when the time comes and that we mustn't miss the chance if one becomes vacant. But I tell you what, Cherry, it will be the strangest thing in the world for me to leave here and be the mistress in my own home, however modest it's going to be.'

She paused for breath again, her voice shuddering a little, and Cherry felt an unexpected sinking in her stomach. If it would be strange for Paula to leave the Melchoir employ, how much stranger would it be for Cherry to carry on here without her? They had never been apart in all their working lives, and it was going to be a terrible wrench. She had never considered it until that moment.

When she didn't say anything, Paula came and sat on the edge of her bed and took her hand in hers.

'You are happy for me, aren't you, Cherry?'

'I'm speechless with happiness for you, you ninny,' she said huskily. 'Who ever thought little Paula would blossom like this and all for the love of a good man! It's wonderful, darling.'

They hugged one another, and then broke apart in embarrassment.

'Now, for goodness' sake go to bed and let me get some sleep, or it'll be morning before we know it,' she went on, pretending to be cross.

But the weak tears that slid silently down her cheeks were as much for the potential loss of a friendship that had lasted for so many years, as for the realization that it was Paula, who had always been slightly in her shadow, who had got the man of her dreams, and not her. She was still chasing rainbows.

It was impossible for Paula to keep the news to herself, and the kitchen staff were all agog at how quickly things had happened for her and the house painter. The other maids were nearly as excited as Paula that a romance had grown right under their noses, while Cook put in a cautionary note.

'I hope you ain't done nothing improper to encourage such haste,' she said in her usual blunt way. 'You know the old saying, "Marry in haste, repent at leisure", and I'm sure I don't need to spell out the meaning of it.'

Paula laughed, still glowing too much at Harold's proposal to take any offence.

'There's nothing improper going on, nor will there be, Cook, so have no fear of that. My Harold's a decent, clean-living man, and besides we don't plan on getting wed just yet. We're courting though, and that much is official.'

'That's all right then,' Cook said, 'and if you want to invite him here on Sunday afternoon next week, I daresay we could manage a special little tea for the two of you to celebrate your betrothal.'

It was all very heady and exciting, and Cherry couldn't help but be caught up in it all, even though she was beginning to feel as though her own heart was breaking. She had lost Lance – not that she had ever really had him – and eventually she would be losing Paula too.

She had no doubt that whatever was said, as soon as a little railway house became available for rent, the couple would waste no time in tying the knot. In fact, whenever she thought of the passion that had flared so quickly between herself and Lance Melchoir, she couldn't imagine it would be long before the lusty Harold found it difficult to keep his hands off his lady-love.

But having a special little tea for the couple next Sunday was a sweet thing for Cook to do, and it would make Paula feel special too. She was glad for her. She repeated it over and over. She *was* glad for her. She was *really* glad for her. She was just sorry for herself.

The day before the party was also the day that Lance was going to come home from the nursing home. In his opinion he had been there far too long. There was nothing wrong with him now. He still had a livid scar on his cheek but he was assured that it would fade in time. His memory had returned almost immediately, and he didn't like the way the staff had kowtowed to him. He was just another patient, damn it, and he didn't want all this preferential treatment. That his mother had insisted on them being paid well for his stay he had no doubt at all, but it didn't help his sense of injustice for those who weren't so well off. For the first time, he had a feeling of empathy with his mother for all the charities in which she had a hand. She meant well, he thought grudgingly, even though he sometimes felt oppressed by her doting on him.

But now he was going home, and he was going to seek out Cherry O'Neil and have a good long talk with her, and to hell with what anybody else thought about that. They had things to discuss, and nobody was going to stop them.

Gerard, in his dual role as butler and occasional chauffeur, was detailed to take Lady Melchoir to fetch her son that afternoon.

'I never thought he was a mummy's boy,' Cook sniffed. 'But I daresay she wants to check that he hasn't fallen for one of the nurses while he's been there. That would be beneath her dignity and put her nose out of joint for sure.'

'I think Captain Lance will marry whoever he pleases,' Paula said, when Cherry seemed to have been struck dumb at the thought of Lance returning home.

'I never said nothing about marrying, and you get on with your work, girl. I swear that since you've been courting with young Harold all you've got on your mind these days is romantic nonsense.'

Paula tossed her head and whispered to Cherry as they went on with their cleaning duties. 'It may be romantic nonsense to her, dried-up old stick, but we know different, don't we?'

'Well, you do, anyway.'

Paula gave her arm a squeeze. 'Don't worry. I'm sure he thinks a lot of you, whatever his family might think.'

Never having had two halfpennies to rub together, they weren't normally in the business of considering inheritances and the like, the way the gentry did, but it had been on Cherry's mind lately.

'It hardly matters what he thinks. It's what the Melchoirs of this world think that counts, and you know that as well as me.'

Her voice was a mixture of bitterness and sadness, knowing that what she desired most in the world could never happen. She wasn't jealous of Paula's new-found happiness, and she was glad for her, but she wouldn't have been human if she hadn't wished with all her heart that it could have been herself. This was what came of moving out of your class, and everyone knew that nothing good ever came of that.

Gerard waited outside the nursing home while Lady Melchoir swept inside with all the aplomb of a queen. No wonder people were more than a little afraid of her regal appearance and her sharp tongue, he found himself thinking. She could scare you into a dose of the trots with one glance from those cold eyes. He didn't normally use such coarse phrases, especially in the company of the kitchen staff where he was a cut above the rest of them, but sometimes they were the only words that described adequately how he felt.

He scrambled out of the car as he saw her ladyship reappear with Captain Lance in tow, accompanied by several of the nursing-home staff as might be expected for such an important resident. Then he found himself having to hide his shock at seeing the still-red scar on the captain's handsome face.

'Not quite the Valentino look now, eh, Gerard?' Lance said jokingly.

'I don't think it will detract from your looks one iota, sir,' he replied loyally.

'Quite right.' His mother was brisk as she sat beside him in the back seat of the car. 'He's been told that it will soon fade and it will give an interesting dimension to his face. There's many that suffered far worse disfigurements during the war.'

Trust her to think of such a thing, Gerard thought, catching a glimpse of brief amusement in Lance's eyes as they settled themselves for the drive home. But it only lasted for a moment. From then on, the mood in the back of the car seemed to become steadily icier, as each of the occupants stared out of the windows in opposite directions and said nothing. In an effort to lighten the atmosphere, Gerard ventured to make a few comments himself, whether or not it was his place to do so.

'If you hear a bit of merriment and music from below stairs tomorrow afternoon, my Lady, it's because one of the kitchen maids has got engaged, so we're having a bit of a celebration.'

He could never have expected the reaction that he got. One minute all was silence from the rear of the car, and in the next it was as if two small explosions were taking place.

'An engagement, you say?' Lady Melchoir exclaimed, for once losing her regal guard and sounding almost animated. 'Well, the girl is to be congratulated for finding herself a willing young man to take her on.'

As for Lance . . . Gerard reported later that he gave an almost choking noise in his throat, and when he glanced back through the driving mirror, he could see his mother's hand pressed firmly on his arm.

He had simply made a harmless remark to break the icy mood in the car, but as Gerard told Cook and the girls some time later, he thought for a minute that the captain was about to have a relapse and pass right out in the back seat.

Cook had made them all a pot of tea before starting to prepare the evening meal for the family upstairs, and they were all having a slice of her seed cake to go with it as he related the story.

'The poor young man,' Cook said sympathetically. 'He must

still be suffering a bit from that concussion. They say it can affect you for quite a while.'

She didn't really know anything of the sort, but she liked to appear as if she did in front of the young girls.

'They didn't object to our having a little party for Paula and Harold, though, did they, Mr Gerard?' Gwen said anxiously.

'Oh no, not at all. In fact, her ladyship even said she was to be congratulated for finding herself a willing young man to take her on.'

Cook gave her usual sniff. 'Well, that sounds as if she thought Paula was never going to get a young man.'

'You don't think . . .' Cherry began, and they all looked at her expectantly when she stopped abruptly.

'What don't we think? Come on, girl, spit it out,' Cook said.

'Oh, nothing. It was nothing at all.'

Lucy grinned slyly. 'I reckon Cherry's got the huff now that Paula's got a young man and she hasn't.'

'Well, neither have you and nor has Gwen, so you needn't start crowing,' Cherry retorted. 'Anyway I couldn't be happier for Paula. She deserves to get out of here and have a little home of her own.'

But in the back of her mind she couldn't help wondering uneasily if Mr Gerard had actually told Lady Melchoir and Captain Lance exactly who had got engaged, or if the two of them had assumed that it was *her*. After all, in her ladyship's mind it would be Cherry who'd be frantically looking for a young man to 'take her on', in order to give her baby a name. The baby that never was . . .

She swallowed a piece of cake too hastily, and started coughing, causing Paula to thump her on the back.

'Lord help us, there's another one choking now,' Cook said. 'You'll be needing to brush up on my first-aid skills before long, Mr Gerard.'

'I'm all right,' Cherry gasped. 'And for goodness' sake stop hitting me, Paula! Something went down the wrong way, that's all.'

'You think he's got hold of the wrong idea, don't you?' Paula asked her, the minute they were on their own. 'You think he believes it's you that's got engaged instead of me.'

'It did cross my mind,' she muttered.

'Well, it solves everything, then. If they all think it's you, they'll stop thinking of sacking you, or even worse, sending you to some quack. They'll think you've found some young bloke willing to make an honest woman of you.'

'It doesn't solve anything,' Cherry said miserably. 'If anything, it makes it worse, because I can't bear for him to think that of me. It's even more deceitful, and I can't go on living a lie.'

'You know what, Cherry? I'm washing my hands of the whole affair. I'm fed up with seeing you moon about because of him, so do what you have to do.'

'I will,' she said.

'Here, where are you going? We've got work to do,' Cook called as Cherry ran out the door.

Cherry didn't heed her. Lance would have been back for more than an hour now, and she guessed that the first place he would want to go was to the stables to check that Noble was being cared for. Like a homing pigeon, she thought . . . And so was she, as she saw him in Noble's stall. There didn't seem to be anyone else around, and her throat felt thick again as she drew near to him. Her heart was beating fast, but she knew exactly what she had to do, and not before time.

As if aware of somebody's presence, he turned around slowly, and Cherry caught her breath at the sight of his injured cheek. She hadn't expected it still to look so livid. She was sad for him, and humiliated at knowing her brother had done this to him. She registered that he wasn't looking too pleased to see her.

'I'm so sorry about what happened, and I have something important to say to you,' she said huskily.

He threw down the brush with which he was grooming Noble's glossy coat. If either of them thought it ironic that this was the place where it had all begun, the place where they had known the greatest, sweetest intimacy between a man and a woman, and that now they stood like two warring strangers, glaring at one another, neither showed it.

'I also wanted to talk to you, but I have already heard something of importance from the butler. You obviously didn't see fit to come to me first with your news.'

'You don't understand,' she said shakily.

He gave a smothered oath, and grasped both her hands in his. It wasn't done with any tenderness, and she winced at the harshness in his eyes now.

'Shall I tell you something, Cherry-Ripe? When I was lying in that hospital bed, I felt like I had had all the guts ripped out of me, and then I saw your face looking down at me. It was the first face I had recognized since your bastard of a brother knocked me down, and all that I could think of was that it was the face of an angel, and the only face I wanted to see.'

'What . . . what are you saying?'

He let go of her hands then and turned away from her.

'I'm saying that I had the craziest notion in the world right then. That I never wanted to let you go, and that come hell or high water, and no matter what the differences between us, I wasn't going to let any other man have you. But you've ruined all that, haven't you?'

Too bemused by what he seemed to be saying, she was also too agitated to think straight. She burst out, 'You've got it all wrong! It's not me who's got engaged. It's Paula.'

Lance looked at her blankly for a moment, and then he spoke slowly. 'Paula . . . you mean the other girl who works with you?'

'*Yes*, that Paula!' Since he didn't seem to be taking in what she was saying, Cherry began to wonder if she was repeating the words to a crazy man. Perhaps the concussion had had more of an effect on him that anybody realized, she thought fearfully. He always seemed so alert, so on top of everything, but it certainly seemed to be affecting his comprehension right now.

'But please listen to me for a minute, because that's not what I need to talk to you about,' she went on hurriedly.

She felt her colour deepen as he continued to stare at her, and she felt deeply ashamed for having deceived him for so long. She had to put things right so that he could reassure his parents that there would be no illegitimate child forthcoming in a few months' time.

'I'm pleased for your friend, but never mind all that. The mis-understanding only makes me all the more determined to say what I wanted to,' he broke in.

After that, she hardly knew how it happened, but somehow she was in his arms and he was holding her tight. His face was close to hers, and she was very careful not to put her cheek against his poor savaged one. She felt faint, because she still hadn't told him, but the moment was too unbearably sweet for her to break the spell. Just for a moment longer . . .

'It doesn't matter about my parents' wishes,' he said in a low voice. 'God knows I've tried to fight my own instincts in order to do right by them, but the hell of it is, I can't get you out of my mind or my heart. So this time I've lost the battle, and my instincts have won, my sweet girl.'

'What do you mean?' she whispered, not fully understanding all this talk of instincts and battles, and unsure whether or not she should be offended by what he was saying about going against his parents' wishes.

'What I mean is that I think you should marry me, Cherry-Ripe.'

She gasped, wondering if she had really heard those words or if all of this was no more than an impossible dream. And then she felt his mouth on hers and all the passion of which she was capable seemed to be released in that kiss, and she was kissing him back as though her life depended on it.

When he finally released her, his mouth was still warm against hers, and he spoke softly against her lips.

'I take it that this means yes?' he asked.

She swayed into him again, too overcome with emotion to speak as she wound her arms around his neck, and let the full-ness of her body against his speak its own words.

Fifteen

The minute Cherry could get Paula to herself, she described as though in a daze what had happened in the stables. It was all a muddle in her head, and she was still trying to accept that Lance had actually asked her to marry him.

'Well, he didn't get down on one knee or anything like that. He just said he thought we should get married,' she repeated. Her voice was still shaking, but she kept thinking that if she said it often enough she might start to believe it had really happened.

'And so this all happened after you told him the truth?' Paula squeaked in disbelief. When Cherry didn't answer, she looked at her sharply. 'You did tell him, didn't you? My God, Cherry, tell me you told him!'

'It was what I intended. I went to the stables, sure that I'd find him there, and I really tried, Paula, but before I could get the words out, it seemed that he and his mother had got the wrong end of the stick about who was engaged, and he thought it was me. When I told him it was you and Harold, everything seemed to happen after that,' she said helplessly. 'Before I knew what was happening, he was kissing me, and the next thing I knew he said I wasn't to say anything to anybody yet because he was going to have words with his parents tonight, and then he would send for me.'

'So if he goes along with your story, as far as they're concerned, the fact that he's asked you to marry him will be to make their grandchild legitimate,' Paula said flatly. 'It's not right, Cherry, and you know it.'

'That may be, but Lance and I know it's because we love each other.'

'Oh, really, and how do you know that? Has he ever actually said that he loves you? How do you know that this won't be little more than a shotgun wedding, because he's decided that if there's a ready-made heir in waiting to the Melchoir fortune, he might as well take advantage of it?'

'It's not like that, and I never knew you could be so cruel, Paula!' Cherry said, tears stabbing her eyes now.

'I'd say it's exactly like that, and if you're daft enough not to see it, then you're in for a bumpy ride in the future. The Melchoirs might accept the kid, but they'll never accept you, and how long will it be before their precious son tires of his kitchen maid bride? I'm not being cruel, I'm being realistic. Please think very hard before you make the biggest mistake of your life, Cherry.'

She was pleading now, giving Cherry a quick hug as she reverted to the gentle-natured Paula she had always been, while trying hard to make her friend see sense.

'Of course I'm going to think hard about the future,' Cherry said. 'And I promise that no matter what we've already said, I won't marry Lance until he knows the truth. I'll know then if he really wants me, or just an heir.'

She was in a state of jitters for the rest of the day, snappy with everyone, and finally Cook told her to get off to the linen cupboard and tidy it, sorting out anything that needed repairing or replacing before she boxed her ears for her insolence.

'And Paula's to stay here,' Cook added sharply. 'I don't know what the two of you have been stirring up with your heads always together, but I swear you're closer than a pair of Siamese twins, and I want no trouble in my kitchen.'

'She'll be getting plenty of that soon,' Paula muttered to Cherry before her friend flounced off, closing the door of the large linen cupboard firmly behind her. She wished she never had to see any of them again, knowing how they would all condemn her for the wicked girl she had been. She wished she didn't have to be summoned to the holy presence of the Melchoirs some time that evening. She wished she could be a fly on the wall when Lance told them what he had to say, and she especially wished she could see Lady Melchoir's face when she heard that her son had proposed to the kitchen maid.

Cherry's momentary fit of nervous giggles faded. He hadn't exactly proposed, she admitted. He had just said he thought they should get married – and Paula's no-nonsense words had put all that into perspective too. Lance thought she was carrying his child, and because he was an honourable young man, he had decided to do the right thing by her. She shouldn't have become so excited and thrilled by his words. If anything, it was humiliating, because he had never said he loved her. Lust wasn't love, even though it had felt so very much like it at the time. She smothered a sob and got on with the task she had been given, trying to blot everything else out of her mind.

Lance waited until after dinner before he spoke to his parents about Cherry O'Neil. Nervous wasn't a word he cared to use with regard to himself, and there had been enough traumatic times during his army career to send any man's guts plummeting, but tonight was different. So yes, he thought, dammit, he was bloody nervous, but he wasn't a man to balk when the situation demanded action.

Besides, his mother was in a remarkably genial mood that evening. He was under no illusions that it was due to the fact that she thought Cherry O'Neil had bagged herself a future husband, and that the party downstairs tomorrow afternoon was to celebrate the fact. He felt briefly sorry for Elspeth, knowing he was soon to wipe the smugness from her face, but nothing was going to deter him now from his resolve. He admitted he'd had a severe shock in the car coming home from the nursing home when the butler had mentioned the kitchen maid's engagement party. He too had believed it was Cherry and that he had lost her. The moment he knew the truth, he knew that nothing on heaven and earth was going to make him back down from his intentions now.

'We'll take our coffee in the drawing room,' Lady Melchoir announced. 'I daresay you'll want to go to bed quite soon after your unpleasant week, Lance dear. You must be feeling very tired.'

'I don't feel in the least tired, Mother, and I want to talk to you both about a very important matter that will affect us all.'

He didn't miss the hopeful glances his parents exchanged. He could read the meanings behind those glances so easily. He had had several visitors as well as his parents while he had been in hospital and at the nursing home, and one of them had been Cynthia Hetherington, the daughter of their dearest friends. They would see this as a sign that the two young people were becoming fonder of each other, and they would be hoping that Lance was going to tell them tonight that he had decided to propose to the dear girl.

He hid a wry smile, knowing that in a very little while they were in for the biggest shock of their lives. After dinner, they repaired to the drawing room and waited until the coffee had been served, and Lance drew a deep breath.

'You've been urging me for some time to find myself a wife, Mother,' he began, 'and of course, it's important for a family such as ours to continue, and I know you will be eager to see grandchildren before you die.'

'Quite right, but we're not thinking of going just yet, my boy,' Francis said jovially. 'My old ticker's good for a few years yet.'

'Don't be coarse, Francis dear,' Elspeth murmured. She turned to her son. 'What is it you want to tell us, Lance?' she said expectantly. 'I can tell you've got something on your mind, and I daresay these few days away from home have given you time to think about your future.'

'They have, but it's only today that it's become crystal clear what I intend to do,' he said crisply.

He hoped they noted that he didn't say it was what he wanted to do, but what he intended. He wasn't a child and he wasn't about to ask their permission, and he wouldn't tolerate any objections, even though he knew there would be plenty at first. But even if he and Cherry had to live in a tent, he was going to make her his bride. But it wouldn't come to that, of course. Even if his father disinherited him, he had money of his own and a good Army pension. They wouldn't starve.

'Well, come on, my boy,' Francis went on. 'Put your mother out of her misery. Are we going to be hearing wedding bells soon?'

Lance felt his face break into a tense smile, knowing his father had given him an unintentional lead.

'You are, Father, but if you're planning my tying the knot with Cynthia Hetherington, I'm afraid you're in for a disappointment. Fond as we both are of one another, we both know she's not the girl for me, and nor am I her knight in shining armour.'

He saw his mother's brow begin to pucker.

'Please stop playing games with us, Lance. I'm not aware that you've been seeing any other young lady, so either you've been very devious indeed, or this is all a bit of nonsense, which I must say is in very poor taste,' she added.

'I assure you it's not a bit of nonsense, Mother. I have been seeing another young lady and I have asked her to be my wife.'

'Well, you young dog!' Francis exclaimed with a short laugh. 'So who is she, then? Do we know her? I take it she's the daughter of some of our friends. The Galtby girl, perhaps? Or that pretty young niece of the Reverend Philips? She's hardly top-notch, but I don't think your mother would object to someone connected with the clergy.'

'Why don't you let the boy speak for himself, Francis?' his wife put in more sharply now. 'Whoever she is, I'm sure she's well-connected, so please do tell us her name, Lance.'

'I'm trying to if you give me a chance. Her name's Cherry.'

Elspeth frowned. 'It's a very odd name for a young lady of quality, although people do choose the strangest names for their children these days. I can't think of anyone we know with such a name.'

'Except for one of our kitchen maids,' Francis reminded her sharply.

In the brief silence that followed his words the only sounds that Lance was aware of were the ticking of the grandfather clock in the corner of the room and his own heartbeats. He cleared his throat. As if he hadn't been on edge before, he was about to shatter all his mother's hopes for a fashionable marriage that would reach the society pages in all the best newspapers.

'Cherry O'Neil,' he stated.

It took a few seconds for his parents to register that he was actually giving them the name of the girl he had been talking about.

Elspeth spoke angrily, clearly refusing to believe what he was saying. 'This silly teasing has gone on long enough, Lance. The kitchen maid may have the same first name as your intended bride, but please tell us exactly who she is.'

He went across to the sideboard and poured himself a large brandy before he answered. He turned back to his parents and looked at them steadily.

'I've already told you. She's called Cherry O'Neil.'

For a moment he thought his mother was going to faint. He poured her a stiff brandy and took it over to her. She swallowed it as if she hardly tasted it, her eyes wide with shock.

'I think we all need a drink,' Francis said, following his son's example, and then he put his hand on Lance's arm. His eyes were like daggers now.

'Are we to understand that you have been dallying with this girl again? If so, then get her out of your system by all means, Lance, but don't come to us with any damn fool nonsense about marrying her.'

Lance slammed his brandy glass down on a side table.

'I have already asked her to marry me, Father, and I have every reason to think she has accepted.'

'Well, of course she would,' Francis said scornfully, since Elspeth seemed to have lost the ability to speak for the moment. 'What girl of her class wouldn't be overjoyed to marry into money? I'm with your mother on this, Lance. Have your fun with her if you must, but that's it.'

'Then you won't legitimize your grandchild?' Lance said.

Elspeth gave a little cry of anguish and Francis's face went a deep and furious red. 'Good God man, have you taken total leave of your senses?'

His wife spoke in a hoarse voice.

'So those terrible letters demanding money spoke the truth. This girl, who works in our kitchens, is going to have a child, and you, Lance, are responsible. Is that what you're telling us?'

'When you put it like that, yes, Mother.'

'What other way is there of putting it, you young fool?' his father snapped. 'You swore to us that that there was nothing in it, and all the time you lied.'

'I lied to save Cherry's honour.'

'*Her* honour! And what about yours? What about the family's honour?'

Lance suddenly became very calm. He drained his glass of brandy and spoke in a measured way.

'I've been honourable enough to tell you of my intentions, and I've told Cherry I will send for her when you know the truth. I intend to do that now, and I will be grateful if you will receive her civilly, since she is to be your daughter-in-law and the mother of my child.'

He didn't wait for any reaction, but strode out of the drawing room and down the stairs to the kitchen where he knew the servants would be having their supper. They all looked up, startled, when he entered the room, and Cherry felt her heart begin to bang uncomfortably in her chest as he walked towards her.

'I'm sorry to disturb your supper, but I need Cherry to come upstairs to the drawing room.'

'Yes, Captain Lance,' she said numbly, her face flushing as she felt all eyes on her. He could have rung down to summon her, but he had come here himself, and that was bound to cause gossip. Only one other person knew what it was likely to be about, and she looked desperately at Paula, feeling as trapped as if she were a lamb going to the slaughter.

Once outside the kitchen, Lance put his arms around her, feeling her tension and wishing he could spare her this. But it had to be done. There was no way he would take the coward's way out and suggest they run away together. He put one finger beneath her chin, forcing her to look into his eyes.

'This is the moment, Cherry-Ripe,' he said tensely. 'We're in for a rocky ride upstairs, but we knew that, didn't we? Just as long as you haven't changed your mind I know we can see it through together.'

Did she hear the smallest note of uncertainty in his voice? Was he giving her the chance to back out? Which one of them was really caught in a trap — herself or him? She took a deep, shuddering breath and her voice was ragged.

'I haven't changed my mind, but you might, because there's something I really must say to you, Lance. Can we have a few moments to talk alone before we go into the drawing room?'

'Of course. We'll talk in the library.'

She followed him with her heart pounding, still not sure how to tell him the truth, still terrified that he would think her as big a rogue as her brother for deceiving him the way she had. But she couldn't bear to go on doing so, and she knew she would have to come clean, no matter how painful, nor what the consequences might be.

Inside the library, Lance closed the door behind them and took both her hands in his. 'Don't be scared, my love. I've already paved the way with my parents, and they have no doubt of my intentions. I know that in the end they will approve of my doing the honourable thing.'

She bit her lip. There was no hint of romance in his words. He was merely doing his honourable duty. This was going to be more difficult than she thought, but unwittingly he had shown her how to proceed.

'What if the situation were different, and I wasn't carrying a child, Lance?' she said huskily. 'When I marry, I always vowed it would be for love, not for convenience, but it seems the upper classes have a far colder way of looking at things.'

'And do you love me?' he said, smiling, not understanding. 'You certainly gave me the impression that you do, my sweet girl!'

'But it works both ways, and you have never said that you love me,' she prevaricated.

In answer, he put his arms around her and pulled her close, aware of the beating of her heart against him. His voice was as husky as hers when he replied.

'Dear God in heaven, you must know that you're in my thoughts a thousand times a day and that I could never love anyone the way I love you. You're in my soul, Cherry, and you're the sweetest girl I've ever known. Is that love enough for you?'

She swallowed a small sob, because she was about to shatter all his illusions about her. Her eyes brimmed with tears as she drew a shuddering breath and muttered against his chest.

'I'm not sweet, or honest, or brave. If I were all of that, I would have told you long ago that I'm not carrying a child, Lance.'

She stopped speaking, because he was suddenly holding her away from him, and his hands on her arms were no longer tender.

'So all of it was a lie,' he said brutally.

'Not all of it. I thought I was carrying for a while, but then I knew it wasn't to be. I even wanted it to be true, despite the consequences for a girl in my position, because then I would have had something of you.'

Would he even care? she thought bitterly. The thoughts rushing through his head now must be of enormous relief, because he would no longer feel obliged to marry a servant. She had relieved him of any noble obligation, and he was free to marry someone more suited to his position in life.

When he didn't say anything for a few moments she began to feel more and more wretched. She would be dismissed, of course. He had already told his parents of the imaginary situation, and they would never continue to employ a girl who was capable of such deceit.

'Why don't you say something?' she whispered. 'I know you must be very angry with me.'

'Angry doesn't begin to describe my feelings,' he said in a clipped voice. 'I thought I knew you.'

She lifted her chin. 'You don't know me at all. You only see what you want to see, a servant girl who had her head turned by a handsome and wealthy young man, and let herself be seduced by him. That's all I ever was to you.'

'You're wrong. Yes, I admit I enjoyed you on that night in the hayloft, and I'm damn sure my pleasure was reciprocated. Are you going to deny it?'

She shook her head. 'Perhaps not, but what good does it do to rake over something that was obviously a huge mistake? But now you know that nothing came of it, so I suggest you go back to your parents and tell them the wedding's off, and I'll go upstairs and pack my bags.'

'Don't be so bloody melodramatic,' Lance snapped. 'That's the last thing I want you to do!'

'Actually,' she said shrilly, hardly heeding his words, 'I'd prefer to wait until after tomorrow. My friend Paula is having an engagement party downstairs, and I'd hate to miss it, if that's all right with you – sir.'

He shook her gently, and now she realized he was laughing at her. He was actually *laughing* at her, and she could have hit him for his insensitivity. Couldn't he see that her heart was breaking? Didn't he care?

'Oh, Cherry, what a mess we've both made of things, haven't we? But with all your bravado and my anger, isn't there something we're both forgetting?'

'Is there?'

His arms went around her again.

'You've already said that you love me, and you know damn well that I love you. Do you think I would have defied my parents and told them I intended to marry you if you didn't mean the world to me?'

'But . . . but now you know I let you go on believing a lie,' Cherry stammered, not sure where all this was leading.

'I also know that I still love you and I still want to marry you – if you'll have me. Will you, Cherry-Ripe?'

'What about your parents?' She was still stammering, her head almost bursting with disbelief at what he was saying.

'I don't want to marry them,' he retorted.

'But they'll never agree. They'll persuade you otherwise!'

'For God's sake, you're turning into the most argumentative woman I know! Just answer me one question. Will you marry me?'

It took less than a heartbeat for her to answer yes.

His mouth was on hers then in the sweetest of kisses, and all her senses were alive with happiness, despite the problems that lay ahead.

'So now we'll go and face the music,' he said, and the very calmness of his voice told her that he was just as aware of how his parents would react as she was.

'I don't think I can,' she said in momentary panic.

'Just be your own lovely self, and we'll get through it together. And for now, Cherry, I think it would be the best idea to let them go on believing they're to be grandparents.'

She looked at him in astonishment. 'But they're not!'

'You know it and now I know it, but trust me, I also know my parents, darling. They may hate the idea that I won't be marrying some long-nosed, blue-blooded girl of their choice, but they'll never be able to overlook the fact that there's a grand-child involved. It will be our trump card.'

In Cherry's opinion, it didn't seem a very savoury way to enter into marriage, but she did trust him, and all her reservations were as nothing compared with the fact that she was going to marry the man of her dreams, the man she loved so much. The full real-ization hadn't sunk in yet, and maybe it would when she had to face the disapproving faces of her future in-laws. At the thought, she gave a nervous giggle.

'What's so funny?' Lance asked.

'I was just wondering how your mother reacted when she realized she was going to be mother-in-law to her own kitchen maid!'

Perhaps she shouldn't have put it so bluntly. Perhaps she would see Lance frown a little, as if the realization hadn't quite hit him so thoroughly. To her immense relief he laughed, and squeezed her hand.

'I can't say it was the happiest moment of her life, and I wish you could have been there to see it.'

'Lance . . . you are sure, aren't you?'

She had to say it, knowing what he was giving up for her, in status, if nothing else. His influential friends would be whispering about them, some might even shun him, and she just hoped and prayed that she would be worthy of him.

'I've never been more sure of anything in my life,' he said simply.

Cherry knew it must have been her imagination that the drawing room seemed very chilly, although it was probably just the atmosphere exuding from the two people waiting for them. Lord Melchoir looked stern and remote, and Lady Melchoir looked at Cherry as if she were something that had crawled out from the nearest stone. Nevertheless, the touch of Lance's hand in hers was enough to strengthen her resolve. He loved her and he was going to marry her, and nothing could change that now.

'Please come and sit down, both of you,' Lord Melchoir said after the tiniest pause.

They sat close together on a sofa opposite the two older people. Lady Melchoir's back was as stiff as a pole, and Cherry felt a momentary pity for her. This situation was so far removed from anything she must have wanted for her son, but love took no account of class, and if it was strong enough to overcome all objections, then it was strong indeed. She was reassured by the thought as she felt Lance's body close to hers.

'Your mother and I have had a further discussion, Lance,' Lord Melchoir said, ignoring Cherry altogether. 'We cannot condone what you are suggesting, and we are agreed that the best thing for all concerned is that the girl is sent to an establishment that will care for her until the time comes for the issue to be born. Since you are accepting responsibility, we will receive it into our care as the child of a distant relative, and the girl will be compensated.'

Cherry gasped, completely shocked at the callousness of the words, and by the way Lady Melchoir sat stony-faced through it all. Before Lance could say anything, she had leapt to her feet and was facing his parents furiously.

'How dare you!' she said passionately, her voice unconsciously slipping into the classy tones of which she was so capable. 'What right do you have to sit in judgement on me, and decide what is to become of me or . . . or the child?'

Lance was on his feet as well now, his face furious.

'You have both gone too far,' he said to his parents. 'You will not play God with us, and nor will you change our minds. The plain and simple fact is that we love each other and we intend to marry, with or without your blessing.'

Lady Melchoir's face had paled at being spoken to in such a way by her son, but it was clear that she had been taken aback by Cherry's outburst.

'Then don't expect your father to pay for your disgraceful nuptials!'

'I expect nothing except a little respect for my own judgement in choosing the woman with whom I want to spend the rest of my life,' Lance snapped.

In the complete silence that followed, Cherry could see what a difficult time these two were having in adjusting to the situation. She took a small step forward and spoke directly to Lance's mother.

'Lady Melchoir, I beg you to understand that we have not gone into this lightly. I know you think little of me, but you know your son, and you know he wouldn't do anything to hurt you unless he felt deeply about it – and about me.'

For a minute she thought she was going to get no response. Lady Melchoir inclined her head just a fraction, and her husband spoke.

'You have a fine turn of phrase for a servant,' he said deliberately and insultingly, 'and you have obviously turned my son's head. But since I can see he is determined, we will all retire for the night and think what's to be done to salvage this reprehensible situation. We will speak again tomorrow.'

With that he and his wife swept out of the drawing room, leaving Cherry drained of all emotion and feeling as though her legs would hardly hold her up. Lance saw it too, and he caught her in his arms and held her tight.

'We should both go to bed too, my love, but have no fear. They'll come round, and by tomorrow they'll be certain that the solution was all their idea.'

'And what solution is that?' Cherry said in a dull voice.

'Our marriage, of course.'

Paula was agog with curiosity by the time she came to bed, to find Cherry already huddling beneath the bedclothes.

'What happened? Have you got your marching orders?' she demanded.

'Far from it . . . I think. I'm not really sure what's going to happen, except that Lance says he loves me and wants to marry me.'

'So you didn't tell him,' Paula said accusingly.

Cherry sat up in bed, giving her a luminous smile.

'That's the most amazing part, Paula. Of course I told him, and he wants to marry me anyway, no matter what his parents think. Not that we've told them the truth, mind. It's the best lever we've got.'

'Blimey, girl, you mean he's gone along with it?'

'Yes, he has. We're going to be married, Paula!'

The realization was suddenly so joyful she could have danced around the room. She leapt out of bed and hugged her friend, and she finally sobered enough to warn her to say nothing, because there was still another uncomfortable meeting with Lord and Lady Melchoir to come.

'You don't think we'll be having a double wedding then,' Paula said mischievously.

'I doubt it, but you're not to let any of this take away the pleasure in your engagement party tomorrow afternoon. For now, this is our secret.'

It didn't stop her dreaming though, of white satin dresses and filmy wedding veils, and living happily ever after. Even if the dreams had no real substance yet, except for the knowledge that she loved and was loved in return, and there was no need to go chasing rainbows any more, for she had found her own pot of gold.

She didn't feel quite so comfortable in her mind on Sunday. She didn't know what she had expected, but there was no sign of Lance, and the family had gone to church as usual in the morning. Later on, the kitchen was all hustle and excitement for the afternoon's party. Harold turned up with a bunch of flowers for Paula, and Cook brought out her old gramophone machine and records to play music for dancing. The entire kitchen was in a cheerful mood, all except Cherry, who did her best not to show her growing unease and bring the mood of the party down.

It was late in the afternoon when they were all dancing around the room and had drunk and eaten their fill and toasted Paula and Harold a dozen times. By now Cook was saying they had best stop the celebrations and begin the evening dinner preparations for the family, when there was a sudden fluster by the door and Lance Melchoir appeared among them. Only Cherry knew why he must be here, and although he urged them all to continue and that he had just come to offer his congratulations to Paula and Harold, she was beset with anxiety all over again. And then he looked straight at her.

'Cherry, would you mind accompanying me upstairs?' he said, in a way that made the rest of the company look at them both in astonishment. She nodded and slipped out of the room, leaving them all to speculate any way they chose. She was aware of that little nervous giggle again as Lance caught at her hand.

'Don't look so worried. A proposition has been put to me, but don't ask me what it is until you hear it for yourself.'

Mystified, she went with him, relieved that at least it didn't sound like anything too serious. It didn't seem as if they were disowning Lance, or throwing her out on the street. And even if it were that, she had a sixth sense and a growing confidence that they would go together.

They joined Lord and Lady Melchoir in the drawing room again, and this time Cherry felt calmer than she had last night. Even if she and Lance were acting out a lie, in time the truth would come out, and by then it would be too late. They would be man and wife. She flashed him a brief smile at the thought and felt a warm glow inside as he smiled back at her.

Lord Melchoir cleared his throat and this time he addressed her directly.

'Miss O'Neil – Cherry – the three of us have had a serious discussion over your future plans, and my wife and I have accepted that in the circumstances our son wishes to marry you. So to save any gossip or embarrassment within our social circle, and also among your companions below stairs, it is our proposal that you marry quietly, with the minimum of fuss, and that you then retire to Ireland. Our family owns various pieces of land there, and you will be able to take up residence where Lance will be a gentleman farmer.'

Cherry was completely taken aback by what she was hearing, and she couldn't have been more surprised if he had said they had landed on the moon. She turned quickly to Lance, ignoring his parents.

'Is this your wish too? Would you be truly happy to be wrenched from your home and the social life you know so well? Your horses and your club, and all the people you know?' she exclaimed, realizing at once what he would be giving up for her.

In that moment she knew she only had to say the word to his parents – that there was no child to force this shotgun wedding – and it would all be over. She was torn between continuing the deceit they were both perpetrating, and the shame of what she was doing to him.

All her life, she had prided herself on being a truthful girl, and this sequence of lies was becoming almost too much to bear. With the words trembling on her lips, she opened her mouth to say more, and then she felt Lance gripping her hands tightly, forcing her to look into his eyes.

'Cherry, I swear by God and all that's holy that I want you to be my wife more than anything. Nothing else matters, so say you agree, and we'll accept my parents' terms and live the quiet life of a gentleman farmer and his lady in the wilds of Ireland. As for my horses, they'll come with us, of course. We may even become horse breeders, and we'll need no other trappings to make us happy. But don't forget that it means you'll be leaving Bristol too, and all the people you know. It will be a fresh start for us both. So please think carefully. Can you agree to sharing the biggest adventure of your life with me?'

She knew he was pleading with her to say nothing more. She glanced at Lance's mother, and saw the lady give an imperceptible nod. It was hardly an acceptance of a kitchen maid for a daughter-in-law, rather a small gesture towards the inevitable. Cherry knew that this offer was a gigantic compromise, removing them from sight in order to preserve the family honour. But, as Lance said, the reasons for it no longer mattered. And suddenly the laughter was bubbling up in Cherry's soul, for this would truly be the adventure of a lifetime, and one that she could never have envisaged in her wildest dreams.

'Then if you want me, I'm yours,' she said huskily to Lance, so softly that only he could hear. The next moment, regardless of the other two people in the room, she was in his arms. His lips met hers in a kiss that was full of promise, and she knew that for them, the future had only just begun.